DANGEROUS MINDS

Xander Weaver

Contents:

Prologue	Pg 7
Chapter 1	Pg 26
Chapter 2	Pg 31
Chapter 3	Pg 35
Chapter 4	Pg 37
Chapter 5	Pg 50
Chapter 6	Pg 57
Chapter 7	Pg 65
Chapter 8	Pg 69
Chapter 9	Pg 73
Chapter 10	Pg 76
Chapter 11	Pg 82
Chapter 12	Pg 101
Chapter 13	Pg 106
Chapter 14	Pg 113
Chapter 15	Pg 128
Chapter 16	Pg 134
Chapter 17	Pg 143
Chapter 18	Pg 154
Chapter 19	Pg 164
Chapter 20	Pg 167
Chapter 21	Pg 175
Chapter 22	Pg 178
Chapter 23	Pg 182
Chapter 24	Pg 191
Chapter 25	Pg 195
Chapter 26	Pg 208
Chapter 27	Pg 212
Chapter 28	Pg 216
Chapter 29	Pg 222
Chapter 30	Pg 233
Chapter 31	Pg 238
Chapter 32	Pg 251
Epilogue	Pg 259
Acknowledgments	Pg 279
About the Author	Pg 281

I dedicate this novel to the love of my life, and the most loving and caring person I've ever met.

I love you, Carrie!

Prologue

Unknown location,
Eastern United States
46 Days Ago
11:14 p.m.

With her heart lodged in her throat, the only sound Keegan Porter could hear was the frantic beat as she slipped from the darkened stairwell and into the main corridor of the building's first floor. She was out of breath, her body almost numb with the panic within, but her determination grew—she would not stop until her escape was made and freedom was won. After all, Keegan knew that if this attempt failed, she wouldn't have a chance at another.

The wide hallway was dimly lit, and being after hours, the building was silent and still. Almost no one entered or exited the facility at the late hour, so she was alone. Every other light running the length of the hall was extinguished, adding to the desolate feeling that chilled Keegan to her core. Even though no shadows moved, she knew she was never alone. They were already aware of her escape and would capture her once more.

The pair of glass doors at the end of the hall was her goal, though they were far from the finish line. Escaping the building was only the beginning of her plan. But if she could make it that far, she stood a chance. It was more of an opportunity than she'd had in the nine months she'd been confined.

Darting for the goal, Keegan focused on the glow of the empty city street beyond. Her bare feet slapped against the cold tile as she sprinted the last forty yards. Only the sound of her own rapid footfalls could be heard in the deafening silence of the building, yet she knew…they were coming. Even without a noise, without a scream or a command, Keegan sensed them as strongly as she sensed freedom. The experienced armed response team was mobilizing just two floors above her head.

As she drew closer to the doors, Keegan's own reflection stared back from the glass. The dark blue of the institutional pajama-style scrubs hung from her thin form like a layer of skin, and her jet black hair framed a face so pale that it barely shown with detail. It was a startling reminder that she hadn't seen her own reflection since arriving in this horrible place.

As her hands slammed against the door's release bar, Keegan's focus shifted away from the image to the street outside, but the barrier was steadfast. Her world spun unexpectedly when the doors refused to budge an inch—the collision of her body against metal and glass sent her ricocheting, skidding down the high-gloss hallway where she slid to a stop on her backside.

Locked—Of course!

In her mind, she was tracking the movements of the men sent to retrieve her. They'd split into teams, with one following her path directly and heading down the stairs. That group would make it to the first floor and be on her in a matter of seconds. The second team was moving through the back of the building, an area she wasn't familiar with. But if Keegan had to guess, they were likely going for the garage and their vehicles, ready to pursue if, by some miracle, she managed to evade the first team.

Still sitting on the cold floor, Keegan looked back at the thick glass doors that separated her from the chance to bury herself in a city that would provide the perfect camouflage with people, lights and noise.

Taking a calming breath, she closed her eyes and let her mind explore the locking mechanism that secured the doors. It was strong and industrial; the sort of lock designed to protect the entire building from the dangers of the streets outside. Ironic, Keegan thought, since there were far more sinister forces at work inside the fortress's sturdy walls.

Her mind went further...dug deeper. The door's heavy metal push bar met with thick, long tooth gears that were hidden behind a heavy plate. She could see it clearly in her mind, as though the components of the door's lock were made of glass themselves. The gears met with another rod that passed behind the plate in the push bar; a rod that ran the width of the door where it met with another set of thick gears canted at forty-five degree angles. Those gears mated with a pair of rods that projected up and down the leading edge of the door where they extended into plates set deep into the door's frame, bracing it in place.

The wrong way, she realized.

Her mind backtracked over the image, studying the schematic in her mind to find the weakness, the way out, desperately trying to block out the men she knew were coming closer with every second. As if walking the mechanical path, Keegan followed the vertical metal bars down, past the canted gears, past the long rod behind the protective plate, through another set of gears, and along another set of solid rods before meeting with a substantial cylinder lined with narrow pins. It was the door's locking mechanism, and its three dimensional form materialized with perfect clarity. Without another thought, the pins inside the lock retracted into the walls of the housing and the central cylinder within the mechanism spun a hundred and eighty degrees.

Keegan launched herself up from the floor, smashed through the door, and skidded onto the sidewalk beyond. Her first instinct was to run, but she had to be smarter than that. She threw a shoulder against the slowly closing door to speed the slow pneumatic dampener that prevented the door from slamming shut. The moment the door reconnected, the lock clicked into place once again, and she was off and running, sprinting down the empty city street like an Olympic champion.

Nearly one hundred yards were behind her when a crash suddenly splintered the silent night. The unmistakable sound of shattering glass brought a renewed surge of adrenaline to her body. Keegan didn't need to extend her senses to know what had happened behind her, or the mistake she'd ultimately made. While she'd assumed the locked doors would slow her pursuers, they'd caused only a second's delay to the team in pursuit. With her lead quickly dwindling, she needed to get off the street and find cover in the darkness promised by the nooks and crannies of the vast city.

Turning right into the nearest alley, Keegan reached the back wall of the narrow corridor before her eyes could fully adjust to the near total blackness. The moon was nearly three quarters full, but the buildings on both sides were four stories tall, doing their part for her by leaving the narrow passage engulfed in shadow. Having no faith that the area would be able to conceal her for long, Keegan cast out her senses, frightened that she'd wasted precious time by cowering and not running further into the world. The shock was too much. The three-man team was headed directly for the mouth of the alley, as if they knew her exact position. It didn't make sense. Even they, with their talents and experience, should've at least had to search—

Oh, no...

Realization struck, leaving her breathless and her mouth dry. Her mind flashed back to the recovery period that followed the brutal medical procedure she'd endured only nine months earlier. Trying to avoid the truth, Keegan raised an unsteady hand. Her fingers carefully probed the scar tissue at the base of her skull as she attempted with all her might to delude herself...forget the painful period of recovery that followed the unorthodox procedure. But it was impossible. Though the pain soon faded, that horrific operation had led to imprisonment, not to mention the onset of her truly unusual abilities. And she tried desperately to deny the fact that the team was coming after her with ease for a reason.

She just couldn't give up. As Keegan's eyes adjusted to the low light of the alley, the fire escape scaffolds suspended from one of the brick walls came into view. There were four different platforms connected by ladders leading up the side of the building. The first floor's platform was raised at least twenty feet off the ground and well beyond reach.

Focusing on the long set of stairs that extended from the bottom of the lowest platform, she saw that the stairs were drawn up flush against the bottom of the fire escape and would extend if someone tried to descend upon them. When that happened, the person would offset a counterweight and lower the staircase. Yet again, a mechanical contraption that could be manipulated. Reaching out, Keegan focused her abilities on the very end of the outstretched staircase. With a horrible shriek from the rusted metal hinge, the end of the staircase dropped quickly to the ground.

The second floor was behind her before Keegan even felt the painful bite of the rough, oxidized iron beneath her bare feet as she climbed. The moment she'd reached the first platform, the staircase's counterweight had kicked in and returned it to a stowed position, leaving no trace of the path she'd taken. It was a small victory, though she knew her attackers were closing in as she climbed higher.

They must have implanted some sort of tracking device while she was under anesthesia, she reasoned. It was a thought that shook her to her very core. After all, if that was the case, how could she ever hope to escape?

Reaching the third floor, Keegan looked through a wide window, taking in the brightly lit hallway. Golden numbers on each door represented the line of apartments.

She tried to lift the window but found it secured, yet another blockade. Looking more closely, Keegan found a pair of latches along the top of the double-hung frame. Bringing her mind to life once again, she triggered both latches simultaneously, and the window slid open without a sound, closing again just two seconds later.

The temptation to barge though one of the apartment doors was great. If she could get to a phone, she could call for help; there had to be someone who would believe her in this world. If they could only see the men who were pursuing her: heavily armed, with two of them smiling wide, looking forward to dragging her back to a windowless locked room. She could sense the desire coming off those men, and it chilled her to the bone.

Desperate or not, Keegan couldn't risk barging into an apartment just to beg for help. Besides, calling for help was out of the question. It would never arrive in time, and the agony of knowing that innocent people would be hurt was too much for her. Especially since she knew her capture would be inevitable if she slowed for even a moment.

Racing to the end of the hall, Keegan located a stairway. Making for the street was out of the question—her assailants had already been joined by the second half of their team. Three men were in the process of picking the locks on the building's front entrance, while the two remaining men had somehow managed to retrieve the fire escape staircase and were already beginning their ascent. She could see it all in her mind as clearly as if she were monitoring the teams via a closed circuit security system, and the image was terrifying.

Lacking a better option, she made for the roof. The door at the top of the stairs was protected by a simple deadbolt lock—trivial, given everything she'd already bypassed. Stepping out onto the asphalt lined roof, Keegan pushed the door shut behind her and heard the deadbolt slip into place with a satisfying snap.

But as she jogged around the open expanse of roof, her worst fear was realized. She was trapped. There was no access to an adjoining building, and her hope of jumping to the fourth floor fire escape below had been crushed. An armed pursuer had already taken up a position, just waiting for her.

It mattered little, she realized. The tracking device made it impossible for her to escape. If there was any chance at freedom, Keegan knew she needed to find the device and disable it.

But how?

She didn't have the time, or the technology. Then again, maybe technology wasn't a problem, considering her abilities. Thinking hard, Keegan considered the easy way she'd been able to manipulate the complicated locks during her escape. With nothing she could do about time, Keegan chose to find the tracking chip and defeat it the same way she'd defeated the locks.

Dropping to her knees, Keegan closed her eyes. With that, the sounds and smells of the world around her slipped into nothingness. She sensed no more than her own heartbeat; nothing else existed except a young woman willing to fight. Starting at her toes, Keegan began a thorough examination, visualizing her body in her mind. The pads of her feet were sliced; the coating of blood was thick and dirty. There was inflammation in her ankles from her reckless run through the dark streets. And in her right knee, what remained of a tree climbing accident when she was just twelve-years-old came to light. Three pins and seven screws were used to rebuild her knee and leg following the accident. Now, she literally marveled at the way the bone had grown, fusing and enveloping the screws over the years, as if her body had chosen to become one with the hardware.

The clarity was amazing.

As Keegan's examination reached the base of her own skull, she took a deep breath, sensing the scar tissue that existed on the surface of her skin. It was hidden beneath her hairline, but the long winding ridge of twisted, pierced flesh reminded her of how recent the surgery had been. What she found beneath the surface sucked the breath from her lungs.

Following the long, deep incision in her flesh as it twisted past deadened nerve endings and penetrated the surface of her brain, she found the nearly microscopic chip buried deep in the tissue. Small wires extended from the chip and snaked in different directions, delving further into her brain. At first shocked by what she was seeing, Keegan realized she didn't have time for distractions. Adjusting her focus and doing her best to set her fear and anger aside, she focused on the chip and assessed its scale. It was tiny, and the fiber-like wires extending from it were even smaller, fractionally thinner than a human hair, and they seemed to twist and turn, running to a half-dozen different parts of her brain.

There!

Tracking one of the thin wires, Keegan found that it headed toward the surface of her brain where it met with a marginally larger flat disc. Though she couldn't be sure why, she felt certain that this was the component being used to track her. The fear sparked inside her as she hoped that severing wire would be enough to terminate the signal she was transmitting. It was a desperate and reckless gamble, but she had no other choice.

A giant blast of air suddenly crashed into Keegan's back, toppling her from her knees, and sending her sprawling to the asphalt roof. She wasn't sure what had happened; all she knew was that her hearing had been erased by a ringing sensation. The world around her spun as she fought to catch her breath. Her mind reached out to the surroundings as her instincts struggled to understand what had just happened.

But there was nothing. She couldn't hear a word, a sound, a movement…her senses were completely mute. It was as if her extrasensory perception had been stripped away along with her hearing, her freedom, and her last glimmer of hope.

Propping herself up on an elbow, Keegan fought to focus. As far as she could tell, she was unharmed. But her mind was scrambled and her body felt numb.

As the tall figure stepped from the dark doorway, time stopped. He cradled a strange looking rifle in his arms. She stared at the small bowl-shaped protrusion at the end where the muzzle of the gun should be.

A sonic weapon, Keegan guessed, based on the dizziness that seemed rooted in her very core.

The man walked slowly closer. Two more men took

positions at his flanks as he advanced. Those men seemed cautious, but the leader exuded confidence and determination, not seeming to share in or care about whatever concerned his friends.

The man's mouth moved as he stood over her, but Keegan had no idea what he was saying. With so many of her senses stripped away, she was shocked to realize that she couldn't even manage to read his lips in her current state.

There was a glint in the man's eyes, and she struggled to understand what it meant.

But with the glint came an anger that made the image even more confusing. His eyes were dark, completely cold and devoid of sympathy. The ridge of an old scar split the brow over his left eye cleanly in two before running down the outer corner of the eye until it disappeared, fading back into his skin. A once vicious war wound was etched into his skin. Professional work had been done to conceal the injury but it was still obvious.

The man studied her as Keegan tried to make sense of what she saw in his eyes. If she didn't know better, she would think that he enjoyed the hunt...

No—he enjoyed hunting *her*.

The contents of her stomach turned at the thought. What could turn a man to such darkness?

One of the other men spoke as he passed the scarred man a cell phone. Taking it, the man remained silent and listened. Keegan saw question flare in the man's eyes for the first time as he moved his mouth in a brief statement. Listening once more, he shrugged his shoulders, then tossed the phone back to his partner.

Keegan fought to understand; she needed to know what had been said. But before she knew what was happening, the two underlings hoisted her by her arms and held her, allowing the scarred man to move in front of her once more. She watched as he retrieved a hypodermic syringe from a pack on his hip. He examined it briefly in the moonlight, and she felt her eyes go wide, trying to struggle against the strong men holding her. But it was no use. She was powerless—as though every ounce of energy had been wrung from her body by the strange weapon.

The scarred man proceeded to eject the contents of the syringe, squirting it into the air. He didn't stop until the syringe was empty. She didn't understand. *Wasn't he going to use the drug?*

But as the man pulled the plunger back on the empty syringe, filling its chamber with air, Keegan understood what he intended. Struggling, willing her mouth to open, she fought to free herself from the harsh, painful grip of her attackers.

The scarred man moved forward. He looked her in the eyes and she saw his lips move once more. This time…she understood.

"Such as waste."

With a shake of his head, the man stabbed the needle into the side of her neck and pushed the plunger all the way to its stop. Pulling the needle free, he stepped away.

The pair of men released her and Keegan crashed to the asphalt in a heap. Her hand slapped at the puncture point, but it did no good. There was nothing she could do now. Her eyes were wide as they jumped randomly around the empty roof before falling once more on the scarred man.

Keegan felt her entire body shudder as if hit by a single violent blow. But there was no pain. Yet another quake passed through her and she realized she was on her back, staring up at the night sky. She couldn't feel or hear anything, but sadness flooded her mind. She'd been so close. She'd almost escaped. She'd almost been free.

The last thing she saw was the scarred man above her. His face was a mask of indifference. He didn't seem to care that he'd just taken her life.

A moment later, everything went black and Keegan Porter was gone.

* * *

New York State
32 Days Ago
9:44 p.m.

The cobwebs and shadows gave way to increasing moments of lucidity as the world around him began to take on a three dimensional quality that William hadn't experienced in far too long. He sat alone in the sparsely decorated room and concentrated on clearing his mind. The chair's threadbare armrest began to feel like something more than indistinct grit beneath his fingers, and the room stank of some kind of antiseptic or cleaning solution. Even the dull, unintelligible sounds that had surrounded him night and day slowly began to slip back into the familiar tones of the psych ward where he'd been imprisoned.

His mind suddenly clearing by a degree, William remembered overhearing someone refer to the facility as a psychiatric hospital. But that didn't make sense. He'd never suffered from mental illness. Shaking his head, William licked his lips with a swollen, dry tongue. Suddenly aware of how badly his body ached, he turned his head and looked around the dimly lit room, trying his best to focus on his surroundings. Sitting in an old, worn out armchair in the corner, he took in the room— the small steel-framed bed against the wall opposite him, and a tall freestanding lamp that looked as aged as he felt. The weak light bulb flickered every few minutes. It was a poor excuse for illumination, and it kept the room in a darkness that matched his clouded mind.

A sudden flash of light outside the small, dirty-paned window pulled William's mind free from its drug-induced stupor. The thunderclap that followed was so close that he felt the reverberation in his chest. It was as if the lightning had struck the building on purpose, just to add to the fear and panic of anyone locked inside. He sucked in a breath and fought the wave of nausea that accompanied the ringing of the thunder in his ears. His heart raced and his ribs burned. It was the first deep breath William had taken in…forever.

How long had they been dosing him with the powerful drugs? It was a struggle just to form coherent thoughts.

While he had no concept of time, the ache in his bones told William that his muscles had atrophied. He felt far older than his twenty-four years warranted.

Pulling himself to his feet, William fought to steady himself on wobbly legs. The room spun around him for several moments, and just when he thought he was going to lose the battle with gravity, his swimming vision settled and his sense of balance returned. Taking a single step required a phenomenal effort of will, he realized. Looking down at the thin fabric slippers that wrapped his feet, he took note of his faded wardrobe—pajama pants with matching button-up cotton shirt. His clothing, much like the upholstery on his chair, was worn and frayed from overuse and long overdue for replacement.

Taking two more steps, William found himself in front of the room's lonesome window. From his second story view, he stared out at the torrent of rain pummeling the shadowed grounds below. His eyes followed three sidewalks as they branched off from the building and disappeared into the rain-soaked darkness. A few scattered lampposts lined the paths making a feeble effort to push back the night. The murky glow they cast and the forking angle of the paths only hinted at the vastness of the world beyond, making William feel far more isolated than he ever had before.

His focus shifting, William suddenly saw the ghost of his reflection peer back at him in the darkened window and felt an incredible shock to his core. Raising a hand slowly, his fingers traced the sallow lines of the reflection, struggling to confirm that it was indeed his own. Several days worth of stubble lined his jaw and neck, but it was the gaunt hollowness surrounding his eye sockets that made him think he was seeing an unearthly apparition.

No, it can't be me…

Following the edge of his jaw, he traced the exaggerated line of his nose before gently poking at the blackened circles framing his exhausted eyes. His hair had grown longer, as well…longer than he had ever let it grow before. Dropping down just past his eyebrows, it was essentially the same shaggy, unkempt mop all the way around. He shuddered, not recognizing the image before him.

My God, he thought. *What have they done to me?*

The reality of his situation set in as his senses returned more fully. William realized that he'd been kept drugged far longer than he had originally suspected. A deep, venomous anger began to well up inside of him. It grew with each passing moment, burning away the residual drugs left in his system.

The drugs…

Now that he could think clearly, he could vaguely recall an unending cycle of faceless orderlies visiting his side at clockwork intervals. They had always remained quiet and administered some kind of…

William glanced down at his left forearm. A catheter had

been taped securely to his flesh, the injection port at the end showing signs of extensive use. He flexed his arm, realizing for the first time how much it ached from the constant repetitive injections.

The sound of rainfall on the roof finally reached his ears. He was exhausted. The desire to drop back into his chair and catch his breath was nearly overwhelming, but doing so would surely cost him his only opportunity for escape. There must have been some sort of mistake—a slip-up in the medication regimen they had forced upon him.

No. He wouldn't squander the opportunity, William promised himself. There was little chance of another. He only hoped he could gain the mental wherewithal to make his escape before they had a chance to dose him once more.

With a concerted effort, William made his way to the doorway of the small room. Each step took substantial strength and concentration, but with each halting step, he felt his blood flow faster, erasing the fog that had blocked the inner-workings of his mind. For each step he took, the next came more easily.

There was no door in the entryway to his room so he stepped close to the opening and listened for any signs of life. Carefully poking his head around the frame, he took in the wide hallway that led left and right. Although the walls had once been handcrafted by artisans who clearly understood the beauty of ornate work, William saw that their efforts had long since been disregarded, left to deteriorate with time and neglect. So, too, had the dark hardwood floors—both looked as if they had once been majestic works, but now decades of use and abuse had all but destroyed the incredible craftsmanship.

Distant thunderclaps came every few seconds as the storm outside intensified. Somewhere, at the furthest range of his hearing, he could identify the sound of a breathing respirator and heart monitor; the beeps and clicks were coming from down the hallway to the left. Whoever was attached to the equipment would require a greater level of attention, he reasoned, so when he exited the room he went right.

By the time he reached the end of the hallway, William had regained full control of his arms and legs. He was able to walk with a near normal gait, even if his muscle deterioration brought pain with each step. Standing at the top of a wide sweeping staircase, he realized what should have been apparent from the very beginning. The building he was being held in was, in fact, some sort of old manor house; an antique mansion that had found its new purpose as a crude and poorly maintained medical facility. The once grand staircase stretched out below him, making nearly a ninety-degree sweeping turn before reaching the dull, scratched floor below. The staircase was eight or ten feet wide, but what had once been beautifully carved treads and risers were now defaced with crude adhesive grip-strips adhered to the stained, splintered wood. Although functional, it was truly a sad shadow of its once glorious design.

William was just about to take his first step when he was startled by a voice from behind. It had been so long since he'd heard the unmuddled words of another human being that he found himself confused by the sound. Placing a hand on the staircase banister, he turned slowly to face the voice.

Mister Waterford? Are you alright? What are you doing out of your room?

The male nurse dressed in medical scrubs looked at him strangely. It was an expression that William couldn't understand. While the nurse seemed alarmed, he couldn't tell if the man was surprised, worried, frightened…or, angry.

What are you doing out here by yourself, you crazy bastard?

William scowled. While he couldn't interpret the nurse's

expression, the man's words somehow didn't fit with the circumstances.

The nurse took a step forward and William felt himself involuntarily stiffen. The nurse must have noticed his movement because he instantly froze, his eyes studying William as if trying to gauge some unknown emotion.

Something's wrong. I've never even seen you on your feet without someone leading you around like a dog on a leash.

Suddenly realizing what was wrong with the situation, William focused on the petulant man's lips. Though he struggled to understand what he was seeing, he was certain that the nurse's mouth hadn't moved, although he'd heard every single word uttered.

"Mister Waterford? Are you okay?" the nurse asked. His voice was soft and quiet, as if not wanting to become the first meal for a hungry bear that had just woken up from hibernation.

Okay, that time it was different, William thought. He had seen the man's mouth move in time with the words. Confused, he looked around, but they were all alone.

A look of severe discomfort suddenly spread across the man's face.

Oh, shit. They warned us about this—someone messed up his meds! The sedative's wearing off!

While William wasn't yet functioning at one hundred percent, he did recognize the sheer terror blazing in the nurse's eyes. The man was about to bolt—and when he did, he would raise the alarm.

Meeting the nurse's gaze a moment before he could turn tail and run, William focused all of his energies on him. And in that single moment of contact, he felt a blanket of calm settle over him. It was as if he was suddenly encased inside an invisible bubble that kept the rest of the world at bay. All of the physical pain, all of his mental disorientation, simply disappeared in that single moment of clarity.

A warm vibration ran through William's body as he felt his mind connect to that of the nurse. For one brief moment, he felt the man's fear—his terror—at the sight of William. William even saw himself through the man's eyes. Standing there at the top of the staircase, his eyes locked on the nurse as if they'd reached out and grabbed him.

Pushing the man's foreboding aside as if it were nothing of consequence to him, William saw the security card that hung from the breast pocket of the nurse's scrubs. William smiled for the first time in what felt like forever. With a completely blank expression on his face, the nurse reached up and released the clip that held the card to his shirt and handed it to William without uttering a word.

No sooner had William taken the card from the man's outstretched hand, when another nurse rounded a corner at the end of the hall. She walked up behind her co-worker; her chin was turned down, reading a clipboard as she moved. Stopping suddenly, the woman nearly collided with the first nurse who stood straight and tall, like a statue in the center of the hall.

"Hey, watch it Gene," the woman snapped. "Why are you just standing—"

With a slight turn of her head, her gaze fell on William.

The woman's eyes grew instantly large at the sight. "Oh, shit!" she muttered in a ghost of a voice.

Making it a half-step back, her retreat came to a swift end as the male nurse pulled a pen from his pocket and stabbed it into the soft tissue of her neck.

Blood sprayed from the wound as the thin weapon ruptured an artery. Her legs instantly folding, she dropped to the floor in a heap. Though her eyes were wide with terror, the expression lasted only moments before a glassy sheen arrived, announcing her passing. A dark black pool spread out beneath her body. The entire savage attack had occurred in complete silence. The only telltale sign was the muffled tumble of her small body as it struck the unforgiving floor.

Taking no pleasure in what he'd just done, or rather, what he'd just forced the nurse to do, William took a deep fortifying breath. He reasoned that there'd been no alternative to the slaying—not if he was going to escape. Furthermore, if he was to complete his getaway, he would have to dispatch the male nurse as well.

With no more than a thought aimed in the man's direction, the command was sent. Without argument, the nurse raised the bloody pen once more and drove it into his own carotid artery. Striking the floor, his head and shoulders were surrounded by a pool of dark fluid even before the vacant look in his eyes was replaced by the glassy stare into oblivion.

William didn't waste another second. Turning quickly and taking careful hold of the rail, he made his way to the first floor of the old building. The front door was an elaborate affair with cracked and neglected scrollwork carved into the coarse grain. Swiping the nurse's key card across the sensor that had been crudely placed in the door's frame, he pulled the door open the moment the lock released. The storm pounded the wide porch on the front of the old mansion, a deluge of water splashing against faded and peeling paint. William didn't hesitate, walking swiftly into the driving rain and disappearing into the windswept darkness.

Chapter 1

Northern Virginia
Present Day
11:14 p.m.

The truck rolled along the endless stretch of country road. With a waxing moon that was nearly full, there was enough ambient light for Cyrus to take in the surrounding countryside. But it was just more of the same, thick forested land mixed with wide open fields planted with what, he had no idea. In truth, his attention was more focused on the man beside him at the wheel of the massive six-wheeled military transport vehicle. Like the truck, the driver was outfitted in pale camouflage patterns. Both the vehicle and the driver's uniform were faded and weathered, having seen their prime years long ago.

It was curious, Cyrus realized. They were so far out in the countryside that he knew their truck was likely to draw unwanted attention; or, at the very least, stand out in the memory of the few people they encountered. It wasn't ideal given the nature of the truck's cargo. And since he was dealing with both skilled and paranoid people, the juxtaposition was disconcerting and warned of the dangers to come.

However, such concerns couldn't have been further from his chauffeur's mind. While Cyrus didn't know a great deal about the man, the few things he did know, he understood with absolute certainty. The man was slouched in his seat, his eyes peering over the truck's wide steering wheel which he held in a near white knuckle grasp. The man looked on edge and defeated, and for good reason.

Cyrus had hijacked the truck some thirty miles back using a scatter of motorcycle wreckage to stop the truck, as well as trick the passenger into exiting the cab. There was never any danger that either of the men in the truck would radio for backup or call for emergency assistance, not with the payload of hardware they'd stolen from the military contractor they'd been charged with protecting.

Capturing the truck had taken less than five minutes. Cyrus was playing the role of the unconscious motorcyclist when the truck's passenger came to check on him. As he suspected, the man was more interested in cleaning the road and moving on than he was of actually finding help for an injured fellow traveler. Because of this, there had been no guilt for Cyrus when he'd laid into the man with a Taser and dropped him right where he stood.

Unfortunately, by the time Cyrus had taken care of the passenger in the glow of the vehicle's headlights, the driver had already been out his door, bringing an M4 assault rifle with him. Cyrus had beaten the man to the punch, though. Drawing a sawed-off double-barreled shotgun from a holster on his hip, Cyrus fired both chambers in rapid succession. The beanbag rounds from the weapon released at short range had caught the driver square in the chest, knocking him off his feet and sending the rifle flying from his hands. Like the Taser, the ammunition was an effective, non-lethal weapon when used at close range.

Cyrus left the passenger bound, gagged, and dumped in the ditch. He temporarily zip-tied the hands of the unconscious truck driver and left him lying in the road. Then, bathed in the vehicle's headlights, Cyrus had cleared the road of the staged motorcycle wreckage.

By the time the driver came around, Cyrus was kneeling beside him in the middle of the still deserted country road. It was the perfect location to hijack a truck. But who would be after a shipment that wasn't supposed to be there in the first place? That was the question the driver must've been asking himself as he looked at Cyrus with a mix of fear and anger in his eyes. Cyrus held one of the driver's boots in one hand and reached deep down into it with the other.

It took only a minute for Cyrus to finish what he was doing, showing the man every step of the process as he pressed a short, wide plug of C4 plastic explosive all the way into the very toe of each of the driver's boots. When he was done, he held the man at gunpoint—a 9mm semi-auto since he had already discarded the beanbag gun. Not giving the man a choice, Cyrus forced him to once more slip on the boots and lace them up tight.

All of that had been about thirty miles back. Once they'd gotten on the road again, the driver, Chuck was his name, had all kinds of questions. But they were the ones you would expect given the unusual circumstances. Why are you doing this? Do you know where I'm going? Do you know who I'm meeting? Do you know what they'll do to you?

At first Cyrus had taken all of the questions as rhetorical. To start with, Chuck had asked them so rapidly that there hadn't even been time for an answer. Secondly, and perhaps more importantly, Cyrus thought the explosives that were currently wedged against the tips of the man's toes should have spoken volumes.

"Well? Do you?" Chuck persisted. He shot a quick glance at

Cyrus before returning his eyes to the road.

So much for being rhetorical.

"Tell me something, Chuck?" Cyrus watched the man, making no effort to hide his amusement. "Are you suggesting that I hijacked this truck at random, on a road in the middle of the night, smack-dab in the middle of nowhere?"

Smack-dab? He chuckled. He was almost certain he'd never used that word before in his life. The rural surroundings were having an effect on him.

Chuck shot him another quick look. He clearly didn't understand the question.

"I think you'd better focus on the road and worry about the C4 between your toes, Chuck. If everything goes well and you behave yourself, you'll walk away from all this in one piece."

Cyrus paused for dramatic effect. "But if you mess with me or you rat me out at the meet? Let's just say walking will be the least of your worries. Okay?"

Aside from stealing another quick look at him, Chuck didn't answer. Since his life would soon hang in the balance, Cyrus needed to make sure that Chuck was entirely clear on his predicament.

"Tell me that you understand, Chuck," Cyrus said. He was speaking to the man with patience, but using the tone of a parent with an unruly child.

After watching Chuck lace up the improvised explosives that had become his military issue boots, Cyrus let the man watch as he'd taken off his own hiking boot. At first, the confusion was clear in Chuck's face…but only until Cyrus produced a small, flat wedge of aluminum. After pulling a long, thin pin from the length of the wedge, Cyrus had squeezed the wedge between his fingers and showed Chuck the pressure sensitive trigger. Then Cyrus slid the wedge into the heel of his boot, slipped the boot back on his foot, and laced it up again. The point was made very clear.

Chuck had looked at him in horror, at first thinking his own feet would be blown off the very first time Cyrus stepped down hard on the heel of his boot. But that wasn't the case, Cyrus had explained. Chuck would be entirely safe as long as he did everything that he was told to do. But it was important for him to realize that Cyrus had the ability to trigger the explosives before anyone could stop him, and use a device that no one would find on him during a patdown.

Between the explosives in his boots and his knowledge of the trigger, Cyrus could understand the man's irritation. But he wasn't entirely sure Chuck had a full grasp of his circumstances.

"I'm just here to make the same deal as you and your buddy," Cyrus explained. "If you play it cool and follow my lead, you'll be just fine. As soon as we're out of that place, you can take your boots off, and we'll go our separate ways."

Taking another glance at him, Chuck seemed like he had something to say. Instead, he settled for a longer, more penetrating examination of his hijacker.

"These aren't nice guys you're messing with," Chuck warned. "If you don't have a damn convincing explanation for why you're here and why Jackson ain't, you're going to get us both killed."

Cyrus smiled. Now they were getting somewhere. Chuck was finally accepting the situation.

"I've got that covered. Just play along and everything will be fine. I don't want to hurt you. Keep in mind that I didn't kill your buddy Jackson back there, I just hogtied him and left him in a ditch. He'll be fine, come morning."

Hogtied? My God, Cyrus mused. *At this rate, I'll say 'yee-haw' before the night's through.*

Chapter 2

District 1198 Garage
11:37 p.m.

Watching from the thick brush of the tree line, Hondo had maintained a visual on the abandoned bus garage for the last seven hours. He was part of a twelve-man team that surrounded the facility in preparation for the operation that was due to kick off at any minute.

The four acre paved parking lot laid out before him had seen better days. The asphalt was cracked, eroded, and entirely washed away in some areas. Likewise, the twenty-thousand square foot structure located in the center of the grounds had been devastated by the elements. The facade was made of brick that once made the structure look like an urban office building. But that thin ornamental finish had since fallen away in small sections, giving way to the elements and exposing corrugated steel walls. The grounds had once been the central location for the storage and maintenance of school buses in the tri-county area; tonight, it would see far more excitement.

Hondo had watched the sad looking building and surrounding grounds for so long that it had given him a lot of time to think. He couldn't understand how the county, or perhaps the state government, could've invested so much in the construction of it all only to later abandon the facility all together and simply leave it to rot. No doubt someone had justified the move, claiming that it made financial sense, but he couldn't see how the math could possibly work out to anyone's advantage—not once the facility had been built and was already operational. The buses, he reasoned, still ran, and they still needed to be parked somewhere. It was just one of so many rusted cogs that were part of a vast machine—a world that seemed forever off-kilter.

Mulling these issues, Hondo had kept his patience, waiting for the information provided in their intelligence report to be proven accurate. And then, two hours earlier, headlights had appeared in the surrounding wilderness. The bus garage sat in a secluded area about a mile off the county highway; not the sort of place people wandered by on accident. A team member stationed near the only road leading to it had radioed in to report the approach of three four-wheel-drive vehicles and a large white box truck.

Hondo had watched as the small caravan advanced on the abandoned bus garage. The lead vehicle stopped before the gate, and a figure climbed out to remove a padlock that secured the eight-foot perimeter fence. With that, their suspicion had been confirmed. When his team first scouted the site, while everything about the location was in a progressive state of disrepair, the padlock and chain securing the swinging front gates had been the only metal within miles that was shiny and completely rust free.

Ever since, Hondo had watched the building—sometimes through infrared binoculars, and sometimes through powerful heat-sensing optics that let him see the silhouettes of the men moving inside the massive structure.

"What have you got?"

The voice came from behind, and while Hondo hadn't been aware of the man's presence, the interruption didn't alarm him in the least. "Hey, Captain," he whispered, as his squad commander belly crawled up beside him and took cover beneath the same short stack of scrub brush. "Nothing new here. But judging by the time, we should be ready for kickoff."

"Hmm," the man grunted. "I hope you're right. I can't say I've got a lot of confidence in this friend of yours. I think we're all just wasting our time."

Looking over at his commanding officer, Hondo pushed the dark, floppy jungle hat back on his head and grinned. "Not to worry Cap'n. He's a good man. He knows the plan and he'll follow through."

"Hmm," the Captain repeated. There was still no conviction in his tone. "Maybe if you told me how it is you know this kid? Give me something to work with here. I don't like putting my men in harm's way over an unknown. All of this is hanging on the likes of a goddamn kid, for God's sake. A kid, I don't know from Adam."

"Sorry, sir," Hondo said. He returned his gaze to the garage. "That's classified intel from another op. You know how it is."

"Yeah, bullshit," the man grumbled quietly. "The kid's, what? Barely out of high school? Classified op, my left nut."

Hondo fought his own smirk. He didn't dare face his C.O. and risk the man's ire. "You know his age is what made him perfect for his job," he reminded the man. "Yormanski was going to take the lead on the operation until he got shot. Without him, we didn't have another operative who was young enough to play the part. It was either Cyrus, or we scrap the mission. How long did you say the boys in intelligence have been tracking this guy?"

"Okay, first of all, Yormanski didn't get shot in the field—or in an operation for that matter."

"Right, he was shot by his girlfriend, the way I heard it. *Shot in the ass*, as rumor has it—"

"That's beside the point," the Captain snapped.

An uncomfortable silence followed. It was one that Hondo knew better than to be the first to break. He understood the Captain's uncertainty and knew that, if he were in his place, he would feel exactly the same way.

"Okay," the Captain finally said in the ghost of a voice. "Yormanski's a putz. If he couldn't keep his girl from shooting him in the ass, maybe we're better off this way."

Both men chuckled.

A voice sounded over the headsets in both men's ears. "We have a personnel carrier on the approach," the voice offered in a concise report. "ETA, three minutes."

"Game time," Hondo whispered.

The Captain was already slipping backward across the ground on his way out of the hide. "Let's see if your boy lives up to all the hype, lieutenant."

Chapter 3

District 1198 Garage
11:52 p.m.

The heavy six-wheeled military transport vehicle rattled down
a mile long stretch of potholed asphalt that had once
constituted the driveway leading to the now abandoned parking
garage. As they rounded the last remaining gentle bend in the
road and the truck's windscreen cleared the thick forest, Cyrus
found the rusted and leaning chain link fence that surrounded
the facility a welcomed site—even though it was guarded by a
pair of men with automatic rifles. It marked the end of that
horrible road. One that would've made for an unpleasant
journey in a well-equipped SUV, it had been a downright
torturous ride in the abused military transport.

Chuck's trepidation at the sight of the armed guards was
obvious. His foot eased off the accelerator, and the heavy
vehicle slowed immediately.

"Take it easy, Chuck," Cyrus warned. "You play it cool or
we're both going to get shot. Keep driving. Pull up to the gate
nice and smooth. There's nothing wrong here—nothing for you
to worry about, and nothing to get these guys upset over. If they
get upset, we're in deep shit. You get me?"

Though he didn't reply, Chuck's foot once more found the

accelerator and the truck resumed its previous pace. Cyrus wasn't sure if Chuck's silence was in response to the explosive that was currently stuck between his toes, or if the man was just normally taciturn. He just hoped they lived long enough to find out.

"When we get to the gate they're going to raise hell," Cyrus explained. "They'll want to know why I'm here and Jackson isn't. Just be cool and play along."

This time, at least Chuck offered a nod in acknowledgment.

The moment the truck reached the gate, they had a pair of rifles leveled at them. And Cyrus's predictions were proven to be entirely accurate when a third man appeared out of the darkness and climbed up to the window on Cyrus's side of the truck. He held a pistol only inches from Cyrus's face and demanded an explanation. Feigning more concern than he actually felt, Cyrus explained that he was a cousin of Jackson's, the man who was supposed to make the delivery. He said that Jackson got held up and couldn't make it so he'd been forced to fill in.

The man with the gun didn't seem to like the explanation, but he looked to Chuck sitting behind the wheel and asked if that was true. Chuck, a man that these people had apparently worked with in the past, confirmed Cyrus's story with a grunt. It was enough to at least get them through the gate. The man with the gun cast an intimidating eye at Cyrus and told him to explain everything to a man named Stills who would be waiting for them inside. But, he warned, if Stills wasn't happy with his story, the two of them would be talking again real soon.

Chapter 4

District 1198 Garage
11:58 p.m.

No sooner had the heavy military truck rolled into the dark confines of the abandoned bus garage than the heavy steel overhead door slammed shut. The wide, empty floor of the structure was cloaked in darkness; only a circle of light marked their destination fifty-feet beyond. A loose perimeter of sodium vapor flood lamps mounted atop temporary tripods highlighted the five armed men awaiting their arrival. Just beyond the glare of the perimeter light, Cyrus could make out the vague outline of a large white box truck.

"Is this what you were expecting?" he quietly asked Chuck without turning his head to look at the man.

Chuck didn't answer. All Cyrus was offered came in the form of a vague shrug seen from the corner of his eye.

Chuck...the brilliant conversationalist.

When the truck reached the center of the circle of light, Chuck stepped on the brake and shifted the manual transmission into 'neutral'. There was a horrible crunching sound as he applied the parking brake, and Cyrus's concern for the questionable maintenance history of the vehicle was once more reinforced. Prior to putting Chuck behind the wheel, back on the remote country road, Cyrus had taken a quick look at the truck, including the undercarriage. It was unlikely that the military base would miss that particular transport any time soon. That, in and of itself, had concerning implications.

"Hands where I can seem them and step out of the truck," came the order.

From the edge of the windscreen, Cyrus could see the man who had spoken. Tall, maybe six-foot-four with short cropped graying hair, he seemed to be the leader. He, and the remaining four men, had a similar look—all military or ex-military. And while each had the hardened look of an experienced solider, there was an edge to the grey-haired man that suggested authority. That, and the fact he was the first of the group to speak up, led Cyrus to peg him as the man in charge.

Making slow and steady moves, Cyrus pushed open the door and climbed down to the cracked concrete floor. Two men, each armed with an M4 rifle, tracked his movements with the barrels of their guns.

"What's going on here?" Cyrus heard Grey-hair grumble from the far side of the truck. Presumably he was addressing Chuck. "Who's the new guy? Where's Jackson?"

Cyrus was immediately pushed forward and marched around the front of the truck where he was met by two more men shouldering rifles. Grey-hair gave Chuck a violent shove toward the front of the truck, and the man stumbled over to stand beside Cyrus.

"I don't like the change in plans," the man spat. "Explain—and make it quick!"

Holding his upraised hands in a placating gesture, Cyrus took a deep breath. "Okay," he said in a dry, uncomfortable voice. "Easy enough. Jackson couldn't make it, so I had to fill in. But it's cool—we've got the shipment. Everything's accounted for."

"That doesn't explain who you are," Grey-hair growled, taking a threatening step in Cyrus's direction.

Instantly taking a half-step backward in response, Cyrus raised his hands once more. "Sorry! I'm sorry. My name's Brodie, I'm sure Jackson's mentioned me before? I'm his cousin."

"Cousin Brodie? Okay, cousin Brodie—tell me something? What makes you think Jackson would share the contents of his 'family tree' with me? I don't know you—never heard of you in my life."

Cyrus shuddered. "Oh," he mumbled. "Well," he looked Grey-hair right in the eye and scowled. "I guess I shouldn't be surprised. Jackson's an asshole—always has been. I should've expected he would try to cut me out of the deal," Cyrus added in a bitter tone. "He's a real sonofabitch, too. I'm his inside man for this transaction, for God's sake. If it wasn't for me, he wouldn't even *have* access to the hardware he's selling."

"Inside man? You're telling me *you* work at Brockmoore? *You're* the guy? That still doesn't explain why Jackson's not here."

Cyrus offered a smug smirk. "Jackson got himself into some trouble with the M.P.'s. He's currently awaiting Court-martial."

Grey-hair's brow creased, and Cyrus noticed the armed men around him go on heightened alert at this comment. Grey-hair looked back at the truck, and when his eyes returned to Cyrus, they were filled with rage. He snatched his weapon from the holster on his hip and took aim.

"Whoa!" Cyrus bellowed, throwing up his arms in a useless effort to protect his face from a bullet that was soon to come. "Whoa! Wait! What's the problem?"

"If you led them here," Grey-hair snarled, "You'll be the

first to die!" He looked to a man over his shoulder and barked an order to check the status of the perimeter team.

"No, wait," Cyrus insisted. "It's not like that. Jackson's locked up on an entirely different matter. It has nothing to do with this any of…of…this!"

Grey-hair looked like he might shoot out of anger alone, causing Cyrus to rethink the way he'd played his hand. He needed the armed men to see him as nothing more than a lab geek, so the mix-up about Jackson had seemed like a good idea at the time.

"Explain," the man barked. "Now!"

"Well," Cyrus grinned. "I told you Jackson was a degenerate. The only difference is, this time he got caught. He went on a bender and ended up AWOL. When the MP's went to collect him, they found him passed out with a big old stash of cocaine, and a hooker named Karl!" He took a breath. "Truth is, I don't think you'll be hearing from Jackson anytime soon."

Cyrus rocked on his heels and offered the satisfied grin of a man taking pleasure in a cousin's misfortune. He pretended to be oblivious to the appraising stare the man was giving him at that moment.

"No shit?" Grey-hair asked at last. "And you say you're his cousin? You seem awfully happy to see him in that kind of shit. Doesn't seem like the sort of response family should have, does it?"

Cyrus shrugged. "Fair enough," he admitted. "But, first of all, you don't know what a mess this family is. And, second of all, we're talking about the rat bastard who was apparently in the process of cutting me out of this deal! Does that seem like a normal, healthy family dynamic to you?"

Slipping his gun back into the holster, Grey-hair scratched his eyebrow and then shook his head. Finally, he smiled for the first time. "Come to think of it, my family's not much better. And you're right. Your cousin is a shithead."

Grey-hair looked at the man with the radio and confirmed that everything was alright with the perimeter team.

"Okay," he said, as if the matter were settled. "Let's take a look at the hardware. As long as everything's in order, you guys can be on your way."

Cyrus was relieved to see the men around him lower their weapons as soon as Grey-hair gave the word. With a wave of a hand, two men were dispatched to the rear of the truck to check the cargo. As far as Cyrus was concerned, the payload should be in order. He hadn't been present for the packing of the shipment, but that Jackson and Chuck might have messed with the load in some way didn't seem likely. Not if they knew what kind of operation they were walking into. Besides, judging by the nervous way that Chuck was scraping the edge of his boot against the dusty concrete floor, he was clearly more concerned with the C4 in his boots than anything that might be wrong in the back of the truck.

"Signal Muntz," Grey-hair said to the man beside him. "Get him out here to confirm the gear. We need to get this show on the road."

At the order, the man stepped a few paces away and spoke a few hushed words into his handheld radio. Within seconds, a short, rail thin man emerged from the darkness. He wore thick glasses and looked horribly malnourished. But his clothes were clean—spotless, in fact—and he moved with a disconcerting confidence. The dark skin and thinning black hair likely made him of some Middle Eastern descent.

Cyrus realized that the new arrival, the one they called Muntz, must be the group's technology advisor, which made his real name Azim Bazzi—the ultimate target of the night's operation. Cyrus knew that, while the mercenaries on the floor around him were a dime a dozen, they were only a small, expendable part of a single terror cell. Bazzi was a much larger prize because he handled the technical needs of multiple cells, therefore, he held vast knowledge of the larger organization.

The local cell knew the man only as Muntz, which made sense. Until now, no one had been able to positively identify the man. Until that moment, he'd been a reputation without a face. When Hondo originally contacted Cyrus, he'd explained that an operation was in the works that would finally cause Bazzi to surface. Bazzi wouldn't pass up the opportunity to take possession of the plasma weapon firsthand. It was the first, and perhaps only, opportunity any agency had at grabbing the elusive terrorist, and Hondo's Delta team was tasked with the takedown. The only snag in their plan was that they needed someone onboard the transport truck—someone who didn't look like law enforcement. And at only twenty–years-old, Cyrus was a perfect fit for the operation.

Bazzi walked past Cyrus without giving him a second look. From the gleam in the man's eye, Cyrus could tell that he was fixated on the treasure in the back of the truck.

Another man stepped out of the darkness and approached Grey-hair. His appearance startled Cyrus because, up until that point, he had counted five armed men inside the building. The presence of a sixth man with an M4 wouldn't be an issue, but it made him wonder if there might be others hidden away.

"We're out of here in twenty," Grey-hair said to the newly arrived man. "Alert the perimeter team. We'll be using the primary exfiltration plan. I want you standing by at the door while we move the load to the civilian transport."

That explained it, Cyrus realized. The newly arrived sixth man had been standing post at the retractable exterior door.

He'd been the one to close it as soon as the truck was inside the building, and he must've stayed in position watching for any signs that they'd been followed.

Six armed men to deal with, Cyrus thought, correcting his plan to allow for the extra gunman. It didn't change the odds, just the geometry, he reasoned. He would just need to move a little bit—

"What the hell is wrong with you?"

Grey-hair was glaring at Chuck who had been neurotically grinding the side of his boot against the concrete.

Shit...

Chuck looked at the man like a deer caught in the headlights of an oncoming car. He stopped moving his foot mid scuff across the floor. "Huh?" was his only response.

"Why do you keep doing that?" Grey-hair demanded an answer to the annoying movement.

Chuck only shrugged in response, but that wasn't the real problem. What was, was the guilty look he gave Grey-hair that spoke volumes, creating instant suspicion where there should've been none.

His eyes narrowed on Chuck, and Grey-hair slowly slid his sidearm from his holster. He didn't seem to understand the threat that Chuck posed, but he seemed certain that something was off. "What. Are. You. Doing." He demanded in slow, concise words.

Oh, shit...

Cyrus stepped forward and did his best to defuse the situation, though he was pretty sure it was too late. "Dammit, Chuck. Are you fooling with your feet again?" He looked over at Grey-hair. "Don't mind him," he said. "He's been bitching about athlete's foot all the way here. Going on and on about it," Cyrus explained, rolling his eyes as if Chuck was an idiot making a big deal about nothing.

The suspicious shift of Grey-hair's eyes made it clear he wasn't buying the act. He brought his gun fully to bear, pointing it squarely at Chuck's chest. "Just the same," he said. "Why don't you take off those boots? I'd feel better if I had a look."

Chuck shot a panicked glance at Cyrus and, with that single gesture, Cyrus knew they were sunk. Grey-hair's gun spun round to take aim at him.

"Better do what he says," Cyrus urged. "Show the man your nasty feet, Chuck."

Chuck's eyes looked like silver dollars. He shook his head emphatically. "Hell no!" he insisted.

In response, Grey-hair's gun shifted back to Chuck. Cyrus didn't waste the momentary reprieve. Stomping the heel of his right boot down on the floor, he ground it hard into the concrete. An instant later he heard the gentle clank of multiple pieces of metal moving across metal and felt a smile spread across his lips.

"Yee-haw," he muttered under his breath. It was the signal for Hondo's perimeter team to move in. It would take 30-45 seconds for them to clear the hostiles at the exterior of the building before breaching the structure.

"Just take your boots off, Chuck," Cyrus insisted in a conversational tone. "Look, I'll take mine off, too."

Cyrus bent down to touch his hiking boot. From the corner of his eye, he saw Grey-hair looking at him in confusion. At the same moment, he heard the sound of half-a-dozen small hollow metal strikes on the distant concrete. He'd just ducked his head tightly to his knee and jammed a thumb into each ear when he heard a man yell in the distance.

The man's scream was cut off as the confines of the parking garage ignited in a blinding rapid succession of white strobes.

Even with his eyes scrunched tight and pressed into the fold of his flannel shirt, Cyrus could still see the blasts in his peripheral vision. But the light was nothing compared to the concussive roar of the accompanying explosions that literally shook the distant walls and ceiling of the cavernous structure. The rapid detonation of stun grenades, or flash bangs as they were more typically known, had a devastating effect. Since they had triggered within a half-second of each other, the effects were amplified. Adding to that was the reverberating nature of the massive empty building, and although he'd taken precautions, Cyrus still felt his ears ringing as he climbed to his feet.

Since flash bangs had no destructive payload, the perimeter of lights had remained largely intact. Only one of the tripod based stands had given way to the force of the painful sound waves. The men around the truck, however, were a different matter. The violent sound and light show had toppled the six armed assailants, as well as Chuck. But the blind and deaf men were already making efforts toward forming an armed response. Unfortunately, while they were effectively senseless, they were still armed with automatic weapons and still had the wherewithal to use them.

Grey-hair was doubled over on his hands and knees trying to pull himself from the floor. Cyrus kicked the man in the side of the head, knocking him out cold, before snatching up the discarded weapon and turning to the gunman closest to Chuck. The man had his rifle in the air and was fighting with the charging handle. Firing a single shot into the man's favored shoulder, Cyrus sent him sprawling to the floor and the rifle clattering off into the darkness.

Cyrus turned in time to find three more men within his field of view. One had just slipped the stock of his M4 under his arm to brace it against his ribs. Cyrus realized that blind and deaf, the man had no intention of taking aim. What he did intend was to use the rifle and shoot from the hip, spraying the entire room with automatic fire. It was insanity, given that there were more of his men in the room than there were actual hostile forces.

Without a second thought, Cyrus raised his weapon and fired a pair of kill shots into the man's chest, only a breath before the gunman could pull the trigger. The blood spatter made it clear that the man wasn't wearing body armor.

Realizing that any of the remaining men could easily attempt the same move, Cyrus raced quickly through the room, his gun barking twice upon each hostile he encountered. In the span of twenty seconds, he had disabled four men and killed two.

At the rear of the truck, he found Bazzi. The little man was lying on his back and clamoring like a turtle beached on his own shell. He cradled his right arm across his chest, a broken shaft of bone clearly protruding through the flesh of his arm. The man had been in the truck's cargo bed when the flashbangs detonated, Cyrus realized. He must have stumbled from the vehicle and fallen to the floor.

"Let's go," Cyrus muttered.

He grabbed the small terrorist by the back of his collar and dragged the man across the rough concrete to the front of the truck where he deposited him, unceremoniously, beside the shell-shocked Chuck. Suffering the effects of the rapid detonations, Chuck wasn't doing much better than Bazzi. He lay on his side, pawing feebly in the direction of his own feet which he could neither see, nor feel. Apparently, even in his stunned condition, he still retained the desire to pull the explosive-lined boots off his feet.

It was funny to Cyrus, considering the gunk he'd shoved into the toes of Chuck's boots wasn't C4 at all—Chuck had nothing more than a couple of wads of silly putty that had been picked up at a nearby truck stop before the action had begun. The trigger Cyrus kept in his boot had been rigged to the flash bangs the entire time. He just used a little misdirection to help keep Chuck in line during a critical stage of the operation. The entire mission would've fallen apart without Chuck's cooperation, and he needed incentive to play along.

When the small service door beside the closed overhead door detonated in a shower of splinters, Cyrus quickly placed his weapon on the floor and kicked it away. He stood in the open circle of light with his hands held high. Two more small explosions sounded in distant parts of the warehouse as additional breaching charges were used.

Men in dark fatigues flooded through the small door closest to Cyrus. They swept into the room, the red dots of their laser sights rapidly probing every surface and crevice of the vast structure.

"Clear," Cyrus called out in a casual tone.

The armed breaching team had poured through the expanse of the large room with impressive precision, but they parted around Cyrus as he stood stock still with his hands in the air. The men treated him as if he were invisible…nonexistent.

"For God's sake, you can put your hands down now."

Turning at the sound of the voice, Cyrus saw a tall man with dark face paint and a floppy, green jungle hat step from the darkness. Pulling the hat from his head, he ran a hand through his short bristle of dark hair. His scalp was thick with sweat; yet another 'tell' that the team's rapid assault on the building's outer perimeter had been brief, but aggressive.

"Hondo," Cyrus smiled. "Good to see you. I've got your bad guys right here. I believe you ordered a six-pack?"

Laughing, the man shook his head. "Bloody hell," he said with a trace of an Australian accent as he looked at the destruction around them. The commandos were in the process of shackling the still-addled hostiles. "You didn't leave much for me and the boys to do," he grinned.

"Yeah, sorry about that." Cyrus shook his head and took a look at his handiwork for the first time. "I'm actually not that used to having backup waiting in the wings. Still, I guess you guys can do the clean up."

Hondo laughed and smacked Cyrus on the shoulder. "That we can!"

They walked outside and into the warm night air where Cyrus could finally take a deep breath of fresh air. His body still tingled from the adrenaline surge, and his ears continued to ring from the grenades.

"Thanks for helping us out with this," Hondo said when they had walked a short distance away from the warehouse. "I owe you one."

"Not at all," Cyrus gave a dismissive shrug. "Just do me a favor and keep my name out of the reports. I don't think my people would appreciate my moonlighting for another outfit."

Hondo laughed and took a long look at him. "Just like that? Do you have any idea what you did here? Do you have any idea who Azim Bazzi is? We're talking about a high-profile collar. This is big! He's got ties that span multiple terrorist cells—some on U.S. soil! With the information in his head, we're going to clean up."

Cyrus shrugged again. "That's great," he admitted. "You'll be able to use him to take more of these thugs off the streets. I killed two of the grunts, but the Grey-haired guy is still in working order. He seemed to be the one calling the shots. Hopefully you can get something useful out of him, too."

"You can bet on it," Hondo said in a very serious tone. "But that's above my pay grade. Still, I wouldn't want to be where these guys are going. They're sure to get everything they have coming to them."

He followed with a grin, "I knew you were up to something when you asked for a half-dozen flash-bangs, but holy hell! I didn't see this coming."

"Yeah, neither did they," Cyrus smirked. "I rigged four of them off the top crossmember of the truck's canopy," he explained. "Then one more from under the front and back bumpers. Since we didn't know how many men I'd be dealing with, I had to make it big. I'm pretty sure my ears will still be ringing this time next week."

"I'll bet! The coms cut out and saved us from the blast. If they didn't have built-in noise suppression, you could've deafened the entire team."

That wiped the smile from Cyrus's face. "Yeah," he muttered. "Sorry about that. The truth is I'm not the best team player. Most of the time, in a pinch like that, I'm on my own. It was actually nice having the cavalry swoop in for a change."

"Just say the word and you've got my support anytime, anywhere. It's the least I can do."

Cyrus laughed. "Speaking of which…Do you have someone who can drive me to the airport? I've got a plane to catch if I'm going to make it to work on time."

Walking away, Hondo called back over his shoulder. "Follow me," he laughed. "I've got just the ticket."

Chapter 5

Hennings, South Carolina
7:46 a.m.

The town car rolled through city traffic making good time despite the storm. Though Cyrus's eyes followed the windswept streaks of rain as they moved laterally across his window, his mind was focused on the words of the man sitting beside him. He'd returned from Virginia late the night before and managed only a few short hours of sleep before his mentor and training officer had arrived, unannounced, at his front door.

"Get dressed," he had said. "A suit and tie, and make it quick. We have a flight to catch."

Thirty minutes later, a helicopter picked them up from a small airstrip in Baltimore, Maryland. The destination, he soon found, was Hennings, South Carolina. There, a town car was waiting to deliver him to his ultimate destination.

"Gertrude Waterford," Greg Boone explained. "Does the name ring any bells?"

Boone was about fifty-years old, though no one would guess it to look at him. At six-foot nothing and nearly two hundred pounds, he looked every bit as fit and capable as any of the men in the Field Operations division. But Boone was cut from an entirely different cloth. He was the Coalition's senior agent and head of clandestine operations. He ultimately oversaw all manner of field operations, both overt and covert. He had also been responsible for Cyrus's recruitment and training only a year earlier.

"Never heard of her," Cyrus admitted. "Are we talking target or asset?" His tone was matter of fact, even though the implications of questions were anything but.

"Asset," Boone said with emphatic certainty. "You'll be responsible for her protection."

That brought Cyrus's attention away from the murky morning darkness outside his window. "Protection? That's a new one. Since when?"

Boone shrugged. "This comes directly from Monica. Gertrude is a high value asset. Some funny things have been happening around her lately, and it's enough to make us think someone's been trying to take her out and make it look like an accident."

"Still, how is this Coalition work? Aren't there private security firms that specialize in this type of thing?"

"You know there are," Boone answered, clearly frustrated. "But there are…extenuating circumstances in this case."

Uh huh, here we go…

"Are you really going to be a dick and make me ask what you're not telling me?" Cyrus said, giving Boone a sharp sideways glance.

He could see Boone working the wording around in his head and realized the explanation was going to be a doozy.

"Miss Waterford was approached through official channels and refused protection," Boone explained. "Whenever necessary, she contracts with the Aragon Group. Since private protection will only make our work more difficult, you'll be providing protection…covertly."

Rolling his eyes, Cyrus took a deep breath and leaned back against the headrest. "I know I'm going to regret asking this," he said without opening his eyes, "but how am I supposed to *covertly* protect a woman's life?"

Thinking about his own question for just a moment, Cyrus suddenly sat up with a jolt and turned to Boone, anxiety written all over his face. "You don't expect me to sleep with this woman—do you?"

Boone's lips pulled into a tight line as he strained to retain his composure. Still, Cyrus could see more than amusement in the man's eyes. He didn't know what it was, but Boone looked ready to burst.

"If that's what it takes to get the job done," Boone said in a calm, collected tone. "Then you are expected to do what needs to be done. Standard mission parameters, kid. Whatever it takes."

Pulling a sheet from a closed folder in his lap, Boone turned it around and held up an 8x10 color photo. It was a press photo, a headshot of an elderly woman with thick glasses and more wrinkles than a Shar-Pei.

"Meet Gertrude Waterford," he said with a wide grin. "And if you think that's what it'll take to get her to accept you, more power to you."

With a laugh, Cyrus took the photo and glared at his friend. "You're a dick," he grumbled.

But to his credit, he then took a closer look at the photograph. Cyrus was the youngest agent ever to join the covert intelligence agency known only as the 'Coalition'. They routinely ran undercover infiltration operations all around the globe. With a fraction of the manpower of the CIA, or even the NSA, it was easy for the group to stay off governmental radar and free from restrictive political red tape. They were a small but effective group that ran tight operations, often with significant and far-reaching effects—though few even knew of their existence.

Cyrus had found his way into the Coalition's sights following an incident he became involved in during his freshman year at Brown University. Boone had worked with Cyrus to resolve the issue, and by the time all was said and done, it had become clear to the powers that be at the Coalition that Cyrus was an ideal fit for their organization. First of all, he was far younger than any of their other operatives. That gave him the unique advantage of anonymity since it is common for people to believe the young to be equally inexperienced, and therefore less threatening.

But Cyrus's number one asset was his eidetic memory. He had near perfect recall of everything he saw and heard. It was a genetic gift that allowed him to excel in his academic career, but it had proven even more effective in clandestine operations. That, and his natural ability to remain clearheaded under pressure, had come in handy nearly as often as his cognitive abilities, making him a true force within the Coalition. As much as his age was an asset in his line of work so, too, was his mind. After a few drinks, Boone had been known to boast that Cyrus was born for this kind of work.

"I don't get it," Cyrus said. He'd committed every detail of the woman's face to memory and handed the photo back to Boone. "Why can't you just talk her into accepting a protective detail? Is it really that big of a deal?"

Looking out the window, Boone nodded as the town car pulled up to the curb. "Trust me. It's a big deal. No one makes this old broad do anything she doesn't want to. She had three different assistants last week alone. Each one was fired before the day was out."

"Three assistants in one *week?*"

Boone grinned and made sure he caught Cyrus's eye for the last bit. "There was a fourth," he admitted. "But she quit before lunch. Miss Waterford didn't get a chance to fire that one."

"Sounds like a real charmer," Cyrus grimaced. He quickly scanned through the last few pages of the report that Boone had handed him after the photograph and was shocked by what he saw. Gertrude Waterford had been nominated for a Nobel Prize in Physics nearly thirty years earlier. For some reason, her current specialty was listed as Applied Neuroscience. Now, at the age of 74, she was working on some sort of unspecified, classified project.

"There's a catch," Boone said with some trepidation. "We couldn't just pull strings and land you the position as Waterford's assistant. She insists on vetting each candidate personally. You'll have to interview for the job. And to get it, you're going to have to impress the old lady."

The hits just keep on coming.

"I don't get it," Cyrus said as he prepared to exit the car. "Waterford's work is classified. That means all of her assistants need to have some sort of advanced security clearance. That doesn't come easy. How is she going through these people so quickly?"

Boone offered a forced smile. "Like you said, she's a charmer. But you gotta make this work, kid. We need you on the inside. There is no plan B. The woman might be a world class battleaxe, but you've got to find a way to make her like you. Well," he decided, "at least get her to tolerate you."

He wanted to ask how he was supposed to do that, but Cyrus knew Boone wouldn't have the answer. Boone wasn't exactly a 'people person' to start with. Cyrus wished he had more time to study Waterford's profile. It would hold the key to making a successful approach. But there wasn't time. He was literally being pointed at the door before getting a shove in the same direction.

"You'll be meeting with Lacy Osbourne from the D.O.D.," Boone said. "She's been stuck doing the background checks on the potential candidates. We've backstopped your credentials. You've got all the necessary clearances, and you'll be happy to know that you aced the background checks. Just use your primary legend, and you'll be set."

He took a breather. "Just one small change," Boone clarified. "This time around, Cyrus Cooper is twenty-six years old. Adding a few years to your resume looks far more credible on paper."

"You don't think it's possible for a twenty year old to have a top level security clearance?"

Boone rolled his eyes. "You just like hearing that you're special. I got news for you kid—it's not a *good* kind of special."

Cyrus laughed. "You're getting cranky in your old age." Then he returned to business. "Lacy Osbourne," Cyrus repeated. "Check."

Cyrus stepped from the town car and into the driving rain. He flipped open an umbrella as he marched up the wide stone steps. A sidewalk led through dense flowerbeds and ended at the wide front porch of the old plantation mansion. As he walked up the short set of steps leading to the front door, Cyrus couldn't help but marvel at the towering granite columns that supported the roof three stories above. The estate didn't belong to Waterford, he knew; it was actually owned by some grizzled old senator. Was the location chosen to impress applicants? No. Most likely, Cyrus thought, it was chosen as some less than subtle form of intimidation. She knew important people, thereby implying that she had clout.

The idea didn't improve Cyrus's developing opinion of Gertrude Waterford. She was already trying to assert dominance by pulling such strings for something as trivial as an interview.

"Sound check?" Cyrus said quietly to himself as he walked across the expansive porch.

"Reading you loud and clear," Boone said to him through the tiny two-way communication device that was set deep in Cyrus's ear canal. "Good luck."

A massive pair of dark oak French doors parted as he stepped near. A man in a tuxedo and tails stood beside the open door and greeted him by name before leading him inside.

Chapter 6

Hennings, South Carolina
7:52 a.m.

Shuffling a stack of folders on the end of the dining room table, Lacy Osbourne realized that her nerves were already shot, and she wasn't anywhere near 9 a.m.. She glanced at the Cellini Cestello Rolex on her small wrist and contemplated, for the third time, whether she had time to grab a cup of coffee before her next appointment.

No, she'd better not. The next poor sucker was due to reach the gallows at 8 a.m. on the dot. If she wasn't there to greet him, he would fail the interview before ever making it through the drawing room door. Not that it mattered, she realized. The first two applicants of the morning had been summarily dismissed before making it past the opening pleasantries.

She added the pair to the eight interviews conducted—perhaps *wrangled* was the better description—the day before, and her pool of prospective assistants was in danger of drying up entirely.

Lacy could already feel the tension headache forming between her temples. At first, she'd found interactions with Gertrude Waterford to be simply frustrating. But the experience had progressed, escalating into the most horrible assignment she'd had in the last ten years; that even included her unfortunate longstanding run as special assistant to an unusually handsy and lecherous Congressman. No, Miss Waterford was her own special kind of hell, Lacy had come to understand. But at least there was light at the end of the long tunnel—her time with the cantankerous old woman would end the minute she was able to locate a suitable assistant for her. At first, it appeared the task was simply beyond her means. Gertrude was relentless, and the single most impatient person Lacy had ever met. While her people skills left much to be desired, the expectations the woman had for her would-be personal assistant defied reason. She had found something unacceptable about each and every applicant, two of them before they'd even managed to speak a word.

A simple cup of coffee seemed so appealing just then. *No,* Lacy thought as the wisp of a smile touched her lips. *An Irish coffee…* That would definitely go further toward curing her woes.

The sound of a man clearing his throat brought Lacy from her musings. She looked up to find a young man in a suit and tie standing on the opposite side of the wide dining room table. He offered a warm smile, then slipped his folded umbrella beneath one arm and extended his hand. "Missus Osbourne? I'm Cyrus Cooper."

Lacy quickly rose and rounded the end of the table to shake his hand. "Mister Cooper! Right on time. That's fantastic. Can I take your umbrella?"

With a swift shift of his free hand, Cyrus dropped the umbrella from under his left arm and caught it in his left hand. His motion slowed and the smile on his face darkened as he offered it to her. "The doorman offered to take it, but then said something about how I might prefer to keep it for my own protection."

Lacy sputtered, stifling an unexpected laugh. She'd been at the residence for three straight days. In that time she'd rarely heard Hamilton speak, let alone make a joke at his employer's expense.

"Don't worry," she said as she set the umbrella aside. "I'll protect you."

* * *

Lacy was a petite woman in her late thirties with delicate features and freckles on her cheeks that had never faded in her adulthood. She wore a dark pantsuit and had long blonde hair draped over one shoulder. The tinge of darkness that had begun to form under her eyes hinted that the long hours and stress of her latest assignment were getting the better of her. Judging by the size of the rock that constituted her wedding ring, Cyrus suspected that she didn't really need to work and wondered if her most recent undertaking was making her reconsider her position. Then again, Cyrus knew what others didn't. Lacy Osbourne worked for the Department of Defense, and not for Gertrude Waterford. However, she'd been stuck with this assignment. She would be out the door as soon as the woman's assistant had been selected.

"Protect him from what?" a harsh voice snapped from beyond the door to Cyrus's left.

Lacy's eyes went large at the sound of the gravely, but feminine voice. She looked as though she might freeze up in the pressure of the moment. "Ah—Miss Waterford, may I present Mister Cyrus Cooper?"

Speaking through the same empty door way off to the side, Lacy seemed unsure how to direct the conversation. Still, given her obvious level of intimidation, Cyrus was impressed with her ability to redirect the conversation.

What could only be described as a disgruntled huff sounded

from just beyond the threshold. "Send him away," Gertrude Waterford snapped. "He's late. I told you before, I'll not abide tardiness."

While the color left Lacy's face in the timespan of a breath, Cyrus also noted that the woman wasn't at all surprised. Still, being dismissed so easily wouldn't do.

"I beg your pardon, Miss Waterford," Cyrus said in a respectful but confident tone. "Perhaps you would permit me to properly calibrate your timepieces. In point of fact, I'm actually three minutes early."

Cyrus's words were met with complete and total silence. Lacy's saucer-shaped eyes shot him a look that announced his grievous error would come with consequences. She looked like she wanted to say something, but the words seemed lodged in her throat.

Finally the old woman stepped through the doorway and entered the room for the first time. She stood five foot five, maybe five foot six at most. It was difficult to tell with the slight hunch that had settled into her back with the passage of time. But even at seventy-four, she still had a thick head of cotton white hair that fell just short of her shoulders. A broad set of bifocals were perched halfway down her nose, and she glared at Cyrus through sharp, observant eyes. The deep set wrinkles of her face were further exaggerated by the venomous scowl she was casting in his direction.

"You mean to say that I can't tell time?" Gertrude Waterford said in almost a growl. Every word seemed bathed in vitriol.

Meeting her gaze, Cyrus offered a confident smile and refused to cower in response. "Not at all, Ma'am. But, as I understand it, you're in need of a personal assistant. Maintaining your schedule, your calendar…these are a must. Therefore, the precision of the timepieces in your home would seem to fall solidly within the parameters of responsibilities for such a position. A position that is currently vacant," he explained. "Which would explain why your clock is running fast at the moment."

Trying to keep his tone affable and professional, he continued, "Not to worry, though. I'm here and I'm more than happy to interview for the position."

For several long moments, Gertrude just stared at him. So did Lacy, for that matter.

"That's alright," Gertrude said at last. Her voice had become calm but still lacked anything that even remotely resembled warmth. "This concludes your interview."

She turned to Lacy, seemingly making a point of turning away from Cyrus. "What time is the next applicant due?" The harsh tone had returned to her voice.

Cyrus heard Boone's voice in the earbud nested deep inside his ear. It allowed Boone to speak to him and was equipped with bone conductive microphone technology that essentially used the wearer's skeleton as the microphone, picking up every sound in the room. Boone had heard everything that just happened.

"Dammit," Boone swore. "We've lost her! And in record time, too."

Stepping forward, Cyrus cleared his throat. "Excuse me, Miss Waterford. I would appreciate some explanation. What's the problem here? You haven't even bothered with an interview."

Gertrude turned slowly to face Cyrus. When her eyes fell back upon him, he realized that he was about to suffer the full brunt of the woman's fury. At the very least he might gain some insight into the discomfort Lacy had suffered through, he reasoned.

"No," Gertrude said calmly in spite of the anger found in her glare. "You've been interviewed, and I've found you wanting. You're not up to the job, young man. Put simply, I just don't like you."

The gentleness of the woman's delivery was chilling. Between her menacing glare and her harsh words, she couldn't have worked harder to hurt someone's feelings if she tried.

"I see," Cyrus said. His disappointment was clear, even in those two words. "You find men intimidating. I understand. But you should make that sort of thing clear for Missus Osbourne. I think it would make it much easier to find a suitable—"

"Intimidating?" Gertrude sputtered. She seemed ready to froth at the mouth with indignation. "Did you just say *intimidating!*"

"Yes. I'm sorry, I'll speak up the next time," Cyrus said with crisp, bell-like enunciation. "I apologize. I didn't realize you were hard of hearing."

The old woman's eyes virtually blazed with electricity, and her pale complexion began to turn pink. When she took two steps in his direction, Cyrus noticed that she leaned upon a cane that was wrapped in the white knuckled grip of her right hand. He hadn't seen it before because she had taken pains to keep it from his sight line once she had entered the room.

"First of all," she snarled, "I don't find you the least bit intimidating. Rude, intrusive, overbearing, and disrespectful— but it will take something much more threatening than you to intimidate me!" Her chin raised in the air. "In addition, I can assure you my hearing is perfectly fine, Goddammit." That last word was muttered, as if chastising herself for Cyrus being right.

Behind the huffing form of Gertrude Waterford stood Lacy;

she had a hand clamped over her mouth and was watching the acidic display in abject horror.

The silence that followed Gertrude's outburst was almost as unsettling as the outburst itself. For the first few long moments, the old woman glared at Cyrus. She seemed intent on staring him down, as if she were some schoolyard bully. But when he returned her gaze with one that reflected neither anger nor discomfort at what had just happened, he saw her eyes finally shift and fall to the floor.

She stared at his feet for nearly thirty seconds. "I find you unsettling," she said at last. The venom had disappeared from her voice, and she suddenly sounded very tired.

"It's been a long time since anyone has stood up to me," she said. Her eyes rose once more to meet his. "To be honest, I don't know if they find my accomplishments disquieting, my age, or perhaps just my demeanor. But you've got backbone. Are you sure you'd be satisfied just being someone's assistant? You seem like you're made of sterner stuff."

"Someone's assistant?" Cyrus said with a curious smile. "Not on your life. But you're hardly just *someone*. You've got four PHD's, a Nobel Prize, and you've been on a first name basis with some of the greatest minds in recent history. I fully expect to get more out of working for you than you will ever get from me," he grinned.

The old woman smiled. "I think he's trying to schmooze me," she said over her shoulder to Lacy.

Lacy, however, just looked back at Cyrus with her mouth agape.

"Sorry, I've never been a schmoozer," Cyrus admitted. "But of all the things you just listed, I'm pretty sure you missed the *real* reason people find you intimating."

Gertrude looked back at him and waited for an explanation.

Cyrus shrugged. "Well, you kind of come off like a mean old lady when you want to."

A hearty laugh burst from Gertrude Waterford's mouth. Cyrus saw the elderly woman's frame rock hard on the support of her cane with the impromptu outburst, and while his first instinct was to offer her support, from what he'd just learned of the woman, she would see that as a slight.

He left her to laugh, and in a moment, she steadied herself. For the first time, a true and honest smile spread across the woman's face. "Alright. You're hired. But be warned—Missus Osbourne, here, may want to bear your children out of gratitude."

She turned to Lacy, who still looked uncomfortable with all she'd just witnessed. "You've been very patient with an unpleasant old woman," Gertrude said. "But I appreciate your efforts, truly. You finally found one I didn't have to throw back."

In an odd display of respect, and possibly support, Gertrude shook Lacy's hand before shuffling off into the next room.

As soon as she was gone, Lacy stepped closer to Cyrus and only dared to whisper the words that were on her mind. "I don't know how you did that, but I can't thank you enough. I just hope you know what you've gotten yourself into."

Boone's voice echoed in Cyrus's ear only a breath later. "You're something else, kid. Good work. *Now the real fun starts.*"

Chapter 7

The Templeton Tower Building
Hennings, South Carolina
8:11 a.m.

Ashley was just pulling her crimson hair into a ponytail as she walked into the sitting room of her condo. Glancing at the clock on the wall, she was relieved that there was still time to spare. There was an online conference call scheduled for 9 a.m., which meant she had plenty of time to open up her laptop and launch Skype before the meeting began. Stopping in front of the sliding glass door on the north wall, she slid the vertical blinds aside and felt the warmth of the morning sun as the room filled with natural light. A massive floor-to-ceiling bookcase consumed the entire east wall of the open plan apartment. It stretched from the corner of the north wall and ended just short of the breakfast counter that marked the boundary of the kitchen.

Drawn by the smell of the morning's freshly brewed coffee, the kitchen was Ashley's next stop. She poured a cup, added two cubes of sugar and stirred the thick blend, while looking back across the apartment and out through the glass doors. It was a bright sunny morning, and she was contemplating the merits of participating in the teleconference from the patio.

There were those who would've harshly criticized Ashley's

lifestyle. At twenty-four years of age, she lived on the sixth floor of a high security apartment building in the middle of the city's downtown. No close friends remained in her life, and she seldom left the apartment. Still, she was no shut-in. Working a full time job from the comfort of her own home, she was a technical editor for a company specializing in the documentation for industrial products. Basically, she was responsible for the accuracy of the documentation that was included with high-end medical and scientific research equipment. It was an ideal vocation for someone with her special needs. She could work in the privacy and seclusion of her home, consulting with professional contacts and using her laptop as a communications buffer. The web, email, Skype, and instant messenger were the tools that made her work possible. As far as the people she worked with were concerned, most didn't even know what city she lived in, let alone that she rarely left her home.

It was a beautiful day. *The patio it is*, Ashley decided. She collected her laptop from the table at the end of the sofa and headed outside. The moment her bare feet met the cool tile of the patio, she knew she'd made the right decision. Placing her MacBook on the wrought iron table, she walked to the edge of the balcony with coffee cup in hand.

The Templeton Tower Building wasn't a skyscraper, by any means. But in Hennings, South Carolina, even the tallest buildings in downtown didn't climb much higher than five floors—which basically meant that the view from her sixth floor balcony was impressive. She could look out over downtown without the rest of the city looking in on her.

Leaving her coffee on the table beside her computer, Ashley glanced at her watch once more. Deciding that she should make final preparations, she headed back inside. Her current work in progress was the literature accompanying a next generation DNA sequencer. And while she found the documentation portion of her work to be dry and boring, chances to play with cutting edge hardware like the sequencer were enough to keep things interesting. Sure, she was only proofing the technical literature, but it was interesting because it hinted at what was happening on the forefront of science. While others could read all day about how something was supposed to work in theory, she immersed herself in the marrow of these high-tech devices and how they actually functioned.

Realizing that today's conference call was a *video* Skype, Ashley stepped in front of a mirror to give herself a critical glance. It wasn't often that she had to worry about making herself presentable, but certain situations were an exception. Not that she was dressed much different most days. On a typical day she donned t-shirt and jeans, or perhaps a sweater depending on the weather. Today it was a dark blouse and matching slacks—and bare feet as usual. She enjoyed the feel of her home's hardwood floors beneath her naked feet. It was a sensation that never got old.

At five-foot-six, Ashley still maintained the same trim 110 pound figure that she had in her teens. Since she wasn't one to leave the house, her daily exercise routine involved alternating between a treadmill and a stationary bike. And although she could be technically classified as a shut-in, she had a personal routine that was well suited for her lifestyle. She was always up with the sunrise for an hour-long workout and a shower before breakfast. Then, an eight-hour workday followed during the week. Weekends started the same way, but in place of work she often read or worked on one of several hobbies.

The only regular person–to-person contact she had was with her grandmother, who she saw at least a couple of times a week.

Aside from her grandmother, she had only her brother. He had been unusually absent though, in recent months.

The few close friendships she'd maintained throughout school had somehow fizzled in the years since graduation. It was to be expected, she realized. It had only ever been a matter of time. She'd never had the type of friends other people did. Given her condition, it was simply impossible. On the outside she was by all rights a very attractive young woman. Had it not been for her affliction, she would've been the same as any other pretty twenty-something woman living in the city. But she'd never been normal. And while her grandmother called it a gift, Ashley had never considered the ability to hear the thoughts of others to be anything but a disorder.

Chapter 8

The Feedmount Building
Hennings, South Carolina
5:22 p.m.

A suit and tie was about as far from his daily wardrobe as he could get, but Cyrus had settled into a routine. His first week-and-a-half had passed without incident. With his responsibilities limited to screening phone calls and managing the few appointments which constituted Gertrude Waterford's calendar, he was beginning to think that the security clearance requirements were in place more to appease Waterford's ego than anything else. So far, nothing he had seen or heard warranted discretion beyond that of a garden-variety office temp.

Still, Cyrus couldn't shake the feeling that Gertrude was continuing to vet him in some way. Certainly nothing challenging had been sent his way, and there was an undeniable feeling that he was being watched. Maybe not directly, but he knew he was being monitored—which mattered little since he had no intention of lowering his guard.

Gertrude Waterford's office was on the third floor of the Feedmount Building in downtown Hennings, South Carolina. Though Hennings was a small city by many measures, it did manage to boast a highly regarded science and technology center that had grown to encompass the majority of five square blocks near the center of downtown. The Feedmount Building was the city's second tallest, boasting sixteen floors.

Sitting at a wide desk immediately outside the pair of French doors that led to Waterford's office, Cyrus could easily overhear any conversation she had on the phone. Interestingly, she seemed to prefer Internet based phone and video conferences whenever possible, choosing to use the speakers and microphone in her iMac in most cases. It worked well for him. Since she never closed the office doors, it made keeping tabs on her that much easier.

Behind him, the wide glass floor-to-ceiling window offered an amazing view of East Dacy Avenue three stories below. A great view, but a potential security issue as well. That was why Cyrus had been forced to sneak into the office on his second night as Waterford's assistant and apply a transparent treatment to the inside of the exterior windows. The result wasn't as good as replacing the windowpanes with fully reinforced bulletproof glass, but it was the next best thing. The treatment added support and stability to even the oversized sheets of glass and would make them impenetrable to anything short of at least the first few rounds as large as 30mm.

Still, for being a week-and-a-half into the job, Cyrus knew that Gertrude was still holding out on him. After all, her specialty was in Applied Neuroscience, and he had yet to hear of any lab or testing group. Her office was all he had seen of her operation. Such compartmentalization proved that she was a cautious, and perhaps paranoid woman. There was a good chance that he wouldn't see where she conducted her actual experiments until he had passed some, as of yet, *unspecified* test. Until that time, he knew that he had to protect a woman who, one, didn't know she was being protected; two, didn't know she was in danger; and, three, didn't trust him any more than she did the mailman or pizza delivery guy.

Waterford walked out of her office and stopped in front of Cyrus's desk. Abandoning the report he'd been typing, he looked up at her expectantly. He'd heard less than usual from the woman over the course of the afternoon and her appearance at his desk was unusual. It was more typical of her to summon him.

"Did the delivery from Wenzeler Labs arrive yet?" Gertrude asked. She pulled the bifocals from her nose and proceeded to clean them with the corner of her cardigan.

"No. I ran the tracking a little while ago. According to FedEx, they are scheduled for delivery tomorrow before 11 a.m." Cyrus could tell she had more on her mind. He had sent her the tracking update when it had come in around noon, so she already knew the status of the delivery just as well as he did.

"Alright," she replied quietly. There was a faraway look in her eye, but it quickly passed, as she slipped the glasses back on and offered a small smile. "I'll be having dinner with my granddaughter this evening," she began. She looked at her wristwatch as if trying to make a decision.

"No problem," Cyrus offered. "Where would you like me to make the reservation?"

Gertrude looked up again with question in her eyes. "Oh, no. No reservation for tonight. Actually, she will be making dinner. She asked that you join us. I'm sorry for the short notice."

Though Cyrus did his best to hide his surprise, he must not have been successful. After their chilling introduction, Gertrude had become significantly more civil in her interactions with Cyrus. Still, he would hardly call the woman friendly. The invitation to dinner caught him entirely off-guard.

"If it's a problem," Gertrude began, "I could phone Ashley. I'm sure we could reschedule for another evening."

"No," Cyrus smiled as he rose from his chair. "No problem at all. I just hate to impose."

"Ashley is interested in meeting you. Since we'll be spending a great deal of time together, I think she wants to know who's looking out for her grandmother. A little over protective, I know, but she's a sweet girl. How could I say no?"

"Absolutely," Cyrus stammered. "That sounds great."

"Splendid. If it's alright with you, we can leave right from the office. Say, six o'clock?"

Chapter 9

Hennings, South Carolina
6:09 p.m.

From her seat in the back of the Lincoln Town Car, Gertrude Waterford watched the city slip quietly past her window. Dusk was already settling over the city streets, and even rush hour wasn't a terrible undertaking in this part of town. Plus, she had the added advantage of her office being only a few miles from her condo.

Still, the last week-and-a-half had been an inconvenience. She wasn't accustomed to spending nearly as much time in the office, preferring to spend the majority of it at the lab. All the same, she knew better than to rush things. She didn't dare bring her new assistant so deep into the fold too quickly. Certainly, all of his clearances and references had checked out. But given her past experience, it was of critical importance not to move too quickly. Even taking the boy to see her granddaughter, Ashley, was a calculated risk. But so far everything she'd seen of the young man was encouraging. Provided that he was everything he seemed to be, she should be able to take the next step and finally get back to work.

That she needed an assistant at all was a concession Gertrude had been slow in coming to terms with. While her mind was as sharp and agile as ever, her body simply wasn't what it had once been. It seemed that the years had finally caught up with her. But having the extra hand would be a good thing, she realized, provided that her latest round of tests went as well in the trial stage as they had in the simulations.

No, she reminded herself. *One thing at a time.* They needed to get through dinner first. She had to be certain that young Cyrus Cooper was really the fledgling ladder climber that he appeared to be. Given his age, Gertrude couldn't imagine him as anything else. Still, it was a strange world and, as often as not, people were not who or what they appeared. That's where Ashley came in. If the boy was anything less than what he'd claimed, Ashley would know it in short order. Her darling granddaughter was also her secret weapon, her ace in the hole, in so many ways.

…And her single greatest accomplishment.

"Why don't you pull over at this little place up ahead," Gertrude said to Cyrus from the backseat. "I want to pick up a bottle of wine for tonight."

Looking up from the steering wheel, Cyrus caught her eye in the rearview mirror. "Costello's Market?" he clarified.

She smiled. The boy didn't waste time or words. It was a precision she could appreciate. And he'd proven himself to have guts. She truly hoped he was on the level. "Yes, that would be perfect."

A moment later, the town car slipped into a recently vacated spot along the crowded curb. Cyrus turned in his seat and looked back at her. "What would you like? I'll run in."

"How about a nice bottle of red?"

The words were no sooner out of her mouth when she saw confusion in his eyes. Or, perhaps, indecision.

"Ah, I'm sorry, Ma'am. When it comes to wine, I'm out of my depth. I can tell the difference between red and white without someone holding my hand, but knowing what's good and what's not? *Not so much.* To be honest, I sort of just cheat and associate the quality with the price."

Gertrude felt a sputtering laugh escape her lips before she had a chance to rein it in. She instantly felt regretful for it, and that sensation struck her as odd. To the best of her knowledge, the only time she'd ever been gentle or anything less than entirely transparent in expressing her opinions was with Ashley. But Ashley was family. Could it be that she was coming to respect this young man? It wasn't like her at all.

Oh, I do hope this one turns out to be on the level, she thought.

"I'm sorry," Gertrude offered with some chagrin. "It's just that most people go to great lengths to offer opinions on wine. It's all very pretentious. I've always suspected that in a blind taste test every one of them would be wrong as often as they were right. Your quip about the price, sadly, is how many of them ultimately make their selections." She explained. "So, I apologize for laughing."

Cyrus offered a grin, not at all embarrassed by her outburst. "It would be a mistake to walk in there and pretend I know what I'm doing," he admitted. "And it would be an even bigger problem if you and your granddaughter were stuck drinking skunk wine all night."

Gertrude found herself unable to deny his simple, practical logic.

"If you can tell me what to look for, I'm sure I'll be fine," Cyrus said.

Looking out her window, Gertrude considered the selection of the small corner market. "It's hard to say what they'll have," she decided. "It would be best if I come along."

Chapter 10

Costello's Market
Hennings, South Carolina
6:16 p.m.

After helping Gertrude Waterford exit the rear passenger side, Cyrus held the door as she entered the small corner market. There wasn't much to the place. It was perhaps a thousand square feet located on the ground level of the three story building that paralleled one of the city's central boulevards. Though clearly a small time establishment, the tile floors were clean and had an impressive shine. The shelves of the shop were covered with the basic sundries when it came to groceries, tobaccos, canned and jarred staples, and other dried goods. And along the back wall, Cyrus saw what appeared to be a rather impressive selection of wine arranged across a lattice-like series of interlocking shelves that stretched nearly to the ceiling.

The shop might be small, but it was clearly well maintained. Likely an establishment run by a family who took great pride in what they had and strived to make the most of it. A short, elderly man of Mediterranean descent stood behind the counter near the cash register, as Cyrus and Gertrude passed through the front door. The clerk offered a warm smile and a silent but friendly nod when Cyrus said "hello."

Making their way through the shop took only a short time, but Cyrus could tell by Gertrude's short steps and the way she leaned more heavily on the cane that she was tired. It also meant that dinner with her granddaughter must be important to her. In the nearly two weeks he'd chauffeured the woman, she'd never gone anywhere but home after a day at her office. She was clearly suffering the effects of a long day.

Cyrus wished he knew more about wine. He could've saved her the trouble of making the trip into the market for something so trivial.

They reached the wine racks and Gertrude began her selection process when the chime on the front door sounded. They'd been the only customers when they'd walked in, and Cyrus was glad to know that the impressive little shop wasn't suffering for traffic as he'd first thought.

Judging by the look of approval in the old woman's eyes and the time she was taking to select a bottle of wine, Cyrus realized that Gertrude was also impressed with the quality of the selection. Stepping back, he allowed her more room as she shimmied slowly back and forth in an effort to narrow her options.

The hair on the back of Cyrus's neck began to prickle. It was a curious sensation, but one he was all too familiar with. His eyes first moved to Gertrude, but she was alright—so focused on the rack of wine that a bus could crash through the front of the store without even drawing her attention. Moving on, Cyrus turned; looking over the tops of the short shelves, he was surprised to find the old man missing from his place at the cash register.

Moving quickly down the aisle, Cyrus reached the end and gained an angle that brought him a clear view of the front counter. The old man lay slumped across it, the small hat he'd been wearing was knocked from the top of his head.

Cyrus felt his heart hammer and his adrenaline surge as he took a step back into the cover of the aisle, only to stop short as he felt the unmistakable sense of cold metal being pressed against the back of his neck.

"Not another step," the voice threatened from behind him.

In an unnecessarily slow manner, Cyrus brought his hands up and held them at his sides. "It's okay," he said calmly. "We don't want any trouble. I'm going to turn around now, very slowly. And then I'll give you my wallet."

Following through on his promises, Cyrus completed his turn and came face-to-face with a wide shouldered man in a black ski mask. The man held a pump action shotgun with a sawed-off barrel. It was raised up to meet Cyrus's eye level, leaving him to look directly down its darkened muzzle.

A second gunman was standing along the back wall, holding the end of a chrome Beretta 92FS semi auto to Gertrude Waterford's head. The second man was shorter; all Cyrus could make out was the ski mask and his upraised gun over the top of the shelves that separated them.

The entire situation frustrated Cyrus instantly. That the two gunmen had gotten the drop on him at all was obviously the first problem. Then, there was the question of what to do about it. If he made a move, what would that do to his cover with Waterford? Would it be blown? There was also the question of what these punks were actually doing in the store in the first place. If they really were punks, they would be focusing on the cash register. But so far, they seemed interested in anything but the cash. They'd taken out the old man at the counter without letting him raise even the hint of an alarm. But rather than grab the money and run, they'd gone out of their way to come after him and Waterford at the back of the store.

Doing the math, Cyrus didn't like the way things were adding up. He didn't think these two were there to rob the store. It might've been an easy assumption with the ski masks and the guns. Especially that chromed out Beretta, he realized. He hated those things with a passion. The 92FS was a solid weapon alright, but *chrome*? He was pretty sure those were only ever made for the movies. Any time he saw one in real life, he felt the urge to slap the owner upside the head. What was the point of a chrome-plated gun?

So while the two men in masks looked the part of street thugs, right down to their choice in weapons, their disregard for the cash register told a different story. Gertrude Waterford seemed the more likely target.

Slowly and deliberately, Cyrus reached into his inside jacket pocket and retrieved his wallet. He held it up between two fingers and watched the reaction in the gunman's eyes. When he failed to focus on the wallet the answer was simple; Cyrus knew he was dealing with a professional. And that changed everything.

The man with the shotgun reached out and grabbed Cyrus by the collar. Dragging him to the end of the aisle, he shoved him up against the rack of wine.

Cyrus looked over at Gertrude who was standing less than two feet away with a bottle of wine locked in the white knuckled grip of both hands.

"You alright, Missus Waterford?" Cyrus asked in a tone intended to inspire confidence.

When she didn't respond, he repeated the question.

Her eyes snapped into focus and swiveled to meet his. "I... I don't know," she admitted in a scared, hollow voice.

"Shut up!" the man with the shotgun ordered, giving Cyrus a painful poke in the ribs with the barrel of the gun.

Cyrus looked at the wine bottle that Gertrude held in her hands. "Is that what you decided on?" he asked. "Did you find something good, or did you just pick based on the price?"

A small smile spread across Gertrude's lips. Maybe it was because of the joke, or maybe the absurdity of the circumstances under which he was making it—either way, it didn't matter. The shorter gunman, the one holding the chrome Beretta to Waterford's head, took exception to Cyrus's casual nature and decided to intervene. He turned the gun and pointed it at Cyrus. That was good; getting the gun away from Gertrude's head was Cyrus's goal.

At the same time the Beretta was being poked at him from one direction, the shotgun was coming at him from the other. Grabbing the pump action handle of the shotgun and stepping back, Cyrus pressed himself tightly against the rack of wine behind him. Simultaneously, he pulled on the shotgun as it was being pushed in his direction. It slipped past his ribs, and he yanked it further.

The shotgun discharged.

The moment the gunman pulled the trigger, Cyrus was already pushing the Beretta aside with his free hand. As the shotgun blast slipped past Cyrus with a thunderous roar, the Beretta rocked and discharged a round that flew uselessly across the store. Cyrus pulled the 9mm from the smaller man's hand and watched the lifeless body skid across the floor. He'd caught the full force of the shotgun blast dead center in the chest.

All of this quick action left Cyrus holding the chrome Beretta 9mm. Lashing out with a brutal front kick, Cyrus sent the man with the shotgun staggering backwards. The shotgun slipped from the man's grip as his arms windmilled for balance as he went flying onto his back.

The moment the shotgun struck the floor, Cyrus placed one

foot atop the weapon. It was his way of accounting for the gun while keeping the sights of the 9mm trained on the man he'd just kicked.

"Don't move," Cyrus warned, "Just stay down."

It didn't matter. Cyrus knew were calculations running through the man's mind. The resulting decision was obvious when it flashed in his assailant's eyes. Covered by the ski mask, Cyrus didn't need to see the man's face to know what was about to happen. Still, he let it come. If only for the resulting police report and an improved chance at smoothing things over with Waterford after it was over.

The gunman reached into a holster secured around his ankle and pulled free a snub nosed .38. "Gun!" Cyrus shouted. He stepped between the gunman on the floor and Gertrude Waterford, who was a few feet behind him.

A single gunshot exploded inside the confines of the small market. The weapon's report echoed off of the cinderblock walls and stung Cyrus's ears.

Cyrus felt a hand on his shoulder and turned to see Gertrude. Somewhere along the way she had dropped her cane but somehow managed to hold on to her bottle of wine.

"Are you alright?" she asked. Her voice was a ghostly whisper as she looked around him and saw the last gunman's body sprawled across the floor, his head split open like a gruesome melon.

"Fine. How about you?"

She offered only a slow but affirmative nod. Her face was pale and she was taking short breaths but she didn't seem hurt. "I think we're going to be late for dinner."

Cyrus smiled. "Yeah… Let's find you a place to sit while I dial 911. Maybe after that, you can call your granddaughter and see about rescheduling."

Chapter 11

The Templeton Tower Building
Hennings, South Carolina
10:04 p.m.

After leaving the town car in the parking garage, Cyrus followed Gertrude Waterford to the main elevator. He was surprised when the woman pressed the button for the 6th floor, since her condo was on ten.

The old woman caught his questioning glance and offered a sly smile. "You're still hungry, aren't you?"

He nodded. "But what's on six?"

"Ashley's apartment, of course." She watched the elevator's floor indicator click from one level to the next. "You're not going to let a little thing like armed robbery interfere with our dinner plans, are you?"

A sense of humor wasn't among Gertrude's many talents. A generous man would describe it as dry, but Cyrus was reasonably certain she was making a joke.

Reasonably certain.

"It's just—" He didn't know where to begin. They'd finished an extensive round of questioning at the hands of one of the police department's senior detectives only twenty minutes prior. That Gertrude would want nothing more than to go home and retire for the night seemed a certainty. Apparently, he'd been wrong. He settled for a change of subject. "Your granddaughter lives in your building?"

At least that explained why he was still carrying the bottle of wine. It was the same bottle Gertrude had clutched throughout the entire harrowing experience at the corner market. She'd made her selection before things had gone *wonky*, as she put it, and was going to drink it if it was the last thing she did.

The old woman smirked. "And why not? I own it."

Cyrus grinned. "The whole building? I'm sorry. You're full of surprises."

He wasn't at all surprised, in truth. The background information provided by the Coalition's research department, along with the rest of the case files, had thoroughly documented nearly every aspect of Gertrude Waterford's life. That included her financial and real estate holdings, as well as her family tree and business contacts made over the last twenty years.

"That's funny," she commented as the elevator doors slid open. "I was going to say the same thing about you. Your behavior tonight wasn't what I would call..." she searched for the proper word. "Typical? At least, given the unusual circumstances."

Cyrus followed her from the elevator. "It's that fight or flight response, I guess," he said dismissively. "I've never really been one for flight."

The apartments on the 6th floor must've been smaller than those on the 10th. The 10th floor was split in half, bisecting the entire level into a pair of condo units. But on the 6th, the hallway around Cyrus contained four doors, two on either end of the hall that more or less faced each other. These four apartments occupied the entirety of the 6th.

And Gertrude owned the entire building.

Taking the lead, Gertrude directed them to the end of the hall where she struck the old fashioned door knocker twice against the door of unit 601, before immediately turning the knob and stepping inside.

The apartment was breathtaking in its open, spacious charm. Cyrus was quickly enamored by the wide sweeping floor plan and the way he could literally see from one end of the place to the other. There was a small formal dining area on the left that was segregated by only a half height wall. To the right, was a comfortable kitchen with granite countertops and stainless steel fixtures. Beyond that, the rest of the apartment opened up into an expansive sitting area with large comfortable couches and overstuffed armchairs. A small flat screen television decorated the wall to the left, while the right was home to a floor-to-ceiling bookshelf that started at the edge of the kitchen and stretched all the way to the rear wall of the apartment. It was covered with hundreds, maybe thousands of books of every color and size.

"I'll be right out," a woman's voice called from a doorway off to the left, past the TV.

"You can put that on the counter," Gertrude told Cyrus, motioning vaguely in the direction of the kitchen. She continued on to the sitting area and promptly deposited herself onto the sofa.

Cyrus placed the wine bottle beside the sink and looked out across the counter into the sitting room. He could tell Gertrude was exhausted, but couldn't understand why she insisted on keeping the dinner engagement after all that had happened.

The police had descended on the corner market within minutes of the conflict's resolution. It seemed that gunshots did not go unreported in that particular part of town, and the response time for emergency services was nothing short of impressive. Of course, by the time they'd arrived, the two gunmen were long past saving.

The questioning that followed the incident wasn't as accusatory as Cyrus originally feared. While he had complete confidence that his credentials would stand up to scrutiny as well as any background check that the local police cared to conduct, it was Gertrude Waterford who worried him the most. She was an experienced, intelligent woman. It was unlikely that she would simply overlook the way he'd dealt with the night's events. In protecting her, he might have already compromised his cover. And while he expected as much to happen at some point, it was crucial that he gain her confidence before that time came.

The store clerk turned out to be alright, if one rated a concussion preferable to a gunshot wound. He was taken to the nearest emergency room by ambulance and was expected to make a full recovery. As close as they could figure, he'd been clubbed on the head by one of the gunman before they'd advanced on Gertrude and Cyrus.

Police detectives had asked the expected questions about the gunmen, and the store's security system went a long way toward answering those questions to everyone's satisfaction. While the surveillance cameras were not ideally positioned to capture all that had transpired, what was shown made it obvious that Cyrus had acted in self-defense. The detective's conclusion was that Cyrus and Gertrude were lucky to be alive. The would-be crooks were obviously rank amateurs who wouldn't be missed.

Cyrus, however, was less optimistic about the 'amateurish' behavior of the night's events. If the gunmen had been there to rob the store, they would've shown at least some interest in the cash register. But the surveillance video had clearly shown the men walking through the front door and striking the clerk before making a beeline straight for them. There'd been no one else in the store, Cyrus knew. Those men hadn't been there to rob the place—they were there for Gertrude and Gertrude only. Such a brazen, public attack was unsettling, and it left Cyrus to question what might come next.

The sound of footsteps across the hardwood floor drew Cyrus's attention. He looked up as Ashley Waterford entered the room. Though he had read her file and already knew a great deal about her, he was still unprepared for the striking young woman who virtually glided across the room on bare feet. She was dressed simply in a dark blue sweater and jeans, but the way her pale porcelain skin was contrasted against soft layers of ruby red hair…well, the effect made his heart beat just a little bit faster. The welcoming smile on her face was amplified by the warm, accepting glint in her eyes. There was something truly remarkable about her, Cyrus realized. She had a presence that brought warmth to the room.

Stepping through the doorway of the kitchen, Cyrus walked slowly into the sitting room. Gertrude pulled herself to her feet, leveraging her cane to pull Ashley into a weary, yet tight, embrace.

"Oh, my dear. You're a sight for tired eyes," Gertrude said in a voice more tender than Cyrus had ever heard from the woman.

"Gram," Ashley said in a near whisper. "Are you sure you're alright?"

"Just fine—just fine. Let me introduce you to my new assistant, Cyrus Cooper."

Stepping forward, Cyrus extended his hand. She smiled as she shook it. "Gram said you were her guardian angel tonight," she said. "I can't tell you how pleased I am to meet you."

When her eyes met his, Cyrus was struck by their iridescent

quality and the way they shimmered when they fell on him. Even in the dimly lit room, they seemed to radiate the most striking green he'd ever seen. He became suddenly very aware of the unusual warmth of her small hand in his and felt his own smile brightening.

Cyrus knew that Gertrude had made a call from the convenience store while he was being questioned by detectives. Apparently that call had been to Ashley.

"Not at all," he said, more quietly than he intended. He was still taken aback by her presence. "Actually, she wouldn't have been there at all if I knew a damn thing about wine."

That brought a genuine laugh from Gertrude, one that was shared by Ashley. "I'm sure you're exaggerating," Ashley said.

"In point of fact, no, he's not," Gertrude interjected. "He's being entirely honest. He doesn't know a damn thing about wine. Of that, you can be sure. But there's hope for him. From what I've seen over the last week, he's a quick study. I'm sure he could pick it up if he puts his mind to it."

Gertrude looked at her granddaughter. "There's a good chance that even you know more about wine than Cyrus," she chided.

"Ashley's not much of a drinker," she said, sending an amused glance to Cyrus. "It's probably for the better, too. Some of the worst mistakes of my life can be traced back to a bottle of this or that."

There was a mischievous grin on Gertrude's face that Cyrus had never seen before. He was surprised what a different person she had become in the presence of her granddaughter. It was as if she'd been infused with...he searched for the right term...

Personality.

Maybe he was seeing the real Gertrude Waterford for the

first time.

"Oh, Gram. You make yourself out to be a lush. Is that the kind of impression you want to make on your new associate?"

Leaning her cane against the couch, Gertrude shrugged. "It's true. It was a bottle of 1904 Dom Pérignon that led to the conception of your mother. But don't you worry, dear, I moved the Dom to the 'happy mistakes' column the day you came into the world."

Ashley laughed at her grandmother's off-color remark. The iridescence of Ashley's eyes was only amplified by her laugh, and Cyrus realized that if he wasn't careful, he might be caught staring like some love-sick teenager. But there was a radiant quality that hadn't been captured in the dossier provided by Coalition researchers. The paperwork had been stunningly antiseptic in its description of the young woman: five foot six, one hundred ten pounds, red hair and green eyes. That loose description had certainly failed to do her justice.

Knowing just the factual data about her, Cyrus suddenly wanted to know more. She had studied veterinary medicine and graduated with honors but had not yet taken up practice in her chosen field. It hadn't been an issue before, but he was suddenly interested to know why. He wanted to know a lot more, he thought. And surprisingly, he was looking forward to a dinner that he'd previously only dreaded.

"Maybe we should eat," Ashley suggested. "Before Gram makes me blush some more. Plus, we don't need the food getting cold for a second time."

A few minutes later the trio settled around the small dining room table. Reheating the dinner hadn't been a major affair. Ashley was a vegetarian and had prepared a vegetable lasagna for the three of them. While not a vegetarian himself, Cyrus could appreciate the dish, and as far as he could tell, it hadn't suffered a bit for having been put on hold.

The conversation over dinner wasn't unusual given the circumstances. There were questions about where Cyrus went to school and what he'd majored in; talk about what sort of work he'd done after graduation—the various nuts and bolts that were covered in his resume, and the security clearance that Gertrude had no doubt already studied. Still, Cyrus got the distinct impression that his cover story was being fact checked as he spoke. It wasn't anything that would've been obvious to most people, but some areas of conversation felt like a heavily veiled debrief. Nothing as invasive as an interrogation, but there was something going on, Cyrus was sure of it.

At multiple points in the conversation, he found Ashley's eyes on him while he spoke. And while most times her gaze was warm and pleasant, there were also times when he would meet her eye and, just for a second, catch a flash of something…different. It happened often enough that he started to watch for it. Partially to convince himself that he was seeing something different in her persona, partially to understand what was happening in front of him. But each time he caught that look—no…it was more of a feeling that he got from her, it was gone just as quick as it had arrived. It was impossible to nail down, and he questioned whether his mind was playing tricks on him.

He might have written it off as a product of his exhausted mind had it not been for the unusual interest that Gertrude was paying to her granddaughter at certain points during their friendly banter. While he didn't understand what was happening, the times he felt a strange vibe coming off Ashley coincided perfectly with the glare Gertrude was giving the girl.

As odd as it seemed, Cyrus had the strange feeling that Ashley was trying to look deep inside of him in some way. And at those times, Gertrude was extremely interested in what Ashley was seeing.

While he couldn't make sense of any of it, the strange glimpses from Ashley were fleeting. And as disconcerting as those brief moments were, Cyrus still found himself strongly drawn to the young woman. It was an indulgence he didn't often allow himself for a number of reasons. But each time he looked into those emerald eyes and saw the corners of her mouth tuck into a pert little smile, those reasons seemed to fade away into nothingness.

* * *

Pushing the last bites of lasagna around her empty plate, Ashley listened to the conversation. She was surprised and impressed with the way the evening had gone. She'd been dreading the dinner in a way that very few would understand, but it had been a rare exception to past experiences. *An extremely rare exception*, she thought to herself.

Strangely, no matter how hard she focused, she wasn't getting anything from Cyrus. It was a one-of-a-kind experience. She couldn't remember the last time she opened her mind to someone's thoughts and heard nothing at all. On any given day it was all she could do to block out the voices of the world around her, but when she centered herself and focused on one person, she could at least push the cacophony of faceless voices living in the city into a hushed white noise that, although was ever present in the background, could allow her to hear the foremost thoughts of her chosen subject.

Except for Cyrus. Definitely a one-in-a-million experience, but Ashley loved the idea. The uniqueness of it all, and the mystery of such a singular encounter, was intriguing.

But it wouldn't make Gram happy. She was counting on her to tell her what she needed to know about her new assistant.

Ashley was her human lie detector, and until that moment, infallible. But it didn't matter how hard she tried; Cyrus was a blank slate. She could talk to him and listen to him, but without hearing his inner voice, it was like she was missing an entire dimension of his personality.

Everyone had that secret additional dimension, Ashley knew. There were the things that people said and did, and then there were the things they thought. Their thoughts were secrets kept to themselves—the things that went through their minds, but they never acted upon. It was a dimension that made some people frightening. It was also a dimension that made most people impossible for her to tolerate.

It was the reason she'd struggled to make it through veterinary school. And when she finally graduated, she'd been unable to bring herself to take a job in the field. Working with animals had been her passion. They were her refuge and saving grace, because they had no separate voice to share. They didn't think one thing, only to do another. She would've been ideally suited for veterinary work, if not for the pet owners. Dealing with the owners had been nearly unbearable.

And so she held up in her apartment most days, content to stay behind locked doors. The further she could stay away from large groups of people, the better. It might be enough to drive a normal person insane, but her sanctuary was what kept her stable. It was her safe haven from the rest of the world.

"Have you heard anything new from William?" Ashley asked, eager to change the subject.

Gertrude shook her head. "Not a word. But I'm not surprised. You know how those people can be. They don't like their *members* speaking with the outside world."

Seeing Cyrus's quizzical glance at her grandmother's venomous use of the word *members*, coupled with the dramatic rolling of her eyes, Ashley decided that she should explain for his benefit. It wasn't a matter she cared to discuss in front of a stranger, but she wasn't feeling her normal, sheepish self in front of him. Plus, Cyrus would be working closely with her grandmother so the subject was bound to come up sooner or later.

"My brother, William, is part of a…church," Ashley explained. "We don't—"

Gertrude interrupted, her irritation evident. "Calling that group a 'church' does disservice to organized religion as a whole," she grumbled. "And when I say that, bear in mind that I'm a lifelong atheist and no fan of organized religion of any kind. *The Order of Origin?* Please! They attempt to propagate their nonsense by claiming that it's science. It galls me that the federal government recognizes them as a legitimate church at all!"

It was Ashley's turn to roll her eyes. She felt her face warming with embarrassment and wished she could turn back the clock and prevent herself from opening the door to the subject. Against her better judgment, she decided to forge ahead and attempt to salvage her family's dignity in the eyes of their guest.

"My brother joined the church some time back," Ashley went on. "Since then, we've seen less and less of him. It's been over a year since I last spoke with him, actually. At least Gram heard from him a few months back. We know he's alright, even if we don't know where he is or what he's doing."

"The whole thing's an embarrassment," Gertrude persisted.

Ashley shrugged. "He's my twin brother," she said with a smile. "Older only by minutes, but I love him no matter what he's doing. I just want to know that he's alright."

Gertrude cleared her throat. "It seems we've forgotten the

wine. After all the trouble we went through to get it, we shouldn't let it go to waste. Cyrus, would you mind getting the bottle and some glasses from the kitchen?"

It was a blatant attempt to change the subject, and Ashley was happy for it. She and her grandmother had never disagreed on any subject the way they did about William, though they both loved him. Once more, Ashley reminded herself that her grandmother just had more trouble showing affection.

Ashley offered to help with the wine, but Gertrude stopped her.

"Why don't we clear the table for dessert?" Gertrude suggested.

As soon as Cyrus was out of the room, her grandmother turned to her with an expectant gaze. Ashley felt like car stalled on the tracks of a runaway train. While she knew what her grandmother wanted, she didn't know what to tell her. She'd never experienced anything like this before. There was no precedent.

"Well?" Gertrude finally urged when Ashley offered nothing. "What's the verdict? Is he on the level?"

Her heart beating faster, Ashley felt the blood drain from her face. She didn't know what to say or do. Her eyes flicked to the door frame leading to the kitchen and thought about what little she knew about Cyrus. She couldn't Read him the way she could others, but she had a sense of him. It wasn't what her grandmother was asking, but it did have value. She liked his smile, and the way he looked at her. She enjoyed hearing him speak and the way he met her eye and really listened when she spoke. Her pulse quickened each time his gaze lingered an extra moment or two, entangled with hers.

Was that enough to make the decision that her grandmother needed?

"I haven't sensed a single lie from him," Ashley finally admitted. It wasn't the analysis that her grandmother was expecting, but the implication was there just the same.

The old woman took a moment to consider the response. In that time, Ashley felt suddenly terrified that her grandmother would ask her to elaborate. Then what would she say? But when Gertrude sighed and offered a satisfied nod, it seemed good enough for both of them. ...At least, for the moment.

Ashley quickly went about stacking the empty plates, then hoisted the pile and headed for the kitchen. Cyrus had found the appropriate glasses and collected the bottle of wine just in time to meet her in the doorway. Setting the wine aside, he took the stack of dishware from her hands.

"What can I do with this?" he asked.

"Just set everything in the sink," she said with a smile. "I'll take care of it in the morning. It's nothing that can't wait."

"You're sure? I'm fairly skilled with a dish towel, and I'm not afraid to prove it," he joked.

Taking the bottle of wine from the end of the counter, Ashley tipped her head in the direction of the dining room. "Thanks, but I'm far more interested in hearing exactly what happened at the market. Don't think I didn't notice how you both avoided that subject entirely."

Cyrus followed her back to the table. Ashley set about removing the cork from the wine bottle, as he passed around the glasses.

"Oh, just the two glasses, Cyrus," Gertrude said solemnly.

"That's alright, Gram," Ashley smiled. She popped the cork and set the corkscrew aside. "Normally I wouldn't. But given what you went through to get this bottle, I can't pass up the opportunity." She continued, "From what you said on the phone, it sounded like a true close call. You could've been killed. And all for a simple bottle of wine?"

Though she waited patiently, it became apparent to Ashley that neither of them was in a hurry to recount the earlier events of the evening. But when Cyrus made a point of deferring the story to Gertrude, her grandmother finally had no choice.

It took less than ten minutes for Gertrude to explain all that had happened, starting with the moment they walked into the corner market and concluding with the final questions asked by police detectives before they were dismissed for the night.

Ashley paid attention to every detail, afraid to interrupt for fear of missing something. The entire story sounded like something out of a spy novel or an action movie. Still, something didn't sit right with her. She wasn't sure what she was missing, but it felt like a vital part of the story.

Sipping her wine, she considered the sequence of events. If she'd interpreted everything correctly, it seemed that the masked gunmen were more interested in targeting her grandmother and Cyrus than they were in the store's cash register. It was a paranoid concern, but given the death of her grandmother's last assistant, she was even more suspicious.

She decided to speak with her grandmother about the idea later, in private. There was no need to worry Cyrus with the matter. He wasn't even two weeks into his new job, for goodness sake.

"So neither of the robbers survived?" She settled for asking.

Cyrus offered only a sad shake of his head.

"And the world is a better place for it," Gertrude grumbled. "Cyrus saved our lives. There isn't a doubt in my mind."

Ashley smiled. She could see a twinge of regret in Cyrus's eyes and realized for the first time that he had killed two men that very night. *How does someone cope with an experience like that,* she wondered?

"If you don't mind me asking," she said in an awkward, tentative voice. "How did you do it, Cyrus?"

He shook his head. "I'm sorry?"

"Well, to hear Gram tell the story, it sounds like you managed some pretty quick thinking and some even faster footwork. You saved her life, and likely your own in the process. That's not exactly something they teach you in the secretarial pool, is it?"

The words had no sooner left her mouth when Ashley realize how they might be construed as derogatory, or insulting. "I'm sorry," she quickly sputtered. "I mean no offense. It's just very...*unusual.*"

She was relieved to see the smile on his face reflected in his eyes. He hadn't taken the comment as a slight. When she studied his expression, if anything, he looked embarrassed.

"It's not nearly as impressive as Miss Waterford makes—"

"Please, I think you've earned the right to call me Gertrude," Gertrude corrected.

Cyrus smiled, perhaps a bit more awkwardly. "Thank you. Yes, it's not nearly as impressive as Gertrude makes it seem. If anything I went with my gut and got lucky. I don't think any of us really knows what we might do in a situation like that until it happens," he admitted.

Ashley felt her grandmother's eyes on her and knew she wanted her to press the issue. She didn't realize she hadn't been able to hear Cyrus's thoughts, and this was a subject that her grandmother was extremely interested in.

Under normal circumstances, Ashley avoided any type of alcohol for a number of reasons. First, it interfered with her ability to filter the white noise that filled her head at any given moment. If she couldn't manage the voices through her own practices of biofeedback, she would first develop a migraine and then her mental state would quickly deteriorate from there. Second, the few brief experiences she'd had with drinking since finding the optimal doses that constituted her daily medication regimen, had been disconcerting. Her medications had unusual interactions with each other when drinking was added to the mix.

But perhaps most of all, she hated being around people who were drinking. People say and do strange, even foolish things when they have full control of their faculties. But after a few drinks, people become capable of exceptionally foolish things. Those same people, after a few drinks, often begin to think things that, very often, made her entirely uncomfortable. It was also enough to wreck just about every friendship she'd ever had.

Still, her decision to sample her grandmother's wine had been a calculated risk. While she couldn't understand her inability to Read Cyrus, she thought that shifting her perspective a little might offer a new insight into the issue. Perhaps if she had a drink or two—or if he did—it would alter the variables enough for her to get a Read. Her grandmother was counting on her, after all.

It seemed like a rational enough excuse.

In truth, Ashley also found herself disappointed in her inability to enter the young man's mind. Setting aside the fact that she'd wished the ability to leave her entirely just about every day of her life since she'd turned fourteen, this was the first time she had felt disappointment at not being able to utilize it. No, if she were honest with herself, her reasons for wanting to Read Cyrus had nothing to do with her grandmother's needs; they were entirely selfish. She just wanted to know more about him.

So she would need to resort to doing it the old fashioned way—by asking questions. It was a unique experience for her.

Typically, she asked questions only to coax someone's conscious or subconscious mind into moving the information that she needed to the forefront. That wouldn't work here.

"There must be more to it than that," Ashley urged. "Based on Gram's account, you managed to use the robbers' weapons against them. That doesn't happen through blind luck."

She watched Cyrus's eyes as they studied her for several long moments. She had the sense that he was trying to make an important decision. When he was done, his glance moved on to Gertrude and studied her in a similar fashion.

"This is personal," Cyrus said in a quiet voice. "But you have a right to know. I did some work on a personal security detail for a high level diplomat a little while back. I picked up a few things along the way. What happened tonight was sort of a hardwired response. It was the kind of thing they drill into you until you act without thinking—which was all part of my job back then."

Ashley realized that the surprise on her grandmother's face easily mirrored her own. And though she was at a loss for words, her grandmother was not.

"That wasn't in your CV. How do you go from a job like that to being the personal assistant to an elderly neuroscientist?" Gertrude asked. Concern was clear in her voice.

Cyrus shrugged. "After you get shot at a few times, it makes you reconsider your career path," came the simple reply. "There wasn't a very bright future in that line of work. Sooner or later, I was going to get myself killed. So I packed it in and decided I would do what I wanted. And my existing security clearance put me in a unique situation.

"There are a few high-level scientific minds in the U.S. who are making a real difference. Landing a job as an assistant isn't prestigious, but there's more to it. Let me ask you—if you had the chance to go back in time and ride shotgun with Albert Einstein while he did his greatest work, wouldn't you take it? If only to have a front row seat for a show that could effect the lives of future generations?"

He smiled wide. "That's a hell of a thing to participate in, if you ask me. Even if in some minimal, inconsequential way."

Sitting back in her chair, Ashley folded her hands in her lap. She didn't know what to say. She certainly hadn't expected such an explanation.

Gertrude seemed taken aback, too. "Just like that?" she asked in a solemn voice. "You strike me as a resourceful and driven young man. Are you really content to sort my mail, and screen my calls? Surely you're better suited for more important work."

Cyrus stayed with the requisite shrug. "Some contributions have more weight than others," he admitted. "Every day can't be the Super Bowl. But, every once in a while, maybe I can contribute something. It doesn't matter if it's small or large. It's just about making a difference."

Gertrude nodded slowly. "Well, you certainly made a contribution today. And I thank you for it."

She raised her glass in an impromptu toast, one that Ashley was quick to join. Clinking her glass against her grandmother's, she then looked expectantly at Cyrus until he, too, raised his in tribute.

The bottle of wine went fast, split three ways. And as Ashley took the last sip from her glass she could see the complete exhaustion in her grandmother's eyes. They all realized that it was time to call it a night. Luckily, Gertrude needed only to ride the elevator up to the 10th floor, and she would be home. Cyrus said he would walk her up and Ashley, anxious to stretch her legs, decided to join them.

Cyrus saw the two women to Gertrude's door and waited outside while Ashley took her grandmother in and helped her to bed. The late night and the unusual events of the evening had taken a lot out of the woman.

While they were alone, Gertrude took the opportunity to question Ashley in greater detail, wanting to know exactly what she had gleaned from Cyrus during the night's conversation. Unable to tell her anything useful, Ashley stuck to her story, saying simply that she sensed nothing deceptive from him the entire night. It was the literal truth, though not the solid vote of confidence that Gertrude believed it to be.

Chapter 12

The Templeton Tower Building
Hennings, South Carolina
2:11 a.m.

When Ashley stepped out the door of Gertrude's apartment, Cyrus was waiting in the hall. She looked at him in surprise. "I'm sorry," she smiled. "I didn't realize you were waiting. I would've moved things along a little more quickly. She's had a long day."

"It's no problem," Cyrus said with a smile. "I thought I'd walk you back to your door. I know it's not far, but I would feel better—if you don't mind."

He realized she was blushing slightly at his overture and wondered if he was making her uncomfortable. The profile he'd read on the young woman suggested that she was something of a shut-in, but that description truly hadn't matched with anything he'd witnessed over the course of the night. Still, if there was any truth to the analysis, she might not appreciate such simple sentiments—old-fashioned as they might be.

When she stepped closer and looked up into his eyes, he was once more struck by their unusual color, as well as the way they seemed to look not just at him but inside him at the same time. She offered a slight shake of her head. "I'm glad you waited.

That's sweet."

The elevator door opened as soon as the call button was pressed. It only stood to reason since the car hadn't been used since they'd exited. They stepped inside, not uttering a word between them, and let the doors close.

The car jolted slightly as it began to descend. Cyrus was keenly aware of Ashley standing directly in front of him. She said nothing but stood close and looked directly up into his eyes once more. He felt her soft hand slip inside his own and they shared a satisfied smile. While he'd been surprised by the gesture, it also felt strangely natural and appropriate. He realized that if she hadn't taken his hand, he would've taken hers. Even after the short time they had spoken over the course of the night, he felt a connection to her that was undeniable. And, he realized, entirely unexplainable. It just seemed right, so he was content to go with it.

The bell chimed, and the doors slipped open once more, arriving on the sixth floor. They stepped from the elevator car, and walked slowly down the hall to the door of apartment 601.

"Thank you," Cyrus said quietly. "For a great end to a very long day. I didn't know what to expect when Gertrude floated the idea of dinner. I was a little nervous, actually. But it was exceptional. I'm glad we didn't postpone after things went a little…sideways on the way here."

She smiled. It was a beaming smile that ignited her eyes and lit up her face. "I was a little nervous about it, too," she admitted. "But I had fun. And you're too kind. It was just some reheated lasagna; nothing special at all, really."

The comment made Cyrus laugh. "No, dinner was nice. *You* were the exceptional part. I can honestly say I've never met anyone like you before. There's just something…" he stopped to search for the right word. "When I look in your eyes, there's something…"

Her eyebrows pinched, and she looked up at him. "You're not giving me a line—" she started. "You feel it too, don't you?"

Cyrus took a step back and pulled away from her, offering a serious look. "No," he said awkwardly. "I'm not giving you a line. I'm not even hitting on you. I can't explain it. I just had this strange sense the first moment I saw you. There's a familiarity—I don't know, something I can't describe."

He looked around the empty hallway, suddenly feeling very uncomfortable, as if Boone was still riding along in his ear listening to everything he said. "The last thing I want is for you to think that it's some kind of come-on. It's not like that at all—"

Stepping very close to him once more, Ashley put her finger on his lips and looked up into his eyes. A tight smile crossed her face. "That's not it," she said quietly. "I felt it. Something I've never experienced before. It's been there the whole night…and you feel it, too?

"There's more," she started. "Some…things have happened tonight that I can't explain. As strange as it seems, I think this is part of it."

Cyrus was sure that he didn't understand all that she was trying to tell him, but he knew what he needed. He wasn't the only one to feel different when she was near. That was enough.

"I think," Ashley began, but stopped short of finishing her thought. Her hand slipped up across his shoulder and around the back of his neck as she pulled herself to him. It seemed she had something left to say in the half second before her lips found his, but after that neither would remember the words they'd been trying to express.

Slipping his hands around her thin waist, Cyrus felt the

warmth of her bare skin where her sweater had pulled away from her jeans. Drawing her in, his body and mind raced with untold possibilities as he caressed the soft flesh at the small of her back and felt the heat radiating from her skin.

While he wasn't sure just how long they stood like that, kissing in the silent hallway, when they finally separated both were short of breath.

He looked down into her eyes and saw indecision there and knew something was wrong. "What is it?" he asked. His voice was only a whisper with her still in his arms.

She bit at the corner of her lip, a subconscious gesture as she sorted through something that had obviously given her pause. While he was concerned for whatever was suddenly on her mind, he found the way she absentmindedly nibbled at the edge of her own lip to be exceptionally sexy.

"Are you alright?" Cyrus persisted.

She nodded. "Yeah," she said quietly. "There are just some things that stand to make this a little complicated, and I'm not sure what to do." She seemed to be talking as much to herself as she was to him.

"I want to invite you in," she explained further. "But I don't want to give you the wrong idea. There's something going on here, but I think it might be more than either of us understands."

She looked away, her frustration clear, but didn't pull herself from his grip. "This is hard to explain," she relented. "Look— let me just put it bluntly, then you can make up your own mind."

He nodded, desperate for her problem to be simple so he could ease her mind.

"I want you to come inside, but it's not what you're thinking." She faltered again, unhappy with her own explanation. "Ah, okay. No. That's not it. I want you to come inside, and it *is* for exactly the reason you're thinking, but it's more complicated than that. There's something you need to understand—well, there's something I need you to help me understand."

Ashley shook her head in frustration and slid from his arms. She walked a short distance down the hall, turned, and paced back. "I'm still not getting this right," she said vaguely.

Cyrus held up a hand and stopped her short. Taking her hand in his, he stared down into her eyes. He could see that she was concerned, and whatever it was, it was important enough that she was tripping over herself in an effort to get it out.

"Why don't we go inside and you can explain it to me there," Cyrus said calmly. "We'll just go in, sit down, and talk about whatever's on your mind. No expectations of any kind, I promise. There's something here," he said with confidence. "It's something…different. I like it, but I want to understand it. Clearly, so do you. So let's just take our time."

She smiled, but the confusion was still clear in her eyes. Nodding, she moved closer and held him tight. "Thank you," she whispered.

Chapter 13

Hennings, South Carolina
8:06 a.m.

The line at the coffee shop was maddening. It seemed that the entire so-called 'civilized' world had only ever agreed on a single fact: that morning coffee was what made the world go round. While Cyrus wasn't sure he agreed, the line at the small corner coffee joint was a clear indication that he was in the minority. He'd started the day off like any other, picking Gertrude up at her apartment on the 10ᵗʰ floor of the Feedmount Building before driving her to the office. This morning, however, his boss had decided that she wanted a fresh brewed cup of coffee to begin her day. Rather than stop on the way in and risk a fiasco like their visit to the market the night before, Cyrus decided to drop Gertrude at the office before running out once more to satisfy the woman's need for caffeine.

It took more than ten minutes for Cyrus to reach the front of the line, order a pair of overpriced beverages, and then retrieve the final product. With a thermal to-go cup in each hand, he headed for the door. But before reaching the exit, he became aware of a man off to his right who was paying him undue attention. With the events of the previous night still fresh in his mind, Cyrus adjusted his course to intercept his observer.

"Can I help you with something?" Cyrus asked, a lack of patience was clear in his tone.

The man sat on a tall stool beside a small bistro table. At first, it seemed as if he might pretend to be ignorant of having any interest in Cyrus. But that idea must have been quickly dismissed because Cyrus saw a shift in the man's demeanor as he became instantly alert; perhaps preparing to react to the confrontational approach. Either way, Cyrus got what he wanted by catching the man off guard.

The observer was of more or less average height and build. Cyrus tried to establish his age as part of his rushed analysis, but it was difficult. He had a shaggy head of brown hair that stopped just short of his eyes in the front, fell over his ears around the side, and nearly reached his shoulders in the back. It was a hair style reminiscent of the music's grunge era. Similarly, the man's jaw was lined with days' worth of unkempt growth.

"I know you," the man said simply as he returned Cyrus's stare from behind a pair of dark wire-framed glasses.

"Then you have me at a disadvantage," Cyrus said. Still not a trace of friendliness touched his tone. "What can I help you with?"

The longhaired man offered a weak smile for the first time, but was slow to respond. Finally he pulled the glasses from his face and laid them on the table. He examined Cyrus more carefully. The observer's eyes were a distinctive bright shade of green that struck Cyrus as immediately familiar. They matched Ashley Waterford's, though this man's offered no humor and radiated absolutely no warmth. Even if the color was a spot on match, the man's eyes lacked the vibrancy and life he had seen in Ashley's.

"William Waterford," Cyrus said quietly. Though the man looked nothing like the images that were included in his dossier, once he was able to pair the man's eyes with the rest of his facial features, there was no doubt.

"Ah," William grinned. "I see you know me, too."

"Only by reputation. I've heard your name mentioned in passing, and you share your sister's eyes."

There was no hiding the look of surprise on William's face. "No kidding? The old crow introduced you to Ash? Well, I guess I shouldn't be surprised. As I understand it, you're her new aide. Ashley would be the best person to vet someone in your position. Still, it's not like Gram to introduce a stranger to the family."

"Who said I was a stranger?" Cyrus was curious to see just how much William knew about him.

With a roll of his eyes, William idly scratched at the scruff on his jaw before responding. Cyrus saw it for what it was, a stall. He was buying time while he considered the best response.

"Please," William said in a disinterested tone. "I've read your file. I think I know you fairly well at this point."

Cyrus's expression offered no hint to his feelings on the matter. "There's more to a man than what you find in his file," he said simply.

"True enough."

"Ashley said something," Cyrus began. "She asked Gertrude if she'd heard from you. I was under the impression that Ashley hadn't heard from you in some time. She didn't seem to know you were in town."

This brought a pointed glare from William. "It seems you've spent more time with my sister than I'd been led to believe," he said finally. "And, no. She has no idea that I'm in town." His gaze became suddenly penetrating, almost as if he were trying to assess the mind living behind Cyrus's eyes. "It's important to me that we keep it that way," he added.

Despite being more than a little creeped out by the sudden glare from the stranger, Cyrus wasn't sure how to respond. He offered a simple shrug. "That sounds like a family matter to me. It's none of my concern."

Though a benign comment, Cyrus was surprised to see confusion on William's face. It wasn't that William didn't understand the sentiment. It seemed more like it wasn't at all the response he was expecting.

Cyrus decided that it was time to end the awkward conversation. He glanced at his nonexistent watch and raised his eyebrows in a mocking manner. "Wow, look at the time," he said. "It's been fun, but I better be going."

His sarcasm seemed lost on William.

The man offered another weak smile. "No problem. I'm sure I'll be seeing you around. Please give Grams my best, and tell her that I'll be seeing her again *real soon*."

Cyrus was surprised when William offered his hand. Though the conversation had seemed benign enough, it had felt anything but. There was something fiercely awkward about it, and he had the sense the man was up to something. He just wasn't sure what.

Setting one of the drinks aside, Cyrus shook William's hand. But the moment his hand was locked in William's grasp, Cyrus felt the man's penetrating stare once more. It was as if William were trying to burn a hole in his eyes.

Frustrated by the act, Cyrus returned the man's crushing grip as well as a stare that was just as withering. This clearly caught William by surprise. He was so unprepared for the response that he did a painfully poor job of masking the look that crossed his face.

The awkward exchange made Cyrus wonder if the man might have the same sort of ability as his sister. Was the odd visual exchange the man's attempt to read his mind? And, if so, had he been equally unable to Read him?

Cyrus could only hope. But judging by the man's reaction, he hadn't gotten what he wanted. That was something, at least.

Retrieving the second coffee from the table, Cyrus offered the man one more glance before turning and walking away without the benefit of another word. There was something about the man. He just seemed *off* in some way.

Cyrus had learned to trust his first impressions, which meant he had a strong suspicion that he would be seeing more of Ashley's brother in the near future.

The next surprise of the morning came when Cyrus reached the car. A cheap, disposable cell was sitting on the driver's seat. He'd left the car locked with the windows only cracked open for ventilation. Under normal circumstances, the arrival of the phone would've been troubling. In this case it had been an agreed upon approach protocol, so it wasn't entirely out of the blue.

Slipping behind the wheel of the car, Cyrus had just set the coffee cups into the drink holders when the phone began to ring. He picked it up before the second chime.

"Who was the guy in the shop?" Boone asked without pretense.

"William Waterford, if you can believe it," Cyrus said. "What's up?" Boone wouldn't be making contact without important news to share.

"That was unexpected. Intel suggested that William has been off the grid for the better part of the last year. He looks like hell!" Cyrus could hear the confusion in Boone's voice and knew the man was trying to read meaning into the young Waterford's surprise appearance.

"There's been a shift in your mission objective," Boone

continued after a moment of silence. "We know that Gertrude's just received confirmation that your credentials are finished. We think you're about to be given access to her lab. We know the location of the facility but haven't been able to get inside. Gertrude keeps all of her research in a digital archive. It's a central database containing reports and records of everything she's worked on for the last decade, maybe longer. We need you to make a copy of the database."

Cyrus didn't respond immediately. He was considering the shift in mission parameters and sensed something he didn't like. "Is Gertrude's protection still my primary objective?"

He heard Boone exhale with frustration. "This comes directly from Monica," Boone clarified. "I'm not saying that I agree, but we have our orders. Your primary objective is the retrieval of the database. Protecting the asset is now secondary. But I don't see any reason why you can't do both. You can walk and chew gum at the same time, right?"

His teeth grinding in frustration, Cyrus wasn't entirely surprised. Waterford's safety had never been the primary objective, he was sure of it. It was Monica Fichtner's way of handling him in these situations. She'd wanted the database all along.

Monica Fichtner was head of the clandestine Coalition, and she was as cold blooded as a snake. He'd have reservations about going in undercover just to steal a copy of a research database. But tell him that he's protecting an elderly scientist, and he would willingly accept the assignment. Being used in such a way galled him, but Cyrus wasn't at all surprised by the turn of events.

"Understood," Cyrus said in a terse confirmation of his new orders before tapping the end call button on the phone.

Gnashing his teeth once more, Cyrus swallowed hard, then

started the car and pulled out into traffic. There were parts of his work with the Coalition that he found less than ideal. Paramount among them was Monica Fichtner—a woman Cyrus harbored an ever-growing distrust for.

Chapter 14

The Feedmount Building
Hennings, South Carolina
9:08 a.m.

Sitting at his desk just outside the set of open doors to Gertrude's office, Cyrus ran through the events of the previous evening. He had gone to dinner with Gertrude and Ashley expecting it to be some sort of test, but there was no way he could've been prepared for what had happened. Boone warned him that Gertrude Waterford took her privacy seriously, but what he'd learned from Ashley simply defied explanation. It was unprecedented, and it only made him wonder what other secrets Gertrude was keeping stashed away.

Ashley's shocking revelation aside, Cyrus was now certain that he hadn't just passed Gertrude's test, but he'd passed it with flying colors. Thanks to a great deal of luck, he realized. But had it been luck? The unanswered question nagged at him. And while those thoughts threatened to occupy his mind, he decided to focus on the predominant matter at hand. He'd navigated Gertrude's unorthodox review process. She would likely lower her guard, if only fractionally. Once she provided access to her lab, he would be able to move ahead with the next phase of the operation.

The fax machine buzzed and jarred Cyrus from his thoughts. He looked at the clunky old device on the table beyond the end of his desk and shook his head. It was shocking that such machines were still used at all. Until taking the position as Gertrude Waterford's assistant, he couldn't remember the last time he'd needed to send or receive a fax, considering the technology the 21st century afforded.

Pulling the newly received stack of papers from the top of the machine, he slipped them into a file folder and walked into Gertrude's office. She was hunched over the keyboard of her iMac, completely engrossed in whatever she was reading when he laid the folder on her desk. "The fax you've been waiting for finally came through," he said quietly, as to not disturb her.

Her eyes darted up from the screen, apparently surprised to see him standing there. They'd been at the office for over an hour and he'd heard barely a word from her.

Gertrude's eyes examined him for a long moment before a hint of a smile touched her lips. "Isn't that the same tie you wore yesterday?" she asked.

He nodded. "You bet. After yesterday, it's officially my lucky tie. I'm not normally a superstitious person, but I couldn't help but wear it again."

Her smile brightened. "Cyrus, if your tie is what got us through yesterday, I'm going to request that you wear it every day. I'm not superstitious either, but why tempt fate?"

She flipped open the folder he had deposited beside her keyboard and quickly thumbed through the pages of the fax. "Splendid," she said with a satisfied chuckle. "Your biometric data and access codes for the lab have been processed." She glanced at the expensive timepiece on her wrist. "Give me an hour, then you can drive me to the lab and I'll show you around."

"The lab?" he asked with all the uncertainty that was due from a new employee who knew nothing of the woman's work routine. "Biometrics?"

"Of course. You don't think I do the bulk of my research here, do you? Not in this cramped little space? The lab has top-notch security. It took some time to get your credentials and biometrics into the system for proper access. That fax was just confirming that everything is now in order. We're all set."

Cyrus nodded his understanding. "Okay," he said slowly. "It's just that I don't recall submitting anything for biometric authentication. Don't you need to take fingerprints or something for that?"

A knowing smile crossed the old woman's face. "All taken care of," she grinned. "And not just fingerprints. Our system has the ability to authenticate via fingerprints, retinal scan, even DNA. But don't worry. I've got it covered."

The expression that crossed Cyrus's face made it clear that he was uneasy with what he'd just heard. He looked at his fingertips and offered a vaguely nauseated expression, just to make sure Gertrude received the reaction she was hoping for. "Okay then," he said slowly, then turned and ambled out of the room. He could just picture the villainous grin that had spread across the old woman's craggy face as she watched him leave.

Dropping back into the chair at his desk, Cyrus was glad to know that his mission was on track. Gertrude was finally satisfied with his credentials and no doubt enjoying the small victory of curling his toes at the invasion of his personal privacy in the acquisition of his biometric information. That was just fine with him. The way he saw it, he had an hour to kill before driving her to the lab and, with luck, moving the mission along.

His run-in with William crossed his mind once more. He'd decided against telling Gertrude about the experience, even though he wasn't entirely sure why. William Waterford remained a mystery—until he knew more, Cyrus refused to be used as a pawn in Waterford family politics. Though, after the events of the previous night, that ship had already sailed.

Cyrus knew he'd dodged a bullet with the tie, but it had only been by sheer chance that he wasn't wearing the same suit from the prior day as well. He had woken up at Ashley's with just enough time to shower and change before taking the elevator up to Gertrude's floor, as he did every morning. It was thanks only to luck that he'd picked up his dry-cleaning earlier that afternoon and had a spare suit in the trunk of the car.

When he'd made a point of walking Ashley back to her apartment, he had planned on calling it a night. But one thing led to another, and the entire night took yet another turn that wasn't anticipated. After what had happened, Cyrus realized he would never see the world the same way again. Likewise, his awakening changed the way he looked at the operation he was working and what it could mean in the grand scheme.

Cyrus thought back to following Ashley through the door of her apartment last night. She headed for the kitchen like a woman on a mission, and he watched her, unsure what to do next.

When he followed and stepped into the kitchen, she was rummaging through the back of one of the cabinets. "I need a drink," she said in an exasperated huff. "Do you need a drink?"

She glanced over her shoulder and gave him a hard look. "Believe me," she warned. "You're going to want a drink."

Still thrown by her odd behavior, Cyrus shrugged. "I could drink," he said quietly.

He was fascinated by what he was seeing. It was like watching someone on a caffeine high rushing around. She rummaged through one cabinet then, not finding what she was looking for, moved on to the next. Finally she went to the pantry in the corner of the kitchen, flipped on the light and stepped inside. He heard the sound of things getting banged around and knocked over. It was almost comical.

When she came out, her eyes were blazing, and there was a wide smile on her face. She held up an unopened bottle of Rey Sol Anejo tequila and a pair of tumbler glasses.

"I've been sitting on this bottle for years," she laughed. "I don't drink, so I haven't had an occasion to crack the seal."

He laughed and looked at the clock on the wall. "And this is the occasion to open it? It's almost two thirty in the morning."

Her look turned decidedly serious. "It'll help," she said in a deadpan voice. "And once you hear what I have to say, you'll be glad it's here."

Her smile then returned, as she grabbed the bottle and glasses and virtually pranced past him. "So we best start now," she said over her shoulder as she left the room.

Dropping heavily on the sofa, Ashley set the bottle and glasses down on the coffee table with a clumsy 'thunk', before motioning him to come sit beside her. He had no sooner taken his place and she was pouring what had to be three generous shots of the expensive tequila into each of their glasses.

Cyrus watched her with rapt fascination. She *was* a woman on a mission. He just wasn't sure what that mission was. Handing him a glass, she offered a toast to *new friends*, she said with a strange glint in her eye. Tipping back the glass, she downed the contents in three quick swallows. He didn't know where this was going, but it seemed that it was headed there fast. With more than a little curiosity, he tipped back his own drink and followed her lead.

It was only a few seconds before Cyrus felt the flutter of the tequila kicking into high gear. The constant and ever-present tension between his shoulders began to fade, and the fatigue he felt throughout his body after a hideous day began to dull. It was moments like this that he realized what a constant state of hyper vigilance he lived in, and the ill effects it had on his body and his mind. The constant pressure and tension he dealt with on an undercover operation was as natural to him as breathing, but moments like this, tiny breaks in his vigilance, were as cathartic as they were dangerous.

Sitting sideways on the couch, Ashley folded her legs in front of her and closed her eyes. She took a long, slow, deep breath and let it out, repeating the routine again and again. It was some sort of relaxation exercise, Cyrus realized. But, for the life of him, he still couldn't figure out what she was up to.

She rolled her head around on her neck very slowly, then stopped and took another deep breath. When she opened her eyes and looked at him, she seemed very much at ease. Her anxious, caffeinated state seemed to have evolved into something more serene and sedate.

Cyrus turned to face her, but waited for her to speak. Up until that point, he had no idea what was actually happening. The drink had hit him like a kick in the ass, and he was feeling better than he had all day. They could sit there like that for the rest of the night for all he cared.

"Alright," she mumbled, mostly to herself. "I can't believe I'm actually going to say this." She looked like she was about to continue, but then stopped once more.

Cyrus could tell that whatever she had on her mind, it weighed heavily on her. But no matter what he guessed at, he couldn't imagine what secret she could hold that would be so enormous that she needed to gird herself so thoroughly before broaching the subject.

"Okay," he said suddenly. "You better spill it. You're

freaking me out!"

Her response was to splash another double shot in each of their glasses. She downed hers before giving it a second thought. Cyrus's response was to pick up his glass. He raised it in a silent salute to her and slowly drank the contents while keeping a curious eye focused on the beautiful woman over the top of the glass.

"I'm sorry for the theatrics," she said at last. "It's just that this goes against everything I know. Still, something inside me is telling me that this is the right thing to do.

"I mean," she hesitated. "I'm not alone in this, am I? You said you feel it, too? Something...I don't know how to describe it..."

He nodded. "I do. I know exactly what you mean. It was there from the first time I saw you." Cyrus's voice was quiet. He knew he was completing her thought. "I feel like I know you, or knew you...or was supposed to know you. I can't quite put it into words. But it's the damnedest thing I've ever experienced."

"For real? You're not just trying to, you know..." she let the question hang.

Sleep with her, he realized.

He laughed. "No. It's something else. Has it ever happened to you before?"

She shook her head. "No, but that's the other part I needed to ask you about. It might be related, or it might not, and this is the part that could really get us in trouble. I need to know that I can trust you.

"It's not a question I ask lightly," she warned. "To be honest, it took a couple of drinks just to work up the courage to give it a voice, so I need your word. This stays between us. It's a lot to ask from someone I just met—and I wouldn't ask if it weren't for—well...whatever *this* is."

Cyrus was taken aback by her sincere request for confidentiality. It was no small request given the real reason that he was there. And in spite of his being a spy by trade, he had always been a person of deep personal conviction. As old-fashioned as it was in the modern age, he was a big believer in people standing by their word. It made it hard for him to offer his confidence in her request. Still, there was an undeniable *something* at play that he couldn't discount; something that told him she was requesting a confidence that he should keep…no matter what.

Cyrus offered a curt nod. "I promise," he said simply.

He could tell from the look in her eye that those two words meant just as much to her as they did to him.

"I need to know if you're a Reader, too," she asked.

Cyrus didn't understand. He watched her eyes for some hint at her meaning. It was a simple question, but one asked with such seriousness that he knew he wasn't grasping her meaning.

He stared at the entire wall of her apartment that was consumed by the gigantic bookcase. No, that wasn't what she meant. That was too simple.

"I'm sorry?" he finally managed.

"A *Reader*," she said again, this time with emphasis. "I've never met another. I thought it might be the reason for our connection."

Cyrus shook his head slowly. "Sorry. I really don't follow. You mean like…books? Novels, magazines?"

Ashley looked crestfallen. She cupped her face in her hands and lowered her head. Cyrus wondered if she was crying. He couldn't imagine why. *A Reader?*

"I'm sorry," she said, sitting back up. "This was a mistake. I shouldn't have brought this up. Can we just forget the whole thing?"

Cyrus watched her eyes. She looked both crushed and exhausted. It occurred to him just how much hope she had riding on that one simple question, and he desperately wanted to understand.

Though he knew it would be a mistake, he was already feeling the full effects of the tequila. Pouring another splash into his glass, he looked to Ashley to see if she was interested. At first she shook her head, but when he started to put the top back on the bottle, she changed her mind.

When he handed her the glass, he took her other hand in his and held it. She met his eye but couldn't offer so much as a smile.

"You're going to make me explain, aren't you?" she asked quietly.

He raised his glass and waited for her to click hers against it before drinking it down.

"There are people with a rare genetic attribute that allows them to hear the thoughts of others," she began. "They're called Readers."

Cyrus laughed. "Yeah, right."

But the look on her face suggested that she wasn't joking.

He took a few moments to process the implications of the idea. It seemed farfetched—like science fiction. But then again, Gertrude Waterford's specialty was neuroscience. Actually, applied neuroscience. So if what Ashley was saying were possible, it made sense that Gertrude Waterford would be 'in the know' when it came to such matters.

"Wait," Cyrus said, suddenly feeling a good degree more sober. "You're serious?"

"I'm one of them."

He looked at her again as if seeing her for the first time. It didn't seem possible. That type of thing, if it were possible, must require some kind of massive mutation, or some other kind of genetic fracture. How could she possibly be so different?

"You're saying that you can *hear* people's thoughts? What—like in your head, it sounds like they are speaking—even though they aren't?"

Ashley smiled. "Actually, that's a surprisingly accurate description of how it works. I can hear them thinking—just like they were speaking aloud. But it's not every thought. It's just the foremost thought process at any given moment."

When she stopped, Cyrus asked her to keep going. He was fascinated and wanted to know more. He still wasn't sure that he bought into it, but it was an intriguing idea.

"It's like when you're about to speak," she explained. "Sometimes you think about what you're going to say, but never actually say it. In that case, you're mind goes through a verbalization process even though your mouth doesn't actually verbalize the words. It's very similar to the way most people process the written word. They see words on a page and process them through the same portion of the brain that's used just prior to speaking aloud. In this case, the words never get spoken out loud, but the brain still runs through the motions. In my case, *I hear those motions.*

"One theory is that Readers pick up on a similar process in the minds of people around them. That's why we can only hear a person's foremost thoughts. It's whatever has the central focus of their concentration at the moment. That's what Readers can intuit."

Cyrus sat stunned for several long seconds. "That's incredible," he said at last. "You're sure you're not just putting me on?"

He suddenly became very aware that everything about his

mission might have already been compromised, and he hadn't even realized it. Was that the reason she had been acting so strangely? Did she know the real reason he was working for her grandmother?

"Are you saying that you can hear what I'm thinking right now?" he said. Even as the words fell from his mouth, he realized they betrayed his nervousness.

The second long delay that preceded Ashley's response felt like an eternity. In that time, Cyrus was acutely aware of the tingling numbness that the tequila had helped to spread throughout his body, and he wondered if he had compounded his mistake.

"That's the really odd thing," Ashley said at last. "You're the first person I've met who I couldn't Read."

Feeling his breath catch in his throat, Cyrus found himself replaying her words in his mind. *Couldn't Read*, she'd said. *Really?*

"It's *never* happened before," she explained. "And I have no idea why. I guessed it might have something to do with the…" she stopped short. "I thought it might have something to do with our connection. I thought you might be a Reader, too, which might explain what was happening between us."

Cyrus smiled. "That's the most incredible thing I've ever heard," he said quietly. "I can see why you would want to keep it a secret. It can't be easy to deal with. Do you have control over it?"

She held up a hand and waggled it in the air. "There are times…large groups of people are difficult; there are just too many people to block out. To be honest, I'm prone to panic attacks. It's pretty lame."

Cyrus noticed he was still holding her hand, and smiled. He hadn't even realized it. It just felt natural. "I don't think its lame," he offered. "It sounds terrifying. Serenity and solitude are rare commodities, and the quiet times are my favorite. It doesn't sound like you get many of those."

"I do when I'm here. It's why I'm pretty much a shut-in."

He shrugged. "I really can't even imagine what it must be like. On one hand, it must be amazing. On the other, terrifying."

Shaking her head, Ashley offered a weak smile. "You can skip amazing and move directly to terrifying. There's really nothing fun about it. Try being a woman walking around the city full of men and hearing everything they're thinking when they look at you. A fraction of what you hear is complementary. But at least 90% have thoughts crossing their minds that range from rude to downright horrifying. Really, really, horrifying."

It would be chilling, Cyrus surmised. It was human nature to have thoughts that were never voiced or ideas that were never expressed in any way. When you look at any given object, you have an idea, an opinion, or an emotional response. The same goes for a piece of artwork or a song. All of those tiny flashes of thought that come and go in an instant are safe and guarded inside our own minds. But what if someone could hear them as clearly as if we spoke every random, errant thought aloud?

The downside to such a talent was decidedly unpleasant, Cyrus realized. But Ashley was an attractive young woman. That raised another question. The things that a healthy red-blooded man thinks when they see a beautiful female are often best left unspoken. Some of those wayward thoughts would be kind, some would be outright rude, and some might be considered entirely offensive, even if no harm was intended. What if that young woman were aware of each of those thoughts?

My God, Cyrus realized. *It was a wonder she ever left her apartment at all.*

"That's why your grandmother wanted me to have dinner with you," Cyrus said. It was his chance to bring the subject back on topic. He didn't like thinking about the unpleasant ramifications of her ability. If it was so bad to think about briefly, how bad would it be to deal with every single day?

Ashley nodded. "I'm sorry for the deception. She takes her work very seriously. I know its overkill, but if it makes her safe, it seems like the least I can do. Still, it's a major invasion of your privacy."

Cyrus decided that his privacy wasn't a rabbit hole that he wanted to jump down at that moment, so he moved on. "What did she say when you told her you couldn't Read me?"

Ashley couldn't meet his eye for the first time all night. "You didn't tell her," he said.

She shook her head. "I didn't know what to tell her," she admitted. "So I just said that you were being honest with her about everything you said. It seemed like a fair bet since you saved her life only a few hours earlier."

It was solid logic, Cyrus reasoned. Still, it was an unusual choice, her going out on a limb for a man she'd just met.

"You really can't Read me?" he asked. "Nothing at all?"

She offered a sly smile. "I'll admit I thought that a few drinks might add an interesting variable to the mix. Since I couldn't, I wanted to know if it had to do with you or me. I was curious if a couple of drinks might lower one, or both, of our inhibitions enough to make it work. But it didn't. You're a blank slate."

"That must be a disappointment," he said with a smile. Still, he was more relieved than words could express. Whatever the explanation, he was happy for it.

"Actually," she said, crawling across the sofa and lowering herself onto his lap. "It's an amazing feeling. You have no idea how hard it is to keep the voices out."

Cradling her in his arms, Cyrus kissed her gently on the lips. Her eyes were looking heavy, and he could see that she was totally exhausted.

"There is something special here, isn't there?" she asked in a faraway voice.

"Absolutely," he replied with a smile.

Ashley was nodding off right there in his arms. "You'll keep my secret?" she asked in a sleepy voice.

"I promise."

A moment later she was asleep.

Cyrus sat there on the sofa for a while, holding her in his arms and watching her doze. It didn't seem possible that they had met only a few short hours earlier. It made him wonder where things might go from there.

Finally, he carried her to her bedroom and tucked her beneath the covers. The effects of the alcohol had hit her hard, and she was out cold. He was feeling it too, for that matter; grabbing a spare blanket from the foot of her bed, he crashed on the couch until morning. Driving in his condition wasn't a good idea and, if he were honest with himself, he wasn't in any hurry to leave.

Before lying down for the night, Cyrus did a quick reconnaissance of the apartment. He made sure that the front door was locked, and double-checked that the balcony was clear before locking the latch on the sliding glass door. Then he made a slow sweep of the apartment. It was unlikely that there were any hidden cameras, but he'd come too far to slip up now. So as he scouted the apartment, he did his best to play the part of the houseguest, interested in the furnishings and decorations. He made a slow examination of the massive book collection that occupied nearly an entire wall of the apartment, and moved on from there.

For the most part, he found nothing of value or interest. One oddity did catch his eye when he did a quick examination of the medicine cabinet in the main bathroom. It contained a pair of prescription bottles labeled as being filled at the local pharmacy only a block away. But it was the names of the medications that puzzled him. They were drugs he couldn't pronounce if he had a gun to his head and his life depended on it. Even with the amazing recall afforded him by his eidetic memory, he couldn't recall ever hearing of either medication before. Whatever they were, they were something specialized. He wondered if they were somehow related to her unusual neurological condition. Given Gertrude's specialty, anything was possible.

He memorized the names of both prescriptions, along with their dosages and prescribed instructions. Oddly, neither label listed the prescribing doctor. Making a note to himself, Cyrus would make sure to look into the drugs as soon as he had access to an anonymous Internet connection.

Chapter 15

Mayflower Lab Facility
Hennings, South Carolina
9:12 a.m.

The car made a sharp left turn leaving the bright and sunny warmth of 18th Avenue behind. Descending the steep concrete ramp of the parking garage, William felt himself swallowed in darkness. A moment later the driver of the vehicle flipped a switch and brought the headlights to life with a glaring flash. Looking across the car, William didn't know much about the man in the driver's seat, other than he was a means to an end— just another faceless bureaucrat in a suit, as far as he was concerned. But at least this bureaucrat was unique in one way. He had the authority to access the lab.

Well, maybe not all the way into the lab, but he could get him past the biometrics and the facility's exterior security. That was far enough. When it came to dealing with the facility's personnel, William was perfectly equipped to handle them himself.

A lot had changed since the night he'd made his escape from the mental institution. William wasn't running anymore. He wasn't afraid of the people who were after him. It was time for them to fear him.

The car crossed the nearly empty parking garage and continued on far into the bowels of the building. Just when it seemed they'd reached the end of the line, the driver turned and drove into what had looked like another dark corner of the garage. Once the car slipped into the corner, however, William realized it had been nothing but a cleverly disguised alcove. Still, a dead end nonetheless.

The driver rolled down the window and pressed his hand against the unadorned concrete wall. At his touch, a small section of wall slid silently aside revealing a large, dimly lit flatscreen display. The man placed his palm securely against the screen, and it blinked to life. A horizontal line flashed once across the surface of his hand. The moment it disappeared, another line appeared on the screen, this one vertical. It flashed beneath his palm as well, scanning his print and capillary response from a second axis.

William leaned forward in his seat for a better view of the lab's high-tech security measures. He'd heard about the system, but seeing it in operation was an entirely different matter. When a thin light projected across the inside of the car in a brief flash, he realized the last of the authentication mechanisms had been triggered. A laser retinal scanner projected out from the wall and scanned the eye of the car's driver.

It was amazing what she did with her money, William marveled. *All of these precautions and she still wasn't safe.*

As soon as the retinal scan was complete, the wall panel slid shut once more. The car jolted, and at first William wasn't sure what had happened. He quickly realized the mild disorienting sensation inside his ear was due to the car's movement. An elevator had been triggered, and the platform on which the car sat was quickly descending.

When the elevator came to a stop ten seconds later, he had

no idea how far underground he had been taken. The driver slipped the car into gear once more and pulled slowly forward, entering a new, smaller parking garage. Like the level high above, this parking level was entirely bare concrete floors, walls and ceiling. It was maybe fifty yards deep and nearly as wide, with regularly placed concrete pillars supporting the ceiling twenty feet above.

There were only three other cars parked in the underground structure, all lined up near the only door visible on the level. The driver angled the car into the next available spot, dropped the gear selector into park, and turned off the ignition.

The man looked at William blankly and awaited instruction.

"What do we face from here?" William asked.

"There's a card swipe on that door," the man said calmly, nodding at the door in the wall before them. "Once through there, visitors are sealed in an antechamber while a member of security authenticates the visitor manually via a window in the wall."

"Tell me about the window."

"Bulletproof, four inches thick; if it's breached, the airlock is depressurized to neutralize any threat to the facility."

"The guard on the other side of the window, will he be able to hear us as well as see us?"

The driver nodded to the affirmative.

"And once we clear the airlock?"

"You'll have access to the facility. Each lab is equipped with auto-locking doors that are automatically unlocked and opened via a proximity sensor that keys off an authorized user's swipe card."

That was fine, William reasoned. He wouldn't need access to the labs themselves. "What about the central computer?"

"The main server room can only be accessed by Missus

Waterford, or the senior security member on shift."

"Which is you?" William asked patiently.

"Which is me," the driver confirmed in a flat, emotionless voice.

"Fine. Let's go."

It took only a moment for the driver to open the lab's outer door by swiping his access card at the panel. A moment later they were inside the airlock. It was essentially a wide hallway that was maybe thirty feet long with another heavy door on the far end. The security window built into the wall to their right was impossible to miss; it was about four feet wide and three feet tall. But if the glass was as thick as the driver had claimed, William couldn't tell it by looking.

"Good morning, Frank," the security guard on the other side of the glass said as soon as the driver stepped into the airlock. His welcoming smile disappeared, however, when he caught sight of the stranger.

"What's going on, Frank?" the guard asked. "I don't have you down for having a guest on site today."

It was obvious that the security guard was already on alert. His eyes moved from William to his driver, Frank, and then back to William. He stepped closer to the control console that was located just beneath the window.

"You better explain fast, Frank," the guard warned. "You know the protocol here—you wrote it."

The guard had already flipped open the large plastic cage that housed a fist-sized red button. William realized instantly that the guard was about to purge the atmosphere from the room. "Hold on," he said to the man.

William stepped toward the window and raised a single placating hand as if the gesture would put the guard at ease. "There's no need for that, friend," he said.

As William stepped forward, he met the guard's eyes and focused his will on the area behind them. His breathing slowed and the world around him dropped from his conscious mind. All he could hear was the sound of his own heartbeat. The time between beats grew exponentially longer, the rhythm of his heart seeming to slow as he focused his will. In truth, it wasn't his heart that had slowed but his grasp of reality as William focused every bit of his will into the singular effort to connect with the man on the other side of the glass.

With a loud 'pop' that only William could hear, his senses snapped back to the present. A small smile turned up the corners of his lips as he looked at the man on the other side of the bulletproof glass. The guard stood stock still with his hand still poised over the large red switch that would seal their fate. There was a faraway look in the man's eye that told William he had accomplished his goal.

"What's your name?" William asked him.

"Sergeant Jason Wilks," the man replied in a monotone voice that was very similar to the driver who had brought William into the facility.

"Would you be so kind as to open the inner door for me, Sergeant," William asked, his grin widening.

The man nodded, closing the protective housing over the red button. Turning to a nearby control panel, he entered a ten-digit access code. The moment he was finished there was a sharp 'hissing' sound and the door at the far end of the airlock swung silently open on its hinges, entity of its own accord.

"Sergeant Wilks?" William said, drawing the man's attention back to the window. "We were never here. Understand?"

"Yes, sir."

William led the way and passed through the airlock ahead of Frank. On the other side of the door, he found himself in an open common area with a small kitchenette to the left and a shallow breakroom with chairs and a television to the right. Frank pushed a button on the wall and the airlock door shut, sealing the way behind them.

"How many men on your security detail?" William asked Frank.

"Six men on the day shift, including the man in the screening booth," Frank explained without hesitation.

"Summon them for me. We need to prepare a proper welcome for my grandmother."

Chapter 16

Mayflower Lab Facility
Hennings, South Carolina
10:16 a.m.

Standing in the airlock entryway of the Mayflower
underground laboratory, Cyrus was glad he'd left his weapon
under the seat of the car when he parked in the underground
garage. As he looked at the security guard on the other side of
the bulletproof window, he knew that the man was reviewing
MWS—Millimeter Wave Scans—of himself and Gertrude
Waterford. The scanning hardware was hidden in the walls of
the short corridor between the two airlock doors and was
capable of detecting guns, even knives that were cleverly hidden
on one's person. The technology was similar to what was used
in the screening processes at most major airports; however,
Cyrus was familiar with the latest generation of cutting edge
hardware being utilized in top private and government facilities.

No one had mentioned the scanning technology, but it was
the primary reason for the elaborate airlock mechanism that was
essentially the last hurdle someone had to jump before entering
the facility. Similarly, the guard on the other side of the glass
was the last line of human defense. Up until this point, all
security measures and counter measures had been automated.

Cost effective in the long run, but no automated system was ever one hundred percent reliable. This was why a flesh–and–blood person manned the facility's final barrier. Where technology might fail, a properly trained operative minding the gate was a wise last line of defense.

"You're clear, Missus Waterford," the guard said from the other side of the glass. "Corporal Thoroe will meet you inside with the proper identification and credentials for your guest."

"Thank you, Sergeant Wilks," Gertrude said; her voice contained a rare warmth that surprised Cyrus.

When the guard turned his head to meet Gertrude's eye, Cyrus noticed the small black dot located behind the man's left ear. It looked similar to the tiny patch that Gertrude wore.

The second door to the airlock popped open with a 'hiss' and Gertrude led him into the next room. While Cyrus pretended to take in the small kitchen area to one side of the entry and the rec-room to the right, he was actually more concerned with Gertrude. He noticed that she was leaning more heavily on her cane than she had most days, and he wondered if the events of the previous afternoon and the subsequent late night had taken more of a toll on her than she let on.

"Good morning, Missus Waterford." A man dressed very much like the guard in the airlock emerged from the wide hallway that bisected the back wall of the rec-room.

He offered Gertrude a brief smile before turning his attention to Cyrus. "I'm Corporal Tony Thoroe," he said, shaking Cyrus's hand. "Pleased to meet you, Sir. I have your credentials here." He handed Cyrus a sealed manila envelope. "Your biometrics are already on file so you're all set."

"Thank you, Corporal," Gertrude said in an apparent effort to truncate any further discussion. "We'll be in the primary lab. Is anyone else inside the facility?"

"Just the security staff, Ma'am. You have the facility to yourself today."

Gertrude offered a satisfied nod before motioning Cyrus in the direction of the wide hall from which the Corporal had emerged. She started off at a surprising clip. It seemed she was eager to get to the lab.

They were fifty yards down the long hallway before Gertrude cast a sideways glance at Cyrus who was taking long strides to keep up with the woman's quick pace. Though she was making efforts to appear like it was business as usual, there was no disguising the rapid 'clank' that resonated from her cane each time it struck the tile floor with every quick step. Cyrus could sense the tension radiating off her.

"Tell me, Mister Cooper," Gertrude said while sparing him a quick glance. Her full concentration was directed on maintaining a rapid pace. "Are you armed?"

Cyrus offered a stoic, but reserved glance of his own. "As your assistant, that strikes me as…inappropriate." His tone was purposefully noncommittal.

She didn't look back. *"That wasn't an answer."*

"After what happened last night, it seemed like reasonable precaution," he said after a few long beats. "But I didn't figure it would fly with security, so I left my sidearm in the car. Why do you ask?"

They turned a corner when the hallway reached a four way intersection. Gertrude led them to the right without a moment's delay. Cyrus could tell that she was winded, but she had yet to slow her pace.

"You're a sharp young man," she said. A wheezing sound entered her voice, but still she pressed on. "Since we've entered this facility, does anything strike you as out of place?"

Stopping in front of a twenty-foot wide sliding steel door,

Gertrude produced a keycard and swiped it across the plate on the wall beside a numeric keypad. A low buzz emanated from the panel indicating that her card had failed to register. Cyrus read the concern in the woman's eyes.

"Can I help you, Ma'am?" Another security guard dressed in the same desert camouflage fatigues arrived, startling them both.

The pair of guards had appeared from out of nowhere.

"Yes," Gertrude said in a raspy, dry voice. "My card seems to have been damaged. I can't seem to access my own lab, for God's sake."

At first, Cyrus found it disconcerting that a pair of soldiers had managed to sneak up on him in the middle of the facility's empty, wide open halls. Situational awareness was of critical importance in the field and absolutely crucial to survival when working undercover. He didn't like the idea of these two men getting the drop on him.

Those unpleasant feelings almost caused Cyrus to disregard the sharp look he saw in both men's eyes as they stepped closer. Having just suffered a blow to his ego, it was easy to dismiss his tingling sixth sense as a momentary flash of paranoia. But as his eyes made an instantaneous scan of the surrounding hall prior to moving back to the guards, he realized what it was that had brought warning bells. The door to a janitor's closet on the opposite side of the hall was slightly ajar, and he realized how the two guards had appeared so suddenly.

There weren't many reasons for a pair of guards to be hiding out in a janitorial closet just then, and Cyrus's senses sprang to full alert.

The first guard had only laid his hand on the gun strapped to his hip when Cyrus snapped out a right cross that demolished the man's nose in a single crushing blow. The man stumbled backward on his heels as a geyser of blood spurted from his face.

The second guard was awarded a second longer to react and managed to free his service pistol from the holster. He was just bringing it to bear when Cyrus locked the man's gun wielding wrist in a vice-like grip and pushed it aside. At the same moment, he grabbed the man by the collar of his uniform with his free hand, jerking his upper body to the right while kicking the man's legs out from under him in the opposite direction. It was a lightning fast move that left Cyrus in control of the man's weapon, and the guard facedown on the tile floor with his arm wrenched violently behind his back.

The first guard was crab walking backwards across the floor to gain distance from Cyrus. As soon as he was safely away, he tried once more to retrieve his sidearm. It was a tricky process with him disoriented from a blow that had left his eyes tearing. He sputtered and coughed as he choked on the blood running down the back of his throat from his crushed nose.

The guard finally managed to pull his weapon free, and Cyrus had a split second to make a life or death decision. He didn't know what was happening, but he'd just been attacked by a pair of United States Marines—Marines who were charged with the safety and security of a top secret installation.

Switching his newly acquired gun to his right hand for better accuracy, Cyrus fired a single shot into the right shoulder of the man who was blindly raising a weapon against him. The violent impact of the round spun the man back to the floor. A clatter was heard as his gun went skittering off across the tile.

Resting his knee on the back of the other guard and applying plenty of pressure to the arm he held wrenched behind the man's back, Cyrus finally had a chance to look back at Gertrude. She'd watched the entire series of events with a shocked, slack-jawed expression. The entire assault had taken place in less than five seconds, and it was clear from the look on her face that she hadn't been prepared for any of it.

"What the hell's going on here, Gertrude?" Cyrus asked in an angry voice.

His words snapped her from her shocked, inactive state. She looked at him for half a breath before turning back to the keypad and striking her card against the plate once more. Once more, the card was rejected.

"Something is very wrong here," she replied without turning around. "I've been locked out of my own lab and, needless to say, this isn't what these men are paid to do."

Frustrated, she tossed her swipe card aside and began punching buttons on the numeric keypad on the wall beside the door. Though Cyrus couldn't see what she was doing, each time she hit a button on the pad it emitted a quiet beep. Whatever she was doing behind him, she was entering dozens of numeric codes.

"Whatever you're doing, make it quick," Cyrus warned. "We need to get out of this hallway now."

"I'm working on it," she muttered.

A moment later there was a loud double 'chirp' followed by a pair of heavy 'thunks' that reverberated through the steel door. Cyrus looked back over his shoulder and saw the massive door to the lab begin to slide open on invisible tracks recessed into the concrete walls.

Flipping the safety on his liberated gun, Cyrus smashed it over the head of the man on which he knelt. The other guard was just starting to pull himself up from the floor when he, too, was clubbed and rendered unconscious.

Turning the guard with the gunshot wound over, Cyrus examined the injury. The man had taken the shot high in the shoulder, and as Cyrus hoped, he was wearing a vest. The bullet hadn't penetrated the skin, but it had spun him and knocked the wind out of him.

While he didn't know what was going on, something was deadly wrong—Cyrus had felt it even before they had entered the depths of the facility. Had the security guards gone rogue, or was there something more happening here? While he wasn't opposed to taking a life in defense of his mission's objective, something about what was happening bothered him, and he felt suddenly reluctant to shoot down anyone until he knew more.

Stepping across the threshold of the massive steel door, Cyrus nodded to Gertrude who stood at the control panel at the edge of the entry. She entered another code into the keypad and the door slid quickly shut behind them.

The lights of the lab flickered on a moment after the door closed, and Cyrus looked at the surrounding laboratory. It was a single open room, maybe a hundred feet wide and twice as deep. There were three elaborate workstations positioned nearest the door at the front of the room. Each system was essentially a small pod that consisted of a large, sloping, ergonomic chair perched before a horseshoe-shaped countertop equipped with three 30-inch flat panel displays.

Beyond the workstations were complex pieces of high end medical equipment, only some of which Cyrus recognized. There were MRI and CT scanning rigs, but they were highly customized compared to the ones he had seen in the Coalition's infirmary.

The lab also contained a pair of long medical tables, stainless steel with built-in drains. They were the same type of tables he'd seen in modern morgues and pathology labs. Along the back wall was a massive walk-in freezer with a door large enough to move in and out of while driving a small forklift.

"What's going on here?" he asked, casting an irritated glance in Gertrude's direction.

Moving slowly across the lab, Gertrude pulled a rolling stool out from under one of the counters and lowered herself onto it. She was clearly in pain from the rapid pace she'd set moving through the complex.

Just like she had following the attack at the corner market, Gertrude was taking this turn of events with a disturbing level of ease. Cyrus wondered what it would take to actually rattle the woman.

"You were going to tell me what you found out of place upon entering the facility," she reminded him.

"I don't know," Cyrus said with a frustrated shrug. He slipped out of his suit coat and draped it over one of the 30-inch computer displays. "This entire place just seems...*off*."

She shook her head. "You can do better than that. You're quite an observant young man. Indulge me. I'm very interested in knowing what raised your hackles."

Cyrus let out an exasperated sigh. "What's the small black dot behind your ear?" he asked, finally cutting through all pretenses.

Gertrude's hand went instantly to touch the small patch behind her ear as if she had forgotten it was there. She looked at him for several long moments, her expression a mix of what he could only guess was self-consciousness and indecision regarding the explanation.

"Alright," he said when her answer was not immediately forthcoming. "Whatever it is, I noticed that the guard at the gate wore a very similar patch. Not too unusual, but interesting. It made me wonder what it was all about. But once we came inside, I saw something in your eye when you noticed that Corporal Thoroe wasn't wearing a patch. At that point you started to become agitated. You were playing it cool, but I knew something was wrong. I figured the patch was some kind of security precaution that wasn't in place.

"Then I started to notice the cameras throughout the facility; first in the rec-room, then in the hallways leading to your lab."

"What about them?" Gertrude asked, clearly concerned with the observation.

"They were all offline. The wall-mounted cameras are from a company called X-Image Systems. The camera is the model A1. There's a small red LED that stays lit in the corner of each, just below the lens. The LED indicates that the system is online, but it's also a part of a sensor array that lets the camera read across multiple infrared and thermal modes. If there's no light, then the cameras are offline. That doesn't happen in a facility with security like this. Not unless someone did it intentionally."

Gertrude's normally grey complexion somehow grew more ashen with that realization. "Then no one knows we're here or what just happened?"

"It's a safe bet," Cyrus said flatly. "So I'll ask you one more time: What in the hell is going on? I think I've earned the right to know."

Chapter 17

Mayflower Lab Facility
Hennings, South Carolina
10:31 a.m.

Though she was seated on a stool, Gertrude leaned heavily against her cane while she struggled to regain her breath. The rapid pace she'd set in the rush to reach her lab was akin to a mad dash given her age, and she was feeling the effects. While she wasn't entirely sure what was happening, it was a virtual certainty that William was behind it. The guards who had attacked them in the hall were veterans of the facility. Every one of them had been stationed there for at least the last nine months. For them to turn on her now seemed to be an impossibility. Each member of the facility's security team had been hand selected for the assignment, and each possessed integrity that was beyond reproach. It was crucial, given the nature of her research.

It had to be William, she was certain of it. How he had managed it was another matter entirely. The facility and its staff had been equipped with all of the necessary countermeasures. Not that she ever expected to be protecting the project from her own grandson.

"Are you alright?" Cyrus asked. His concern for her

wellbeing was plainly visible in his eyes.

The young man was another variable that Gertrude had been trying to qualify. There was something about him, but she had consistently failed to put her finger on the exact quality that brought about her concern. By all accounts he seemed perfect for the position. Over qualified, in fact. For a time, she'd attributed her concern to that over-qualification, but now the 'disconnect' had become painfully apparent. The way he handled the pair of armed assailants attempting to rob the market was one thing. However unlikely, that *could* be attributed to a fortunate confluence of opportunity and luck; not to mention, how he claimed to have worked with a high-profile client and had learned many things regarding protection. But the way he had disabled the pair of armed guards, Marines no less, outside of her lab? That was another matter. Lightning didn't strike the same place twice, and no one was *that* lucky.

Still, she pushed those concerns aside for the moment. They had made it to the relative safety of her lab, but they were still cornered. The Mayflower Laboratory was located eight stories beneath the foundation of the city's central post office. In here, they weren't just cornered—they were cornered in a very deep dark hole.

"I'm alright," she said in a voice that was so weak that she surprised even herself. "I just need a moment to catch my breath."

But the look he was giving her indicated he was anything but convinced by her explanation. Plus, there was something more in his appraising stare; an unasked question of some kind that she was starting to dread.

"Okay, out with it," she said with a flagging sense of patience. "Speak your mind."

"I think it's time you leveled with me," he said without

hesitation, and in a tone that no longer deferred to her as a superior. "Running into a pair of thugs at the corner store was odd, but easy enough to write off to chance. But now you have trained Marines gunning for you. That's twice in twenty-four hours."

Gertrude stared at Cyrus, unhappy with his tone but entirely unable to argue with his concerns. "Is there a question in there somewhere?" she asked, with no hint of amusement.

Shaking his head, Cyrus turned and walked away. There was clearly more to the young man than she had expected. Gertrude was suspicious of everyone and everything, so finding out that there was more to him didn't shock so much as annoy her. Perhaps troubled was the better word, she realized. Whoever he was and whatever he was there to do, he had somehow managed to subvert Ashley's attempts to Read him.

That, more than anything, made no sense. Ashley had never been wrong before, and she'd never met anyone who she couldn't Read. Not unless they wore a neuro-dampener, of course. But Gertrude had developed that technology herself, and she knew with absolute certainty who had been equipped with one of the tiny devices. Each patch was no larger than the eraser at the end of a pencil, almost invisible unless you were looking for it, and they were foolproof—the only protection against Ashley's ability to glean thoughts, or William's ability to Push thoughts upon people.

That was it, Gertrude realized with absolute certainty. Though she didn't know how, William had gained access to the facility and turned the security team against them. It should've been impossible since neuro-dampeners were standard issue to all members of the security team. They were required to wear the patch night and day as it was the only guaranteed way to safeguard their minds.

But somehow William had subverted the technology. That idea alone was nearly as terrifying as the six trained Marines who were waiting to kill her.

"Marines?" Gertrude said suddenly.

Cyrus turned to look at the old woman. He clearly didn't understand the comment.

"You said Marines," she clarified. "How did you know that our security team was comprised of Marines? They wore no designation beyond rank. There was nothing to tell you from which branch of the military they'd been recruited."

"No trick there," Cyrus said. "Marines have a way about them. They sort of carry themselves differently. I have some friends in Delta, too. They're another distinctive bunch."

He seemed eager to dismiss the line of questioning.

"You're quite the enigma, Mister Cooper," Gertrude said with a slight grin. "Just full of surprises, aren't you?"

"All the same, I would appreciate it if you would fill me in on what's going on here. Why are American soldiers trying to kill us? I can't keep you safe if you don't level with me."

"That's it, isn't it? The explanation for your over qualification? You're not my assistant at all. You're here as some kind of bodyguard. Who sent you?"

The penetrating stare she received from Cyrus made it clear that his patience was running out far more quickly than hers.

"We can have that talk once we're out of here," he snapped. "Now spill it. What's going on?"

Though it was the last thing Gertrude wanted to explain, she realized that her back was almost literally against the wall and Cyrus represented her only plausible hope of escape. He was smart, too. He wouldn't settle for some watered down version of the truth. She would have to be honest and hope for the best. Besides, once they were clear of this mess, measures could be taken to insure that he never disclosed what she was about to share.

"Very well," she agreed. "As you surmised, those men outside are not acting of their own volition. They are being manipulated by an outside influence."

She levered herself up and into a standing position with the help of her cane, and crossed to a nearby station. There, she opened a cabinet door to reveal a small safe with a digital keypad. She entered the combination and swung the door open. Moving quickly inside the safe, she retrieved what she needed and closed the safe again before Cyrus had a chance to see inside. Turning around, she held out a small flat box about the size and shape of an old audio cassette.

Flipping open the lid, she showed Cyrus the inside. The box was lined in white felt but contained eight tiny round raised platforms. On top of each platform sat a small black patch just like the one she wore behind her ear.

"One of these is for you," Gertrude explained. "It's the final component of your security clearance package. You place this behind your ear. Once you do, you must never remove it. It's our most vital and sensitive security precaution."

She handed the case to Cyrus. "Take one and place it on the skin at the base of your skull directly behind one of your ears. It won't hurt, and once it's in place you'll actually forget that it's there."

Cyrus took a long look at the box, and then moved his gaze to her. She could virtually see the wheels moving behind his eyes, but she didn't understand what he was thinking.

Taking the box from her hand, Cyrus closed the lid with a solid, audible click. His eyes remained fixed on hers the entire time. Finally he took the entire case—all eight of the tiny patches included—and slipped them into a pocket inside his jacket.

"You don't understand," Gertrude snapped in ill temper. "You must apply the patch now. It's a safety precaution."

Pulling a second stool out from beneath the nearby counter, Cyrus sat down without reply.

"Cyrus," Gertrude snapped. "You must do this *now*."

"You can say it as many times as you like," he said calmly. "But until you explain what that patch is and exactly what it *does*, I'm not touching it.

"You have a choice to make," he continued. "Because I'm not doing anything until I get answers that satisfy me."

An exasperated huff was the best Gertrude could offer in response. She wasn't accustomed to conceding to the demands of others. But even as much as she found him insolent, she also knew he was her only chance at escape.

"You won't find any satisfactory answers," Gertrude said, lowering herself onto a stool beside Cyrus. "In all honesty, the truth is something you won't be inclined to believe, even if I share it."

"Share it," he demanded. "Let me make up my own mind."

Taking a moment to gather her thoughts, Gertrude decided that she was in a position with nothing to lose. "The man behind all of this is my grandson, William. He is manipulating the men charged with guarding this facility. By now, he will have full control of the complex. And now that he has taken control, I'm afraid I don't see a way out."

"There's always a way out," Cyrus said in a reassuring tone. "But the first step is to fully understand what we're up against. You said that he was manipulating the security team? You're talking blackmail, or some sort of coercion?"

"William is very *unique*," Gertrude began. She was having trouble finding the word. Actually voicing them proved even more difficult. "William has an unusual ability. He can make people *do things*."

Cyrus offered only a quizzical glare.

"Put crudely, his ability is mind control," Gertrude responded in a grating voice. "He needs only focus on what he wants from another person and he can *Push his thoughts* into *their minds*."

Cyrus laughed at first, but quickly realized she wasn't joking.

"We refer to it as *Pushing*," she explained. "He can literally influence the thoughts of others."

Cyrus sat quietly for several minutes, obviously taking time to process the unexpected revelation.

"He just has to think it, and people will do what he wants them to?" Cyrus asked finally. "That's incredible."

"It's not quite as simple as all that. It's not as easy as a passing thought. Thank God, it actually requires a concerted effort on his part. Otherwise, he might go around influencing the actions of everyone near him."

Her frustration and anger grew as the thoughts raced through her mind. "No, it's not entirely that easy. He had to try to do it—make a very specific effort. But, that said, the difficult process unfortunately comes easy to him, and makes him dangerous."

"No kidding," Cyrus snapped. "As illustrated by the armed men outside the door waiting to kill us. Actually, that raises a good question. Why *are* they trying to kill us?"

Gertrude realized that she had grown suddenly very tired. Somehow explaining the gravity of their situation felt as though it had lifted some sort of psychological burden from her shoulders. With that, exhaustion was setting in.

Cyrus must have noticed this as well because he left her to collect her thoughts while he went to retrieve a pair of bottled waters from the refrigerator. When he returned, she explained how William's ability hadn't manifested until shortly after his eleventh birthday. At first his ability to influence others was minimal, and it had taken her some time to realize his potential. But by the time he reached the start of his teenage years, it was clear that his gift was going to be a problem. He had become quite adept at manipulating the people around him to get the things he wanted.

Gertrude had realized it to be a slippery slope, but one that she was ideally suited to help him navigate. Since her field of specialty was applied neuroscience, she was already one of the world's foremost experts on the mind as well as the human brain. It hadn't taken her long to locate the portions of his brain that gave him the unique ability; after that, she was able to design a tiny implant that could be inserted into an adjoining portion of his cerebral tissue. It had taken some time to get the software properly calibrated, but once both the software and hardware were complete, a tiny capsule was embedded into his brain tissue. It was no larger than a small wood splinter, but it proved to work perfectly. William's ability to influence the thoughts and actions of others had been neutralized.

Though the procedure was a success, William's reaction to it was anything but positive. He'd become dependent on his ability. It was a type of sixth sense—a living part of him that was suddenly stripped away. And while everything Gertrude had done was for his own good, it had taken years for William to finally adapt and realize that she had kept him from the destructive path his ability was leading him down. In time, he worked around his reliance on his ability. He also came to understand just how destructive his careless use of that ability had been.

"I don't understand," Cyrus interrupted. "You make it

sound like William was doing well. Like he was a normal, functioning adult. But what I'm seeing here today seems anything but. What aren't you telling me?"

"At some point William realized how to disable the implant," Gertrude explained. "It was designed so I could modify the settings as needed. It was likely that some degree of fine-tuning would become necessary as he grew older and his brain moved through various stages of maturity.

"Somewhere along the line, he realized it was possible to interface with the implant. He found a way to access it and managed to shut it down. Since then, he's been running unchecked. He's become a danger to himself and everyone around him."

"Why don't you just reactivate the implant? Wouldn't that take away his ability all over again?"

Gertrude suddenly found herself unable to meet Cyrus's eye.

"What is it?" he pressed.

"I tried that; twice in fact. William killed both of the men I sent to deal with him."

Cyrus nodded, seeming to understand the potential danger. "It's funny," he said in a faraway voice. "He seemed off, but not anything like the man you describe when I ran into him."

Gertrude felt her heart catch in her throat. She struggled to catch her breath even as she stared at Cyrus through wide, unblinking eyes. "You've *met* William? What are you saying?"

Cyrus shrugged. "It was this morning when you sent me for coffee. He was at that little shop you like down on Fifth. I was walking out the door when I realized this long–haired, hippie-type was staring at me. It sort of set off alarms in my head after what happened yesterday, so I went over to see what his problem was. As soon as he took off his sunglasses and I saw his eyes, I knew he had to be related to Ashley. They have virtually identical eyes. It was odd."

"What did he say to you?" she asked, fighting off a claustrophobic sense of panic.

"Not much," Cyrus said when he thought about it. "It was more about what he didn't say. He seemed really…I don't know, *off* in some way—like the things that he *wasn't* saying were dangerous. He had this really intense, driving focus that just sort of rubbed me the wrong way. I don't know exactly how to describe it, but the way he met my eye struck me as violent. I've never seen someone look at me like that before."

Releasing a stifled breath, Gertrude suddenly realized she was holding her hand in front of her mouth and striking a pose every bit as terrified as the way she was feeling. But when her rational mind kicked in once more, she noticed parts of the story didn't add up.

"That's it?" she finally managed to ask. "Why didn't he use his ability right then and there? It would've been so easy. You were coming back to the office and he knew it. You could've killed me and no one could've stopped you…"

Her eyes narrowed as she glared at Cyrus. "You said he seemed off when he looked at you? That you found him intense, but off-putting?" She slid off the stool and walked slowly around the lab as if her mind where somewhere else entirely. So much so, that she had left her cane still leaning against the counter when she began hobbling around.

"Is it possible?" Gertrude muttered to herself. "But…how?"

She turned quickly and looked back at Cyrus. "I think he tried to Push you but it didn't work." Even to herself the statement had a wavering sense of conviction. It had never happened before, and it felt odd to even suggest it.

Cyrus only shrugged. "Okay," he said simply.

"You don't understand," she said. Her voice was growing

more agitated. "In all of my testing, that's never happened before. There's never been a subject who William couldn't Push."

Cyrus said nothing. Clearly he didn't understand the significance.

"*Never!*" Gertrude snapped.

The analytical portion of her brain was already spinning with questions and ideas. This offered an entirely new dimension to her research.

"Roll up your sleeve," Gertrude demanded. "I need to draw a blood sample!"

Chapter 18

Mayflower Lab Facility
Hennings, South Carolina
10:48 a.m.

Gertrude sat at one of the counters on the far side of the lab running Cyrus's blood sample through a series of processes that meant absolutely nothing to him. Moving closer to the lab's main door, Cyrus listened to the faint buzzing sound that was coming from the other side. He glanced back at Gertrude, satisfied that she would remain distracted. So far she hadn't realized that the security team was attempting to cut their way into the lab. From what he could tell, the sliding steel door was some variation on the old-fashioned blast doors that had been used in Cold War era bunkers. It was standing up to the security team's attempts to gain access to the lab, but it wouldn't last forever.

Cyrus knew he needed a plan.

The lab had no secondary entrance, so they were literally cornered. When he had asked Gertrude why she had led them to the lab once she realized the facility had been compromised, she said simply that she couldn't allow her research to be taken. She would destroy it before letting it fall into the wrong hands.

He still didn't know what constituted *the wrong hands*. The fact that her grandson was behind the attack on the lab seemed more like a personal matter than anything relating to her work. But that this was happening at all suggested that William was after far more than just a personal attack on his grandmother. Confronting her here clearly indicated that his goal involved the hidden research facility.

In light of current events, Cyrus had given more thought to his chance meeting with William earlier that morning. While it was obvious that the encounter was anything but accidental, Cyrus had been slow in coming to his ultimate conclusion. The awkward encounter had been William's attempt to use his gift to Push Cyrus into doing something; perhaps even killing Gertrude, or possibly manipulate him to take control of the underground lab. Whatever his plan, all Cyrus knew was that he had proven himself immune to William's influence—and without the aid of the strange patch that Gertrude and the security force had worn. Since that patch had suddenly proven ineffective, he had a unique advantage.

Forcing those thoughts from his mind had proven more difficult than Cyrus would've imagined. Even though the analytical portion of his brain told him that he needed to focus on the more pressing threat posed by the armed men attempting to breach the lab, he still had trouble wrapping his mind around what he'd learned in the course of the last twenty-four hours. William was a violent threat with some sort of supernatural power that allowed him to Push his thoughts and will into the minds of those around him. And his sister, Ashley, had the ability to Read the minds of people in close proximity. It was just too strange to believe.

No, Cyrus realized, as he looked back at Gertrude who was still busy at the far side of the lab, there wasn't anything supernatural happening here. There was a common thread and she was it. It wasn't a coincidence that she was a neurobiologist and neuroscientist, with two family members exhibiting exceptional neurological traits. There was more to it. But he needed to escape the lab before he could look into the matter more carefully.

Though his careful examination of the lab hadn't turned up any viable escape routes, the lab's ventilation system had caught his eye. The ceiling was about twenty-feet overhead with row after row of lighting ballasts suspended from lightweight chains that were anchored into the face of the concrete ceiling. Suspended in the space between the lights and the ceiling was a network of tubular eighteen-inch aluminum ducts. Some led to vents which brought fresh air into the lab, while others were part of a heavy duty exhaust system.

Gertrude had explained that the lab could have its entire atmosphere vented in less than a minute. In case of a dangerous chemical spill, all of the labs inside the facility had been equipped with identical emergency exhaust systems. It was necessary, particularly since they were located so far underground. Without it, a potent enough chemical spill or gas leak could render the entire facility permanently unusable.

Fresh air would be pumped into the room through vents situated along the floor while exhaust panels along the ceiling voided the atmospheric contents of the lab. It was an interesting system, Cyrus thought. But not for the way it functioned. He was more focused on the mechanics of the system itself.

Each of the ceiling vents opened into a wide four-foot by two-foot screen that hung from the ceiling, just beyond the overhead lights. The vent led to an eighteen-inch circular aluminum tube. But, most importantly, each vent and tube in the room backtracked to the same large aluminum box that was suspended from the ceiling in the back corner of the room. The box was cube shaped, measuring about eight-feet in each direction. It contained the fan unit that generated the vacuum needed to suck the air from the lab.

A system capable of moving such a massive amount of air in such a short amount of time would require both a powerful air draw and tubes wide enough to move the requisite volume of air. Cyrus quickly decided that the ventilation system was a potential way out.

A few minutes later, he had positioned a wide table beneath the massive ventilation box. Atop the table he placed another smaller table, before positioning a tall lab stool at the apex of the pile. The improvised ladder provided him hazardous, but adequate access to the panel on the bottom of the exhaust system's main housing.

Gertrude had been working at a nearby computer station, entirely consumed by her work on his blood sample. But as Cyrus prepared to climb his ladder, he saw her tap the same key on the keyboard repeatedly and with increasing frustration. "What is it?" he asked. "What's wrong?"

She entered several additional commands before responding. But when she finally pushed the keyboard away and slammed her fist on the table, it was almost as good as an answer.

"I just lost access to the server," she snarled. "The central database is offline."

Cyrus had a fair guess, but he needed to be sure. "What does that mean?"

She glared at him as if it were a monumentally stupid question. "I would say that William has just breached the server room. He won't get whatever he needs, but he'll want to make sure I can't stop him, so he's disabled remote access." She practically seethed, "He can't access the encrypted data without my help, but he's apparently crafty enough to keep me from accessing what I need from here."

Gertrude retrieved a small USB thumb drive from a drawer under the counter and inserted it into a port on the side of the keyboard. "I can't run a full analysis of your blood sample until I get back into the central server," she said through clenched teeth. "I'm storing the raw data on this drive until the server's back online. If you're right and they're about to enter my lab, I don't want them accessing this information. William will want to know why he couldn't Push you. I don't want to give him anything to work with."

Cyrus was surprised to find out that William would even be interested. Was it really that unusual for him to encounter someone with a natural immunity to his neural abilities? It was a subject Cyrus planned to raise once they had reached safety.

Though he had managed to construct his ladder without drawing Gertrude's attention, once she pulled the flash drive free from the computer keyboard, she regarded him on the primitive perch through bulging eyes.

"What in God's name are you doing?" Gertrude snapped.

Cyrus didn't look at her or stop his effort to free the access panel. There wasn't time. "We need a way out of here," he said simply. "I figure we have fifteen to twenty minutes before they breach. We have to get moving."

Lacking the tools to properly unscrew the access panel on the bottom of the large aluminum box, Cyrus slipped his fingers under the edge of the thin sheet metal and simply tore it free; it peeled back, offering a minimum of resistance.

"What are you talking about? We're perfectly safe in here," Gertrude said with gritty frustration. "The integrity of this lab is monitored off-site. I'm sure that a team has already been dispatched to recapture the facility."

Cyrus stopped what he was doing and looked down at Gertrude. She stood at the base of his improvised tower and leaned heavily on her cane with both hands. A deep scowl decorated her wrinkled face.

"William took control of the facility without firing a shot," Cyrus explained calmly. "If what you say is true, he's the puppet master, and he's now pulling the strings of the men who previously guarded this base. That means no alarms have been triggered, and no help is on the way. And it might be for the better. If William is as powerful as you say, the last thing we need is to hand him control of even more armed soldiers."

The scowl on Gertrude's face darkened.

"So no help is coming," she admitted. Judging from the sound of her voice it was as much a realization to her as it was to him.

"But we are safe in the lab…at least for the time being, so what are you doing?"

"They're cutting through the door," Cyrus said, pointing to the far end of the lab. He could already see an orange tint appearing along two separate sections of the wall. They were using cutting tools and torching a small access port, creating two separate lines which had started from the floor and were now working their way vertically. Before long, the lines would converge and complete a single breach in the door. "It won't take long."

Five minutes later, Cyrus had managed to tear the guts from the inside of the ventilation system exhaust box. He'd torn a powerful impeller motor from its mounts with his bare hands, and then proceeded to rip away the aluminum and stainless steel ductwork surrounding the air exhaust. By the time he was done, a pile of sharp metal wreckage had collected beside his stack of tables below.

Climbing down from the improvised ladder, Cyrus wiped the sweat from his eyes and took a deep breath. It had gotten hot, working inside the metal box suspended from the ceiling. And tearing the ventilation apart with his bare hands had taken its toll. His hands were lacerated; a spider web of small to medium-sized cuts now dripped blood on his clothes and the concrete at his feet.

Gertrude passed him a clean rag. "We need to put some antiseptic on those cuts," she said simply, before staring up at the jagged hole that was their only chance at freedom.

Cyrus saw a concern in Gertrude's eyes that wasn't related to his well being, and he knew something was wrong. He asked her what the problem was.

"The computer network is offline," she replied quietly.

So? He wondered, offering a shrug.

"All of my research is stored on the facility's main server," she explained. "At first I thought William was after me, but he could get to me anywhere. If he's gone through the trouble of coming here, he must be after the database."

It was a concern that had been bothering Cyrus for some time. Why would William go to the trouble of attacking the lab when he had the power to attack Gertrude anywhere, and at any time?

"Why would he want the database?"

A frown crossed the old woman's face, but she said nothing.

"I think the answer is pretty damn relevant right now," Cyrus insisted.

It was several long moments before Gertrude spoke. Cyrus was just about to accept the idea that she wasn't willing to discuss the matter when she finally gave in. "I think he's working for someone who's after my research," she said at last. "My relationship with William has been strained for some time.

We have certain…issues. I think that undermining my work is his way of striking back at me."

That confused Cyrus. "So which is it? Is he trying to kill you, or is he trying to undermine you? There's no point in doing both."

The question brought a penetrating stare from Gertrude. "What are you talking about? What makes you think he's trying to kill me?"

Cyrus rolled his eyes. "Well, the men with guns who are currently trying to break down the door, for one! Plus, I was told that your last assistant died under suspicious circumstances. It's currently believed that her death was actually a botched attempt on your life."

Another scowl from Gertrude appeared. He was getting those a lot lately.

"Sometimes an accident is just an accident," she corrected, and not very convincingly.

Cyrus was content to let that part of the conversation drop. It wasn't going anywhere useful. Either it had been an actual accident, or it hadn't. They had reached a point where it no longer mattered.

Looking back at the dark hole in the ceiling, he shook his head. "We need to get out of here."

"We can't leave without the data," Gertrude said in a tone that left no room for discussion.

"You don't have an off-site backup?"

She let out an audible sigh. "Not at the moment. The off-site backup was scrubbed while you were being vetted. Until I knew you were on the level, I couldn't risk having the information compromised. We were coming here today so I could reinitiate the upload and get the data replicating once more."

Cyrus felt his temper begin to flare. She was paranoid to an extreme. But was that the case, or was there something legitimate that she needed to hide? The more he learned of the woman, the less certain he felt.

"What if William already has your data? What if he's wiped it from the system and has already left the building?" Cyrus asked.

"He *can't* access the system without me," she practically shouted. "I'm the only one with the passwords. That's why he needs me alive."

Great!

What would William be willing to do to her in order to get that information? And what would he do with her once he had the data? Perhaps just as importantly, what had happened to that family to put them at such odds? The more he learned about this case, the more questions were raised.

"Okay, so we get the data and then we get the *Hell* out of here," Cyrus grumbled. "But step one is getting out of this lab."

Gertrude's eyes followed the stack of furniture leading to the dark hole in the ceiling. "How in God's name do you expect me to get up there?" she asked quietly.

Cyrus smiled. Running his hands under cold water in the lab's sink, he settled for wrapping them in thin white rags. The cuts in the exterior door had progressed, and they didn't have time for additional first aid. His only concern was that the wraps didn't interfere with his mobility, so they had to be kept thin; just bulky enough to stem the flow of blood. William's men would gain access to the lab in a matter of minutes. He had just enough time to prepare the next stage of his plan.

Pocketing a long shafted, flat-tipped screwdriver that he found at the back of a drawer while searching the lab, Cyrus also retrieved a pair of extra large latex examination gloves from the dispenser on the wall. Wrapping the wrist opening of a glove around the stem of the gas valve in the wall along the back of one of the counters, he feathered the release mechanism until the glove was inflated to just short of its rupture capacity. Then, twisting the latex at the wrist end of the glove as he slid it from the gas valve, he created a temporary seal that held long enough for him to tie it off as one would a child's balloon.

It took only a matter of seconds to complete the procedure with the second glove. Once his work was complete, he and Gertrude were ready to make their escape. She was already standing by, ready for the next step in his plan. Her scowl made it obvious that she had doubts regarding their chances for success, but for once she kept the thought to herself.

It was just as well. The orange line in the steel door had turned from a warm sunset into a burst of flame…they had only seconds left to make their escape.

Chapter 19

Mayflower Lab Facility
Hennings, South Carolina
11:08 a.m.

Clutching her cane in the darkness, Gertrude was afraid even to breathe. Her heart pounded in her chest, and she realized at that moment that it was a good thing she didn't need to stand. She wasn't sure she could; her entire body was shaking. She couldn't see anything, but she sensed Cyrus beside her. Reaching out a hand, she touched him just to be sure. How could he be so calm in this situation? She swallowed hard, a difficult task given how dry her mouth had become.

Finally, a thundering crash arrived, just as Cyrus had warned. Still, Gertrude felt her breath catch in her throat once more. This time it felt like her heart had actually stopped. The clamor of boots across the floor reached her ears, and she realized the guards were moving quickly. She struggled to discern how many there were based on the sounds of the footsteps, but the metallic rattle that accompanied each step made it impossible.

What struck her next was how quietly they moved. Aside from the footsteps and the slight crackle of a distant handheld radio, she heard no voices. Still, the rattle of the footsteps made their general location obvious. She could also tell when, one by one, the men left the floor. Feeling the line of cold sweat on her forehead, Gertrude knew that they were ascending Cyrus's improvised ladder one at a time.

The silence that followed the last rattle of the floor tiles seemed to last an eternity. Still, Gertrude waited for the command.

"Okay," Cyrus whispered in the darkness. "Watch your eyes, and remember to move as quickly as you can."

Out of nowhere a searing light blinded Gertrude, and she raised a hand to shield her eyes. She didn't have the luxury of letting her eyes adjust, so she accepted the discomfort as light flooded their hiding place. She watched as Cyrus pushed the large heavy tile away and sat up, sticking his head through the hole—gun drawn, ready to fire.

When no shots rang out, Gertrude counted her blessings. Their hiding place had been a gamble, but so far it seemed to be paying off. She pushed a bundle of network cables off her leg and propped herself up on both elbows. Cyrus had already extracted himself from the eighteen-inch recess beneath the laboratory floor. A moment later, he pulled another of the three-foot square tiles free, allowing her to stand.

The entire lab sat on a floor of metal tiles. The tiles were raised eighteen inches over a recess in the concrete floor that made it easy to route plumbing, electrical conduit, and network lines as needed, anywhere in the lab. Every lab in the facility was configured similarly for ultimate flexibility. The raised floors were common in computer network data centers, but proved equally flexible and effective in a laboratory environment.

Accepting Cyrus's hand, Gertrude allowed him to hoist her up from where she had lain flat on her back beneath the floor. With surprising ease, he lifted her out of the hole in the floor and set her aside. A moment later he had retrieved her cane from the recess and was already replacing the floor tiles to mask their escape.

Looking at the crude hole that had been cut into the steel door a few feet away, Gertrude realized for the first time just how much effort it had taken for the soldiers to cut through the door. Though she had never considered it before, she now saw that the exterior door was more than four inches thick.

Glancing over her shoulder, she looked at the tower of furniture leading to the gaping hole in the ventilation system along the ceiling in the back corner of the room. She wondered how many of the security team had gone into the ventilation system on the wild goose chase, and how long it would take for them to realize they had been duped.

"Let's go," Cyrus whispered.

With those orders, Gertrude watched him duck through the steel door's crude hole. She followed quickly behind the man who would lead her to safety.

Chapter 20

Mayflower Lab Facility
Hennings, South Carolina
11:22 a.m.

Stepping through the hole, Cyrus noticed a small pool of blood a few paces away and recognized that he must've hit one of the guards harder than he thought. Regardless, he had no doubt that both of the downed guards were once more back in the game. It was the down side of his reluctance to kill the Marines on duty. But as much as letting them live flew in the face of his primary instincts, taking their lives was still far more of a violation of his personal beliefs. While he was accustomed to dealing with enemy combatants in situations similar to this, he now faced American soldiers: Men who opposed him through no fault of their own. The fact that they had been stripped of their free will was an inexcusable abuse he wouldn't compound.

Though he wasn't sure how many of the guards had followed his false trail into the ventilation system, a quick glance at the camera mounted high on the wall reminded him of two things; First, there would still be one guard left to man the security feeds; second, the men following the false trail wouldn't be fooled for long. Whoever was monitoring the cameras would soon radio the rest of the team to expose his deception.

Cyrus drew the weapon he had taken from one of the guards he'd disabled prior to taking refuge inside Gertrude's lab. A carefully fired shot permanently disabled the watchful eye of the camera as they moved down the hall. He did the same with each camera as they moved.

After taking out a total of nine cameras, covering several hundred yards of surrounding adjacent hallways, Cyrus doubled back and stashed Gertrude in one of the many unlabeled utility closets that lined the halls—positioned between massive steel doors leading to labs similar to Gertrude's. Odds were good that she would be safe there while he took the majority of the security team out of play for the duration of their visit.

Along the way, he stopped at one of the fire suppression stations that were built into the hallway walls at equal intervals. They were simple utility panels that reflected the level of preparation that had gone into the design of the facility. Being secreted so far underground, emergency response efforts were simply not an option. So, like the ventilation systems in each lab, the halls were equipped with stations containing a section of heavy gauge fire hose wound around a thick spool, a pair of oxygen masks, and a massive red headed fire axe.

Shattering the glass panel on one of the fire stations, Cyrus left the rest of gear behind, retrieving only the heavy red axe. Heading down the hall on his own, he stepped into one of the half-dozen labs they had passed that had its security doors wide open. Those labs seemed to be unallocated—prepped and configured with basic laboratory equipment, but not in use.

Just inside the door he flipped the half dozen light switches that were arrayed directly beside the numeric keypad that controlled the heavy rolling security door. While the keypad was recessed into the concrete wall to avoid tampering, the light switches were part of surface mounted electrical boxes that were affixed to the face of the wall. A thick metal conduit ran from the row of light switches up into the darkness beyond the light fixtures above. He was relieved to see that this lab had been wired exactly as Gertrude's had, and that his plan was still sound. Quickly, he moved deeper into the lab as the overhead lights blinked to life with a flickering buzz.

Near the back wall, Cyrus pulled the few free standing lab tables into a defensive perimeter and upended them, creating a barrier by protecting the back wall from the positions the security team would have when they entered the room. Then, driving the screwdriver into the seam between the wide tiles on the floor, he pulled back the first panel and revealed the recessed space beneath.

Cyrus assumed that his opponents would have realized how he had evaded them in Gertrude's lab. After all, even though the men were in some way under the control of William Waterford, they were also professionals who retained their high-level tactical awareness and the ability to operate independently. They weren't mindless drones obeying a single-minded command, so there was a very good chance that they would be on the alert of another deception following the wild goose chase through the ventilation system.

Pulling back another floor tile, Cyrus set it aside with the first. He dropped down into the shallow cubby and stared at the tangled mess of haphazardly placed flexible conduits and loosely run network lines. He kicked the cables and conduit away, creating enough room for him to move around. Once he had the space, he ducked under the floor and crawled beneath the tiles. It took only seconds to fashion a small open area in the thornless briar patch of tangled cables and wires.

The decoy complete, Cyrus quickly rose from the hole in the

floor and darted back to the lab's entry. Using the screwdriver once more, he began prying the conduit tube that ran from the bank of light switches and up into the darkness beyond free hanging light ballasts. He needed to separate the conduit from the wall just enough to fit his fingers behind the pipe without making his modification obvious.

As an extra measure to ensure later efficiency, he slid the bladed tip of the screwdriver under the corner of the metal switch plate and applied *just* enough pressure to bend back the plate's corner and create a jagged little barb.

Cyrus pocketed the screwdriver and retrieved the fire axe from where he had left it leaning against the wall. He knew there wasn't much time left. Whoever was running the cameras would've recalled the security team by now, and they would be searching and hungry for blood.

With a single swing of the axe, Cyrus severed the conduit just above the light switches and plunged the lab into darkness. Sparks flashed and several of the overhead bulbs popped, sounding like minor explosions in his silent surroundings. It was for the best; he needed to draw the security team to him sooner rather than later.

With a jump, Cyrus pulled himself up along the wall of the lab using the wiring conduit as an improvised rope. He'd only been able to pry the tube away from the wall as far as he could reach while standing on the floor, so he quickly ran out of hand holds when he reached the next point where the conduit was still anchored.

Planting his feet against the wall, he levered slowly and pulled the tube away from the wall as needed while he moved higher into the darkness of the ceiling beyond. As soon as he began his ascent, he missed the comfort and grip of the hiking boots that he typically wore. His dress shoes not only offered no support in his climb, but their slick soles made finding traction on the smooth surface of the concrete wall almost impossible.

Once he climbed past the height where the light fixtures were suspended from the ceiling, Cyrus reached the maze of ducts and tubes that constituted the elaborate ventilation system.

By the time he reached the appropriate height, his eyes had adjusted to the near total darkness. Grabbing hold of one of the anchoring assemblies that supported the duct work, Cyrus shifted his weight so he was no longer hanging entirely from the conduit. Placing one foot on the small steel flange that supported a major section of the duct, he eased into a comfortable crouch that left him with a bird's eye view of the room's entry below.

He didn't have to wait long. It was likely the popping of the light bulbs that helped reveal his position. Cyrus didn't like the idea of hanging suspended from the ceiling in the awkward position any longer than necessary. Hanging from rigging that wasn't designed to bear his weight, he was already becoming uncomfortable in his stooped position, and his proximity to the aluminum duct work was precarious at best. Any movement on his part could cause the metal work to flex and, if it did, it would most certainly make a terrible racket.

When the security team arrived, they did so with silence and precision. Cyrus didn't realize they were there until the shadows of three figures crossed the threshold beneath him. The first moved to one side of the door and took up a kneeling position, his rifle raised and ready. A breath later, two more men swept into the room. The three men fanned out and moved slowly into the darkness. Cyrus watched, nearly afraid to breathe considering any movement might give away his position. He needed to get the men as far into the lab as possible before making his move.

As the trio moved out of his field of view, Cyrus wondered if that was the extent of the force moving in on the lab. An answer to his silent question came a moment later as a pair of additional shadows appeared at the corners of the darkened doorway. They were being cautious, likely more so after what had happened in Gertrude's lab.

All Cyrus could do was wait. If he had to take out the two men at the door, things would get messy. Worse, his escape would be delayed—likely long enough for the first three men to attack him before he could seal the lab.

Just before he had to make the tough decision, Cyrus noticed a simultaneous change in the posture of both remaining shadows at the door. The last two men quickly swept into the room, each sticking to their respective walls as they moved deeper into the lab and out of Cyrus's line of sight. A smile spread across his face and he exhaled a slow, silent breath. The first part of the team had found his burrow beneath the floor. In the darkness, they weren't able to establish the extent of it, and radioed the men at the door to tighten up their perimeter while they took a closer look.

Cyrus knew he didn't have long before they realized his hidey-hole was only a diversion; so, taking a deep breath, he swung his weight-bearing foot from its balancing point on the ventilation duct platform and placed it against the wall. Finally, the lack of traction his shoes brought to the party actually worked in his favor. Slipping his cloth-wrapped hands around the vertical wiring conduit, he slid silently down to the floor. The short burst of friction quickly passed through the wraps on his hands and he felt the cuts on his palms burn. Still, he didn't lose a step.

The moment his feet touched the floor, his eyes fell on the lights of the numeric keypad that was mounted into the wall. The tiny display was lit with a message that said simply, READY. Those tiny letters seemed glaringly bright while his eyes attempted to come back from the near pitch-black world in the ceiling.

According to Gertrude, the lab was equipped with dozens of sensors that monitored for any kind of contaminant leak. Even a small issue with a chemical spill could quickly grow catastrophic for a secret lab located so far underground, particularly in a major metropolitan area. While most of the chemical sensors would be impossible to find without knowing where to look, it was a near certainty that one such device would be located in or near the door's control panel.

Retrieving the pair of inflated sterile gloves, Cyrus simply gashed them both open on the tiny bend of jagged metal he had created at the edge of the light switch plate. The first glove deflated with a muffled pop, followed immediately by the second glove. A heartbeat later, a large red light flashed to life at the center of the lab. It began to spin, mimicking the familiar light on top of a police car, alternating between red and blue, as a blaring klaxon sounded from seemingly every direction.

A large 'hiss' burst from the far end of the doorframe beside him, and Cyrus moved without conscious thought, leaping through the entrance just before the massive steel door rocketed across its rails, coming to an explosive halt when it met the frame on the opposite end. A violent noise shrieked and gas vented into the hallway as the perimeter of the door began to glow with some kind of chemical reaction.

The lab was now sealed in a very literal way, Cyrus knew. While he had expected a similar automated response when he sent a healthy dose of natural gas into the chemical sensor near the door keypad, the fact that the doorway was now effectively welded shut was unprecedented.

Five of the six-man security team had been taken out of play without any loss of life. The ventilation system would've purged what was thought to be tainted atmosphere from the lab and replaced it with fresh, clean air. But the doors were not likely to open again until some sort of administrative override was used to ensure that the precipitating issue had been properly dealt with. That pleased Cyrus. Now he just needed to locate the last remaining member of the security detail and find out if William Waterford still lurked in the shadows of the Mayflower Laboratory.

Chapter 21

Mayflower Lab Facility
Hennings, South Carolina
11:47 a.m.

With five of the six security guards locked up tight, Cyrus had more freedom to move through the facility. He didn't have to worry about rounding each corner only to catch a bullet in the face. It took him less than a minute to double back to the supply closet where he'd stashed Gertrude. Unfortunately, when he entered the small room to retrieve her, she was nowhere to be found.

It seemed like a long shot that the roving security patrol had found her, at least until he took a closer look at the strike plate on the door jamb of the supply closet. It was wired with a sensor. He realized that the moment they'd entered the closet, it must've tripped a signal back in the facility's security office, alerting one and all that the room had been compromised.

After all that had happened, it seemed a safe bet that William now had Gertrude in his possession. And if he needed her help to gain access to the central database, thanks to his ability to manipulate the minds of others, it was only a matter of time until he had exactly what he wanted.

Cyrus realized he needed to act *fast*.

The first order of business was to locate the security office. Since William was now short on manpower, there was a very good chance that the office would be unguarded and would offer Cyrus the same omniscient view of the facility that William had enjoyed while stalking them. Cyrus hoped to locate William and the last remaining guard and gain a tactical advantage by using the cameras prior to making his move.

As he rounded the corner and sprinted down the hall, Cyrus passed Gertrude's lab. The familiar hole in the lab door caught his eye, but then the pool of blood on the floor outside the door drew his attention. Stopping dead in his tracks, Cyrus stared at the dark patch and realized it had been disturbed. Though he couldn't tell it by looking at the congealed puddle itself, he found a pale pink semicircle marked on the tile a few feet away. Looking closer, he found another mark a few feet further down. A path…

Cyrus smiled. Studying the markings, he realized that Gertrude had intentionally plunged the base of her cane into the pool of blood while being led past the location on the way to destinations unknown. It was her attempt to leave a trail for him to follow.

Not bad! The trail would certainly come in handy since it would make navigating the warren of hallways that zigzagged the underground structure much, much easier.

Afraid of wasting more time, Cyrus pushed the improvised trail of breadcrumbs from his mind and focused on first locating the security office. He needed to gather intelligence before he could stage a rescue. As luck would have it, finding the security office didn't prove to be a difficult matter. Each intersection in the wide halls was labeled with a series of highway-like road signs denoting the proper direction to labs, maintenance areas, and offices. The paths to the administrative and security offices were equally well designated. Cyrus took a deep breath, hoping that very soon the hunter and prey in this scenario would be reversed, and William Waterford would meet his fate.

Chapter 22

Mayflower Lab Facility
Hennings, South Carolina
11:52 a.m.

Sitting on the wheeled stool, Gertrude couldn't help but lean the bulk of her weight on her cane. She was exhausted, and the day had only just begun. Now, more than ever, she was feeling every last hour of her seventy-four years. But all of that paled when compared to what she experienced when she looked into William's eyes. They contained so much anger and pain that she scarcely remembered the young boy she had once bounced upon her knee.

William stood only a few feet away dressed in a dark t-shirt and jeans. His hair was long and shaggy, more so than she had ever seen it, and she wondered if it had grown that way by his own choice or through the neglect of his previous caretakers. She wanted to voice the concern but feared for her own safety, and the bitter, malicious feelings that were sure to come to the surface. William was her grandson, but she had substantial reasons to fear him.

Not the least of which would come if he gained access to her project archives. If William harbored harsh feelings for her now, he was sure to come unglued if he learned the truth of his birth.

"I'll ask you one last time," William said with a patience that was not present in his penetrating stare. "Then I'll tear into your mind and take what I want."

Gertrude shook her head sadly. "We both know that isn't true, William." She placed her finger on the tiny circular patch behind her left ear to ensure that the small device was still in place. "Even if you take this from me now, it will be days before the compound is clear of my bloodstream. And we both know you can't wait that long."

A smile spread across William's face, as if he knew a secret and was deciding whether or not to share it with his grandmother. After letting the disconcerting grin last for several moments too long, he turned to the other man in the room and motioned him forward.

"This is Frank Hubbard," William said. "Otherwise known as the Chief of Security for the Mayflower Facility."

Twirling his finger in the air, William signaled for Frank to turn around slowly.

The man made it only half a rotation before Gertrude realized the point of William's display. First, she thought it was to illustrate that the man was entirely under his control. As part of the screening process, security personnel on staff at the lab had undergone an extensive battery of psychological examinations. Due to his rank and position, Frank Hubbard would've been among the best of the best—the cream of the proverbial crop. The objective was to staff the facility with capable individuals who already had some sort of natural immunity to various forms of neural manipulations. That Frank had become William's puppet was deeply troubling, but it turned out not to be the primary scene in William's twisted theatrical production.

Gertrude felt the breath sucked from her lungs when Frank turned far enough for her to see that his patch was still in place behind his left ear. Her jaw fell slack, and she found herself staring wordlessly at the man before her. Certainly it was possible that William had compromised the man in another way—perhaps through bribery or blackmail. But it was the look in Frank's eye that told her that wasn't the case. When a subject was Pushed it brought a slightly different look to their stare. It wasn't something most people would notice in a complete stranger; it wasn't even something a close friend or family member was likely to notice in another, but it was something that Gertrude recognized with practiced precision. She'd been around enough Pushed subjects over the years to understand what she was seeing.

What she didn't understand was *how?*

"Thank you, Frank," William said, waving the man a few paces distant to stand guard.

"You sent me away," William said, fixing his grandmother with a chilling glare. "You had me medicated and locked up. But you can't put me in a cage, Grams. As it turns out, the more drugs they pumped into me, the harder I had to work to maintain control of myself."

His eyes produced a manic gleam and his grin turned into a toothy smile. "It turns out that you only made me stronger! Tell me, how does that influence your precious research?"

It took a moment for Gertrude to find her voice. "You mean to tell me that the compound no longer inhibits your control?" It was terrifying to even contemplate the question. The threat of having it confirmed chilled her to the bone.

"From the look on your face, I'm guessing you don't have a plan B?" William mused. He looked over his shoulder at the floor to ceiling glass wall that separated them from the server room beyond. The room was dark but seemed alive with the random pulsing of a variety of tiny colored LED lights that blinked on the faces of dozens of servers and rack mounted components.

"Give me what I want," William said, meeting her eye once more. "Or, I swear to God, I *will* take it, and I'll make you wish you'd treated me differently while I'm at it."

A nauseous churning was gathering momentum deep in her gut. Gertrude knew that, not only did William mean to make good on his threat, but he was also looking forward to the opportunity to bring her pain. Still, she reasoned, whatever he might do to her now was nothing compared to what he would do to her if he accessed the database and learned the truth.

Chapter 23

Mayflower Lab Facility
Hennings, South Carolina
12:01 p.m.

Cyrus listened to William's threats as he tried to coax his grandmother into giving up access to the database. He couldn't understand why William didn't just dig directly into Gertrude's mind and extract the information; based on all that he had learned, it seemed the man was sufficiently capable of such mental manipulations. So why was he going through the trouble of questioning his grandmother at all? *There's something more going on.* Something that William wasn't saying that made him reluctant to engage his grandmother on such a level.

After locating the security office, Cyrus had made a quick sweep and confirmed that the area was clear. The security server had been smashed in an effort to prevent exactly what he was attempting. Luckily, whoever had done the job hadn't been thorough enough. The power supply in the computer that operated the cameras and recording devices had fried, taking down the surveillance system. But the machine had redundant power supplies, which was typical of high end, mission critical hardware. Cyrus simply swapped out the power supply. It took the computer longer to boot up than it did to reconfigure the hardware, but after that, he had the base's camera system functioning once more.

Locating Gertrude and William in the server room had been a simple matter. Cyrus retrieved a couple of party favors from the weapons locker of the security office before ducking back out the door and sprinting through the hallways. Actually locating the server room would've been the hardest part of his task, had it not been for Gertrude. Each hallway intersection was clearly labeled to make navigating the underground structure easy, but the location of the server room wasn't designated by any of the posted signs. Nor had the server room been listed on the building schematic diagrams that were posted on the wall of the security office. It seemed that the only personnel allowed access to the central server room were those who knew how to find it for themselves. It was a curious security precaution, but no less strange than some of the other things Cyrus had seen since accepting his current assignment. Had it not been for the faint scuffmarks of dried blood intentionally left by his so-called employer's cane, Cyrus would've wasted precious time searching for the location he'd seen on the surveillance displays.

Now Cyrus crouched at the corner of the last solid wall that separated him from his target. Thankfully, this wall was fully framed and clad in drywall. The next room and its adjacent rooms were walled entirely in glass. He realized he was lucky enough to get as close as he had, because he remained in earshot of the conversation William was having with Gertrude. Had they been one room over, Cyrus would've been unable to approach without giving up his position.

The conversation he'd overheard had confused him. It was like seeing a puzzle from a distance. There were large portions of the bigger picture that were missing, but the few portions of the greater whole that Cyrus *had* understood were bone chilling.

Cyrus shifted the gun to his right hand and was just about to make his move when he heard William speak again, but this time around his voice was different. Cyrus realized that the man was speaking to someone new, evident by a more patient and softer tone.

Tipping his head around the corner of the doorjamb, Cyrus quickly learned that William was using the phone from a nearby desk. It made sense. Wired lines were the only hope he had of communicating with anyone outside of the building. They were too far underground to have cellular access.

"You were right," William said into the phone. "She won't talk. I'll have to extract the information personally."

William went silent, obviously listening to the voice on the other end of the line.

"I understand. It's not a concern. I can do this. To be honest, I think I'll enjoy it."

He waited once more.

"No," William said. "I understand. Minimal breakage."

Lowering the phone gently onto the receiver, Cyrus saw a smile cross the man's face before he turned back to his grandmother.

"That's it," he told her. "If you won't tell me what I need to know, I'll take the information by force. Your last line of defense just gave me the 'all clear'."

All clear? What did that mean?

"So you're not in this alone?" Gertrude spat in an acidic tone. "That shouldn't surprise me. You've never done anything ambitious on your own; just ridden on everyone else's coattails. Why should this be any different?"

Wow, Cyrus marveled. *These people take family issues to an entirely new level.*

Stepping around the corner of the door, Cyrus walked into the glass office with his gun held high. Gertrude was the first to see him, her wide-eyed expression prompting William to turn and face him. It also prompted Frank to go for his weapon.

Cyrus beat the man to the punch, firing a single round that didn't strike Frank but also didn't miss him by much either. The bullet shattered the glass wall behind the mind-controlled guard and caused him to halt in the midst of drawing his weapon. The gun was halfway out of his holster when Frank regarded him with wide eyes.

"Drop it...or, the next one won't miss," Cyrus warned. His voice was level, and he had a surprisingly conversational tone given the spiking tension in the room.

Frank's eyes remained locked on Cyrus. He shifted his grip on the gun, holding it between the tip of his thumb and forefinger before slowly stooping and placing it on the tile floor.

"It's nice to see you again, Mister Cooper," William offered, with a tight smile. He had Gertrude's arm tight in his grasp and kept her positioned between himself and Cyrus. Still, he made little effort to use her as a human shield.

Cyrus turned his gun toward William but held it in a position that showed he was less prepared to fire. "You've gone through a lot of trouble just to get here," Cyrus said. "If you'd been more forthcoming at the coffee shop this morning, maybe we could've cut to the chase."

"It's funny you should say that. That was, in fact, my intention. But you proved surprisingly immune to my...*charms.*"

The comment brought a smile to Cyrus's face. "Don't flatter yourself. You're not that charming."

"Evidently not," William admitted. "But, in fairness, it's not often I meet someone such as yourself. The only people to ever give me trouble are the one's wearing that damned patch." He twisted his grip on Gertrude's arm and forced her to turn so that Cyrus could see the tiny dot that was still in place behind her ear.

It was beyond troubling when Cyrus caught a quick glance at Frank, standing silent with his hands raised, and realized that he wore the same patch as Gertrude.

"It doesn't seem like you have trouble with the patch, after all," Cyrus commented. He hoped to get William talking. He was playing catch-up, and had no solid idea what the patch accomplished in relation to William or why William couldn't Push him like he did the others. He was hoping to sort it out in the process.

"Seems you're right. There's been a reversal of fortune," William said smugly. He was practically beaming, impressed with himself and his triumph. "Gram's miracle patch is no longer a problem for me."

"Clearly," Cyrus acknowledged in a dry, passionless tone. He would admit the man had succeeded, but stroking his ego was entirely unnecessary. "But why break into a maximum security installation? What's here that's so important to you? It can't be your grandmother. You could've gotten to her in a hundred different ways that were easier than this."

"Very true. This isn't about her so much as it is her work," William explained. "You work for her—"

Stopping cold, William cocked his head and looked at Gertrude. He seemed confused at first, and then smiled with understanding. "Oh, I see," he said. "You're still new here. She hasn't shown you what dark secrets lie behind the proverbial curtain." He laughed. "Don't worry Grams. They won't be secrets for much longer.

"It's only a matter of time before grandmother gets what's coming to her," William met Cyrus's eye as he continued, "For now, this is about her research and the atrocities she's committed. You really have no idea what she's done, do you?"

Cyrus raised his gun and took careful aim at William. "She's not the one trespassing and taking hostages," he warned.

Shifting his angle by several degrees, William brought the semiautomatic handgun held in his free right hand into view and pressed it squarely into Gertrude's back.

Movement to his left drew Cyrus's attention and he spun, turning the gun on Frank. The man had pulled a secondary sidearm from a hidden holster. Cyrus had the man squarely in his sights and his finger had already pulled the slack from the trigger; now, sending the round would require fractional effort. But when he saw that Frank wasn't pointing the weapon at him, Cyrus backed off the trigger—both Frank and William had their weapons trained on Gertrude.

"Don't look so surprised," William said. He was now careful to use Gertrude as a human barrier. "The thought is practically screaming in her mind. She knows you don't want to shoot a United States Marine. And, by the way, she's pissed. If she had it her way, you would kill me and Frank right here and now. Does that sound like the kind of woman you should be working for?"

He made a good point, Cyrus realized. And as much as he didn't trust William, nothing the man had said since he'd entered the room had struck him as a lie. Once this was over, Cyrus planned to make a point of looking into William and Gertrude Waterford more thoroughly. But this time he wouldn't use the information provided by his people at the Coalition. Something was going on here that wasn't detailed in the mission briefs he'd been provided.

The most interesting point at the moment, however, was why both William and the Marine named Frank were currently pointing their weapons at Gertrude. He was the most obvious threat in their current situation, the man with the gun, and it made sense for at least one of them to be threatening him. But since William was effectively in control of both weapons at the moment, it could only mean one thing.

"Why don't you want me hurt?" Cyrus asked. The question fell from his lips before he realized he'd said the words aloud.

Surprise registered plainly on William's face. "Can you Read me?" he asked.

Cyrus shook his head. "No, but you're reluctant to shoot me, which means you have a reason. You want to know why you can't Push me, and you can't do that if I'm dead."

William's smile widened. "Are you sure you're not a Reader?"

"I don't need to be."

"To be honest, I'm a little on the fence about killing you," William admitted. "Did you know that she ran an extensive workup on your blood? She prompted the computer system to do a full DNA analysis and genome map right before I knocked the network offline.

"She's even more interested in what makes you tick than I am. And if you let her get her hooks into you, you'll wish I'd shot you right here and now." His voice grew deeper, as if his mind was traveling back to a time of pain. "You don't know what this woman is capable of."

Cyrus fixed William with a penetrating stare. "I said it before and I'll say it again, she's not the one taking hostages."

"Tell that to Keegan Porter," William spat. "Or any of the other—"

Movement in his peripheral vision told Cyrus that Frank was making his move. Even now, killing Frank seemed too wrong.

Dropping the sights of his gun in a sharp angle toward the

floor, Cyrus fired a single shot. The weapon's report sounded like an explosion inside the fish tank-like walls of the glass room. The fired round struck William's foot, the only clearly exposed portion of his anatomy. Blood splattered across the tile as the man shrieked in pain.

Cyrus charged forward, tugging Gertrude aside, at the same time as he drew a solid bead on William's torso. But he needn't have bothered. When the man recoiled in pain and shock from the gunshot to his foot, the gun in his hand was sent flying. William was already slumping to the ground, his hands prodding the new, fleshy hole in his body.

With William momentarily immobilized, Cyrus stepped in front of the still stumbling form of Gertrude and spun to bring his weapon to bear on Frank. But, again, he needn't have bothered. The gun had already fallen from the man's hands; William's mental hold on him had shattered along with the bones of his foot.

Frank looked around slowly with unblinking eyes, likely without seeing anything around him. It was as if his brain was rebooting. The effort was apparently too much for him, as his knees buckled and he collapsed to the floor where he landed hard on his butt. There he sat, silent and still like a punch-drunk fighter who had gone one round too many.

Cyrus forced William face down on the floor and pulled the man's hands behind his back. He began slipping a pair of flex cuffs, liberated from the security office, around his wrists.

Cyrus shot a harsh look at Gertrude. "What sort of proximity does he need?"

She didn't answer. She only looked confused, likely stunned by the rapid violent display.

"Proximity!" Cyrus snapped. "How close does someone need to be for him to put the whammy on them?"

Gertrude's eyes snapped back to a sharp and ready stare. "Fifty meters, last I knew. But he's changed," she said with concern. "He's more powerful now. Let's say one hundred for safe measure."

Cyrus offered a curt nod. "It looks like his boy Frank is snapping out of it. Take him and head back to the security office. That will put you at a safe distance."

"Right," she said, heading for the door. "Wait—what about you?"

"It's like you said, I seem to be immune to whatever he's doing to people. I'll be fine. I figured a serious shock would be enough to knock out whatever he was using on everyone. If we dose him with a sedative, will that keep him offline?"

"Absolutely. I know just the cocktail. Give me ten minutes."

Gertrude helped the frazzled and hapless form of Frank Hubbard to his feet and guided him from the room. Cyrus sat with a knee on William's back and pinned him to the floor until Gertrude and Frank had reached a safe distance. If worst came to worst and he thought William was trying to work his magic on someone again, it shouldn't take more than a kick to the man's shattered foot to put things right.

Chapter 24

The Feedmount Building
Hennings, South Carolina
2:06 p.m.

Cyrus waited in the living room of Gertrude's spacious 10th floor apartment. He hadn't realized how much larger units on the 10th were compared to Ashley's place on the 6th, but the difference had now become apparent. The room held a pair of massive sofas and three large chairs arranged around a regal fireplace. Expensive antiques, the likes of which Cyrus had seldom seen outside of a museum, were on casual display all around the house. A large terrace, complete with a wrought iron table and matching set of chairs overlooked the city below.

In the next room, Ashley was tending to her grandmother. Gertrude had called in ancillary security teams to lock down the underground lab once William had been subdued. An intensive debrief had followed in which Cyrus had been thoroughly questioned about everything that had happened as well as his involvement in it.

After all was said and done, Gertrude insisted on returning to her office so she could get back to work. Recognizing the woman's exhaustion, even if she didn't, Cyrus had suggested that stopping by her condo briefly would give her a chance to freshen up. He'd phoned Ashley with hopes that she might convince the woman to settle down and recuperate. As he suspected, the moment Gertrude stepped into her home, the full weight of the morning's events settled in, and she was willing to take the remainder of the day off. Ashley took Gertrude to her room and put her to bed.

Cyrus bided his time and waited for Ashley to finish with Gertrude; the events of the morning ran through his head in a constant loop. He still had trouble reconciling William's ability to literally control the thoughts and actions of the people around him. If that wasn't strange enough, his apparent *inability* to influence Cyrus was as much a shock to the young man as it was to Gertrude. By both accounts, William had never encountered an individual who he couldn't Push. The thought was as curious as it was chilling. That there were people out in the world with such a talent was beyond frightening. They could literally be capable of anything.

"It sounds like the two of you had quite a morning," Ashley said as she walked into the room.

Cyrus had been pacing, taking in the eclectic collection of antiques while he considered the unanswered questions of the day.

"It's not what I expected when I got out of bed this morning," he said with a tired shake of his head.

"You mean when you rolled off my couch this morning?" she corrected with an awkward smile. "I wanted to apologize for last night. That was embarrassing. I don't usually drink. I'm terrible with liquor."

"I hope you're not sorry. I enjoyed last night. It was a long day, and it was nice to end it with some good company."

He noticed her cheeks flush with the compliment and felt confident that she had enjoyed it as well. She slipped her hands into the hip pockets of her jeans and shied away from his glance.

Definitely embarrassed, Cyrus thought.

"The truth is that I'm on medication," she explained. "It doesn't mix well with alcohol. I pretty much go from zero to smashed with no time in-between."

"I know what you're thinking," she said with a roll of her eyes. "Why was I drinking at all, right?"

He offered only a shrug and a grin.

"The truth is, I'm not sure. I had a glass of wine and it was nice. Then it got me thinking about all that I've missed out on over the years. That bottle of tequila was a gift from my best friend. She always said I didn't let myself go enough—that I was wound up too tight for my own good.

"Well, unfortunately the bottle of tequila lasted longer than the friendship. She just couldn't relate to what I was going through and we drifted apart. I think that, meeting you last night and the stress of the last few months, just sort of put me over the edge. As soon as I remembered the damned bottle, it seemed like the perfect chance to break the seal and shake things up a little."

"It was excellent tequila," Cyrus offered. *Shockingly good tequila.* At over four hundred dollars a bottle, it should've been. He had more questions but it wasn't the time, yet, when she invited him down to her apartment and offered to make lunch, he saw an opportunity to ask what he wanted to know.

"I should probably stay and keep an eye on your grandmother," Cyrus said. It was his primary mission objective, as far as he was concerned. Even if the Coalition was really more interested in Gertrude's database, his focus was on protecting the woman behind the research. It seemed like the better long-term play no matter what the orders he'd been issued. Then again, maybe there was something to be said for what he could learn about Gertrude from Ashley.

She nodded her understanding. "Yeah. But I just gave her something to help her sleep so I don't expect to hear from her until morning. Plus, we can activate the alarm system, and we'll only be a few floors down."

Cyrus considered the idea.

"I make a mean cheeseburger," she urged.

He smiled. "It's a deal."

Chapter 25

The Feedmount Building
Hennings, South Carolina
2:17 p.m.

Ashley greeted Cyrus at the door of her apartment. The moment she saw him, a smile spread across her face and she realized just how relieved she was to see him. Leading the way, they passed through the wide sliding glass doors. Her bare feet touched the cool tile floor of the wide balcony, and she took a deep breath, reminding herself that everything was finally alright.

"You had another interesting day," she said over her shoulder as she looked over the balcony railing and into the city streets. She wanted to sound conversational, but in truth, she'd been terrified about the outcome of the morning's events.

Gripping the rail tightly, she continued without turning to face him—if anyone could find the residual uneasiness in her eyes, it was him. It had proven harder than she first anticipated to set her anxiety aside. "Trouble seems to seek you out," she said with deliberate calm.

As if in response to her reluctance to look at him, Cyrus didn't respond until she finally turned and met his eye.

"It's starting to seem that way," Cyrus admitted with a

bashful grin. "I think your grandmother's the one you need to worry about, though."

An uncomfortable silence stretched between them. Ashley felt Cyrus's eyes on her the entire time. Finally she walked closer to him, only meeting his eyes as she stepped within arms' length. "Thank you for not killing my brother," she said quietly.

His eyebrows arched in response to the statement. "Gertrude told you about that? I was under the impression that it was a sensitive subject. 'Need to know', she called it."

"William can be...*overzealous*. And it might be hard to understand, but he had a good reason for doing what he did. While I don't agree with his methods, he went to the lab looking for answers, and he found what he was looking for."

"He went there to kill your grandmother," Cyrus said flatly.

Even as he said the words, Ashley was sure that Cyrus didn't believe the statement he made.

She shook her head. "Don't you think someone with William's talents could've gotten to her a dozen different ways? Why go to that much trouble?"

"He sent two armed thugs after her in that convenience store. I think his actions speak for themselves."

He was right about the store, she realized. But the armed men who had attacked them at the market had been William's attempt to evaluate Cyrus while putting a scare into their grandmother at the same time. It was a major mistake. One that had resulted in a concussion for the innocent store clerk and one that could just as easily have cost Cyrus his life. The entire incident frustrated Ashley. She would never have allowed William to take such action if she'd known his intention.

Ashley had spent the majority of the morning sitting on her balcony at the wrought iron patio table working on her laptop. A wide foldout canopy had been extended from the side of her building, covering the entire expanse of the veranda, providing comfortable shade. She moved back to her chair in front of the closed laptop and motioned for Cyrus to take a seat opposite her at the table.

In hindsight, it would've worked better if she and William had recruited Cyrus to their cause in the first place. Now she wasn't sure how to proceed.

"What is it?" Cyrus asked, sensing her trepidation.

Taking a slow, deep breath, Ashley leaned forward in her chair and rested her elbows on the edge of the table. "William's *actions* at the market—his sending those men into the store? He wanted to put a scare into Gram, yes, but his primary goal was to observe you."

Shocked, Cyrus leaned forward and glared. "What?"

"Is it really that surprising? You were her new protector," Ashley explained. "Her assistant, at least on paper, but it was clear that you were there to protect her from him."

With a shake of his head, Cyrus waved the thought away. "No," he said simply. "Even I didn't know about William, or the threat he posed. I was asked to watch over Gertrude, but that's the extent of it. Until you told me about your...*ability*, I didn't know anything about you or William beyond the fact that you were her grandchildren. There was a vague hint of some kind of threat against her, but nothing specific. I was just supposed to keep an eye out and discover if there was, in fact, a credible threat."

A scowl crossed Ashley's face. It would be so much easier if she could just Read him. The ability was so much a part of her that she hadn't realized just how often she had come to rely on it. How did normal people know if they were being lied to? She needed to be sure.

Ashley settled for asking straight out. "Who sent you?" The

words came out quieter than she expected, forcing her to realize just how afraid she was to voice the question. No, that wasn't right. She was terrified to hear his answer. Truth or lie, it wouldn't matter. It wasn't going to be good news.

Cyrus's wordless reply came in the form of a disapproving stare.

An unexpected pang of sadness rang through Ashley's body. Her eyes dropped away from Cyrus and fell to her lap where she silently folded and unfolded her hands. No answer seemed somehow worse. But rather than lie to her, he'd chosen not to say anything at all. Perhaps that meant something.

An abrupt shift in her glance brought Ashley's eyes to rest on her closed laptop. It lay on the table between the two of them. She felt a shiver run down her spine when she considered the report she'd read only minutes before Cyrus had arrived.

"*What are you?*" she asked, her voice a hoarse whisper. Her eyes moved from the laptop and met his. She could do nothing to mask the question, concern, and confusion that she was feeling.

All of that seemed to catch Cyrus off-guard. He stared back at her, looking entirely unsure how to respond. It was a raw, exposed expression that she'd never seen on his face before, and it made her realize she had just witnessed an honest to goodness crack in his ever-steady armor.

"Are you a Reader?" she pressed. "Is that why I can't Read you? I knew there were others—I've just never met one."

"Wait—What the hell are you talking about?" Cyrus interrupted. He looked sincerely confused.

While she had him off-guard, she decided to press the point in hopes of learning something new. She had so many questions. He had already proved unwilling to answer some of them, so she had no choice.

"You," she urged. "I can't Read you. William can't Push you. I didn't know what that meant until Gram did a blood work-up on you. So what is it? What can you—"

"Wait!" Cyrus was on the verge of losing his patience; she could see it in his eyes. "What are you talking about? Gertrude told you about the blood test? But how? She never had a chance to see the results."

In a flash, the confusion in his eyes was replaced by suspicion. His gaze shifted to the laptop on the table. A moment later, his penetrating stare met her eyes, and she knew that he had guessed correctly.

William had accessed the laboratory database prior to Cyrus catching up with him. But rather than steal the data and attempt to escape with it, he had transmitted it to Ashley electronically. William hadn't had the time to examine the data onsite, but Ashley had plenty of time in the hours that followed.

And the things she'd said about William attacking them at the market to evaluate him? That made sense now, too. He'd taken her comments as assumptions but he was wrong. She'd been in communication with her brother prior to they day's events. William might not have told her about each plan to attack Gertrude, but she'd spoken with him after the fact. That much was now clear.

Cyrus sat back in his chair and rubbed his eyes. "You were in on it together," he concluded. "Gertrude said that William couldn't access the database without her, but you'd already taken care of that. You Read your grandmother prior to William's attack on the lab. You'd already provided him with what he needed to access the computer network. By the time he finally had his hands on Gertrude, he had already transmitted the database to you."

Taking a deep breath, Ashley considered how best to

explain. She hadn't expected Cyrus to sort things out. At least not so quickly. It was another reason she should have approached him about all of this after their first meeting. If she could just make him understand the truth, she felt certain he would see that everything that had happened was entirely justified.

"William and I are fraternal twins," Ashley explained. "And we've been close for as long as I can remember. It's almost like we share a mind.

"A little over a year ago, William went missing. He just up and disappeared without a word. That wasn't like him. We've always been close. He never left town without telling me, and we always kept in touch on the rare occasion when he was away. But this time it was as if he just fell off the face of the planet.

"There'd always been a sort of link between us. We each had a tangible awareness of the others presence. It was something we took for granted as children. It wasn't until we became older that we realized our bond was unique. It made it very obvious to me that, when William disappeared, something had happened."

Cyrus settled into his seat. Ashley saw the impatience of his stare, but was relieved that he was giving her the time to explain. This was her best chance to get it right so she decided not to hold anything back. She would be putting a great deal of trust in him. It was a substantial leap of faith, trusting someone who might yet side with her grandmother and put an end to everything she and William were trying to accomplish.

"I knew something was wrong right away and I told Gram about it," Ashley went on. "I explained that I was sure something had happened to William. But she told me that Will was an adult and could do as he pleased. She couldn't make him stay in the city any more than she could make him do anything he didn't want to do. She promised me that he would come back one day and I would see that all of my worry was for nothing."

"And William did come back," Cyrus urged her on.

Ashley offered a slow shake of her head. "No, he didn't. But a few months ago he managed to make contact. He was being held against his will. He was being kept drugged by his captors; captors who knew about his ability to Push and had him on a drug cocktail that kept him too fuzzy to use his ability and too out of it to make contact with me."

By now Ashley knew Cyrus well enough to understand what he was thinking. Whoever had taken William had to know of his ability and have an intimate knowledge of neuro and biological triggers, which narrowed the pool of suspects significantly.

"Once he reached out, I knew that William was still somewhere in the city. We've never been able to communicate over distances of more than a hundred or so miles…"

"You can communicate with William? What—like, telepathically?" Cyrus said quietly, as if testing the idea aloud. After all he had learned over the last week, it shouldn't be too much of a reach.

"You planned the attack on the lab together," Cyrus said pointedly. "Why?"

"William and I grew up with these abilities. We were raised like this," she offered in a equally tempered voice. "I was taught *never* to Read my grandmother, and William was taught *never* to Push her. It was a core part of the way we were brought up, so we never thought anything of it. Gram always had her work. She took care of us, and we took care of her. William and I never knew our parents, so Gram was all we ever had.

"And that was fine until we had a family dinner about a year and a half ago. I had a couple of glasses of wine with dinner, and I wasn't as careful as I usually am. It wouldn't have been a problem, but Gram took a call from the lab that night. Something had gone wrong and she was really worked up. I didn't mean to, but I started to overhear random thoughts."

Thoughts of that eye-opening night made Ashley's stomach knot, and she found it hard to continue. But when she looked for some kind of judgment from Cyrus, rather than a look of criticism she was expecting, she found only patient concern. The truth of that simple, caring gesture warmed her heart and pushed back the curtain of dread that had felt so suffocating only moments earlier.

Taking a short breath, Ashley flashed Cyrus a slight but appreciative smile before forging ahead.

"We weren't supposed to be able to influence Gram. That patch she wears behind her ear? It's called a neuro-dampener. It's specifically designed to prevent people with abilities like ours from influencing anyone wearing it. She worked on that device for *years*. She said that someday it would be necessary to protect ourselves from less scrupulous people with abilities like ours.

"But something was wrong. That night, I don't know if it was my drinking or if something went wrong with the neuro-dampener, but I couldn't help it. Her thoughts just kept surfacing in my mind.

"Cyrus, what I heard…it just wasn't right. It was about her work and the tests she'd been running at her lab. Tests on people—*invasive* human tests. Vivisections on people! It was part of some new gene sequencing program she was working on.

"It was all I could do to make it through the rest of the night with her. The next day, I told William what I'd heard and he didn't believe me. He decided to prove me wrong. He

Pushed Gram and made her tell him what she was doing. That was the day he disappeared. It wasn't until he contacted me almost a year later that I actually realized the two events were related.

"Gram's people were the ones who took William, Cyrus," she choked on the truth. "Gram had him locked up and drugged for almost an entire year!"

Feeling tears welling in the corners of her eyes, Ashley realized that her story was over before she was ready. Whatever case she was trying to make to Cyrus now rested on the information she had placed before him. He was in a position to shut them down if he chose. But if he did, her grandmother would continue her horrible experiments in secret. Appalling things that Ashley couldn't abide. Not from anyone—and certainly not from her own flesh and blood.

Still, the die had been cast. Ashley swallowed her desire to sob and sat silently back in her seat instead…waiting for the next round to begin.

* * *

The story was hard for Cyrus to believe. Unfortunately, not as hard as it should've been. It explained the coincidence between Ashley's and William's abilities and Gertrude's specific field of study. But could the woman *really* be capable of such atrocities?

Of course, Cyrus realized. He'd seen the best and the worst from people, with the most extreme examples coming since taking his job with the Coalition. Add to that Gertrude's less than angelic disposition and, no, it wasn't a stretch of the imagination by any means.

"The proof is right here," Ashley said, placing her slightly trembling hand on the closed lid of her laptop.

Cyrus wondered, and not for the first time, about the Coalition's true interest in Gertrude's research. Though he was originally tasked with protecting the woman, he had no doubt that the shift in mission parameters had always been the ultimate end game. The Coalition was more interested in the research than they were in making sure Gertrude was kept alive.

"You and William are connected," Cyrus said. There was something about the things she'd said that was bothering him, apart from what he had just learned about Gertrude. "Gert didn't tell you what happened at the lab, did she?"

Ashley watched him closely but didn't reply.

"You saw it all, didn't you?" he continued. "Everything William did? Everything that happened?"

She offered a nearly imperceptible nod.

"So you know I shot him."

"I also know that you could've killed him. But you didn't. It was always a danger of William's plan and one of many reasons I was against it in the first place."

It was Cyrus's turn to watch Ashley carefully. He felt certain that she was sincere. She wasn't angry that he'd shot her brother.

"You were never part of his plan," Ashley explained, "except for testing you at the coffee shop, which only proved to him that you were the one person he ever met that he couldn't Push. Still, he wouldn't change the plan when you proved more of an obstacle than he anticipated. He's lucky to be alive.

"Drugging him was a good idea," she continued. "For someone new to all of this, you're picking it up rather quickly. But then again, we both know you're not entirely *new* to all of this."

Cyrus was confused by the accusation. She couldn't Read him, but could she possibly know what the Coalition had tasked him with? Even he wasn't sure of his ultimate goal anymore. Only that it no longer aligned with the mission passed down to him by the powers that be.

"I've seen the results of your blood workup," Ashley explained. "Your genetic markers have a great deal in common with William and me. In fact, genetic analysis found chromosomes and components of your make-up that the system wasn't able to classify. So...I'll ask again. Who are you, Cyrus? And what do you really want?"

Caught off-guard by Ashley's accusations, Cyrus wasn't sure how best to respond. He was almost positive she was trying to distract or confuse him. Biology wasn't his strong suit, but he was well aware that the human genome was fully mapped by scientists back in 2001. Her claim that analysis of his genetic make-up had turned up unknown genes was impossible.

Opening his mouth to respond, Cyrus realized that he had no idea what to say. He leaned back in his chair once more and tried to make sense of Ashley's comment. It had to be a distraction of some kind.

Maybe she was mistaken?

"Wait," Ashley said curiously. The furrow of her brow and the scrunch of her short nose mirrored his confusion. "You didn't know? You really didn't know? *Then why are you here?*"

For the first time, Cyrus became very interested in Gertrude's database, understanding that it might hold entirely different interests for different parties. Certainly the Coalition wanted it. For what, he couldn't even guess. Ashley and William wanted it. For them, it held the key to their past, and possibly even their origin. But for him, it could very well hold the answers to questions that he hadn't even known to ask.

Ashley looked equally concerned by the revelation. It seemed that she had certain preconceptions about him when they met that afternoon, and those beliefs were now equally in question.

"We should wait for William," Ashley said. "He's studied genetics extensively. He'll be able to help us sort this out."

Cyrus met her eye with a questioning glance. What was she thinking? William was in custody following the violent attack on a secret and secure installation. He wouldn't be going anywhere for a long time.

Unless...

It was the casual way that Ashley had made the comment, as if it were a done deal. If she really had some kind of sensory link with her brother...

Cyrus bolted from the chair and headed into the house. Even as he stepped through the sliding glass door, he had his cell phone in hand and the line was ringing. He heard the connection and was just about to speak when Ashley gently pulled the phone away from his ear.

"You can't," she said in a desperate but hushed voice.

Something about her tone and the steely look in her eye made him reconsider. He tapped the screen and ended the call.

Stepping forward, she placed her lips close to his ear. "My apartment is bugged," she whispered. "Come outside so I can explain. *Please?*"

Cyrus knew that the sedative he'd used on William had worked. He was certain of it. It was either that, or the pain resulting from the gunshot wound had been enough to prevent the use of his ability. That meant once William was in custody, something had changed. Either his guards switched to a different sedative that wasn't strong enough, or there'd been a gap between doses. Either way, William had regained control of his ability. With his talent for manipulating the will of others, having his cell door opened would be a simple matter. Escaping the facility, too, would be trivial. He would literally have the help of the entire security staff. They would open the doors for him, delete the security footage and, in the end, likely retain no memory of the events.

Pocketing the phone, Cyrus turned to find Ashley standing in the wide doorway, silhouetted by the afternoon sun. She motioned for him to follow.

Reluctantly, he decided to go with it for the time being and see what he thought once the dust settled. Though he'd been tasked with a job, he wasn't a mindless drone. With no clear answer as to who was in the right, all he could do was give the case more time and sort things out as he saw fit.

Chapter 26

Undisclosed location
Hennings, South Carolina
2:40 p.m.

William heard the key enter the lock on the outside of his cell door and knew what was coming next. Sitting on the edge of the metal framed cot, he looked at the thick wrap of white bandages that engulfed his right foot like a massive sock stuffed with cotton. The sedatives they'd given him had done a better job of dulling the pain than they had at disabling his auxiliary senses. He knew that there were five men currently inside the building with him, and that the next shift wasn't scheduled to arrive until twenty-one hundred hours. 9 p.m., William realized. He would be long gone by then.

A tall man with a short military-style buzz cut moved through the door and stepped into the room. He showed indifference to William, neither meeting his eye nor avoiding it.

They should've been better prepared, William thought with a smile as he pushed himself onto unsteady legs for the first time since his capture. Taking a tentative step and placing weight on his right foot, he winced as the shot of pain rocketed through his foot and up his leg. He wondered what the pain would be like once the drugs had worn off entirely. His vision still swam from their powerful effects as he hobbled across the small room and out the door.

Stepping into the hallway, William saw an orderly line of four additional men dressed similar to the man who had released him. While these men varied in height, they had similar haircuts and sturdy, muscular builds. They were the remainder of the security team charged with William's temporary incarceration.

The four men moved single file into William's cell, the last man turning and pushing the solid steel door shut behind him. The original guard had left his set of keys hanging from the lock on the outside of the door. William turned the key; there was a satisfying 'thunk' of metal on metal as the mechanism's massive bolt slid into place. But rather than withdraw the key from the lock, he placed his palm against its wide surface and applied lateral pressure. The key quickly snapped, leaving its shaft stuck inside the lock's tumblers. Pocketing the rest of the key ring, William ambled down the hall and headed for the main exit.

When he stepped from the front of the building, he was surprised to see that he was still in Hennings. They'd brought him to an abandoned railroad yard just outside the city. The sun was high in the sky, and while half-dozen rundown and dilapidated old one and two story buildings surrounded him, there wasn't another living soul in sight.

After retrieving a short steel pipe from a nearby pile of discarded junk, William leaned on the pipe, using it as a cane, and stepped off the curb. The asphalt was cracked and shattered. It had once constituted the main path through the center of the railroad depot. From here, he would head north and make for the first major road where he could acquire a ride and put some distance between himself and his captors. It wouldn't be long before they realized he was missing. The next shift wasn't due for hours—it was information willingly divulged upon William's simple request. Unfortunately, it was the team's procedure to check in with their command station every hour on the hour.

Once he found a place to hold up, William's first order of business would be to contact his sister. He had transmitted the entirety of his grandmother's research to Ashley before his encounter with Cyrus, and he was anxious to find out what she had learned from examining the research. All they knew at the moment was that their grandmother was not who they believed her to be. She was not at all the loving and caring woman who had raised them, supposedly interested only in their wellbeing. Their entire lives had been a lie, told by a woman who was only interested in observing them like rats in some endless lab experiment. The truth was that they meant nothing to her beyond the time and effort she had invested in them as living and breathing biological experiments.

William had long since been convinced of the truth—the revaluation had resulted in his year-long incarceration in a mental hospital, drugged beyond rational thought. Ashley had been right. If he'd listened to her from the start, things would've gone very differently. It was just as well in the end, William realized. Seizing Gertrude's files was the best way to expose her for the monster that she was. Without those files, they had no proof of the atrocities that had been committed.

William limped on, focused entirely on reaching the regional highway nearly a mile away. But when an uneasy tingling crept up his spine and brought a throbbing pain to the base of his skull, he stopped his aggressive hobble mid-stride. Leaning against his improvised walking stick, he turned slowly and looked down the length of street he had just walked.

Something was wrong. He could feel it. But whatever sense

was triggering the alert was either foreign to him or impeded by the effects of the sedative still making its way through his bloodstream.

His eyes roamed the weathered and destroyed features of the old buildings that lined the short stretch of pavement. Siding peeled from the face of some buildings, nearly every window in sight had been shattered, and some structures even had walls that had partially collapsed, giving up to both time and gravity. It was difficult to locate an anomaly in the sea of broken and disjointed components.

It was a presence, William sensed...someone was out there. He wasn't alone at the railway yard after all. And though he reached out with his senses, he couldn't pinpoint the presence he was feeling right to his very core. He couldn't even be sure it was a single person, he realized. It could be kids wasting time in the wreckage of the old trains, or it could be a support team moving in to assist the men guarding his cell. And with the sedatives still playing havoc with his mind, he wasn't going to be able to reach out over any distance to discover who or what was watching.

Turning quickly, he began limping once more. Redoubling his effort, he focused on the only thing he could—escaping the rail station and finding refuge as quickly as possible.

Chapter 27

Undisclosed location
Hennings, South Carolina
2:44 p.m.

Sitting on a small metal folding chair that was surrounded by piles of junk, Sam Turner watched the time pass without incident. He was due to be relieved by the next shift in just over two hours, and the thought of stretching his legs was already growing on him. Still, at least he had shade in his improvised blind. And as uncomfortable as the folding chair was, it beat lying prone in the mud for days at a time. He only wished that his vantage point on the rooftop at the edge of the abandoned railroad depot had afforded him the benefit of a breeze. Some fresh air would've been a welcome refreshment to help the hours pass more smoothly.

It wasn't his hide that bothered him so much, though. It was the futility of his task. He was watching the front door of a building six hundred yards away on the off chance that the prisoner in custody was able to slip past the half-dozen men guarding him, and make a run for it. It didn't seem likely. Actually, the idea was absurd. Sam had seen the man they were sitting on. He was in his mid-twenties, a little over six-feet tall, and in the neighborhood of two hundred pounds. But for all of that, he didn't have the bearing of a trained operator. Sam had worked with plenty of that type in his day, and he knew the look. Sometimes their physical appearance was the giveaway, in other cases it was the look in their eye that showed you the man knew how to handle himself. But the man down there offered neither indicator. He wouldn't be escaping his cell, let alone getting past the six men guarding him.

Needless to say, when the door of the distant building opened and a lone figure stepped onto the sidewalk, Sam's first thought was that one of the guards was breaking protocol for a smoke. But even at six hundred yards, there was no mistaking the target's haggard stance or the trouble he had walking. When the man bent over to retrieve something from a nearby pile of trash, Sam brought a set of field glasses to his eyes for a closer look.

"Sonofabitch," he mumbled, watching the distant figure limp out into the street, steering wide of another pile of twisted and rusted metal wreckage.

The figure had his back to him, headed away from Sam. And though he wasn't in danger of losing his shot anytime soon, Sam's orders had been explicitly clear: He was to neutralize the target immediately upon acquisition. Failure to act decisively could sacrifice the entire mission.

That had been the part of the assignment that stuck him as unusual. While Sam had executed dozens of sniper assignments over the years, the particulars surrounding this op had been unusual. First of all, the job was on American soil. That was a first in his experience. But more interesting had been his CO's insistence that it was critical to take the kill shot as quickly as possible.

But why? Sam couldn't see how a single unarmed individual limping down a distant street could possibly pose an imminent risk. At his current rate of movement, Sam expected the target to remain in range for at least another three minutes. Still, orders were orders, and he was nothing if not an obedient soldier.

Bringing the rifle to his shoulder, Sam rested the bipod on the improvised stand he'd prepared for just such a situation. The pair of short metal legs protruding from beneath the barrel of his rifle took the full weight of the gun off his hands and offered a rock solid and steady view through the scope. The crosshairs centered on the base of the distant target's skull when the target suddenly stopped walking. His finger, already wrapped around the rifle's trigger, eased a bit as Sam watched what his target would do next.

The man turned in a slow circle. Even at the great distance, Sam could see his target's eyes scanning his surroundings. The man knew that something was wrong. But how?

When the distant figure turned north once more and began limping again at an increased rate, Sam took a deep breath. It was a strange experience, and it sent his CO's explicit orders echoing through his mind once more.

Placing the crosshairs on the back of the target's head for a second time, Sam's fingertip slipped into place on the trigger. A gentle squeeze let loose a single round, and the weapon's massive report seemed somehow intensified in the silence of the surrounding area.

Sam's target toppled to the cracked pavement like a felled tree. Through his scope, he could still see the telltale pink cloud that drifted in the air a moment after the body had fallen away. It was unpleasant work, Sam thought, as he folded the legs of the rifle's bipod. He hated shooting down an unarmed man. Furthermore, he had no idea what terrible wrong the man had committed. But, it was the nature of the job. And he followed orders, no matter how unpleasant they might be.

Zipping shut the soft-sided rifle case, Sam pulled the strap over his shoulder and headed for a ladder that was leaning against the east side of the building. He would evacuate to his fallback position before reporting what had happened, and then once more bury the slight guilt he felt for taking down an enemy without giving him a fighting chance.

Chapter 28

The Feedmount Building
Hennings, South Carolina
2:40 p.m.

Sitting on the terrace alone, Cyrus watched Ashley through the sliding glass door. She was inside, walking back and forth across the kitchen as she prepared hamburgers for lunch—vegiburgers for herself. The grill was already preheated, located away from the furniture, off by itself in the corner of the balcony.

He took another sip from his beer bottle and thought about what Ashley had explained after ushering him outside and away from the prying ears that were apparently on high alert within the confines of her home. Her awareness of the bugs had come only hours earlier, along with the information William had sent from inside Gertrude's hidden lab. At first she'd been shocked, she admitted. Surprise quickly gave way to anger. But after moving further through the information that William had transmitted, Ashley said the surveillance of her home paled in comparison to the other outrageous things her grandmother had done.

Even while Ashley was explaining the broad strokes of her grandmother's wrongdoings, Cyrus could see the pain grow in her eyes. While Ashley was aware that her brother had gone missing a year earlier, the database contained a detailed account of everything that had happened and everything he had been subjected to during that time. It seemed beyond reason, but there was no question that their grandmother had been responsible for William's disappearance. However, the reason for it was still unclear. Having had only a few short hours to examine what amounted to tens of thousands of pages of records, reports and raw data, it was evident that it would take a great deal of time to connect the dots.

Cyrus took another sip of his beer, concentrating on Ashley as she pretended to go about her normal routine. The laptop containing the full contents of the database sat on the table beside him, ripe for the picking. His orders were simply to acquire the information. And while the change in the mission objective had struck him as troubling at the time, it seemed even more wrong now. Understanding the nature of Gertrude Waterford's work, he wasn't confident that bringing the data back to the Coalition was the right move. The outfit served a purpose, and his people did important work, protecting the United States and the American's who lived there. Still, there was something about their commanding officer, Monica Fichtner, that had never set right with him. It was a feeling that had only grown more pronounced with time.

Fichtner was a cold-hearted, seemingly robotic woman who had run the Coalition since its inception. She was so devoid of human emotion that Cyrus had taken to calling her the 'Red Queen', a name taken from the malevolent artificial intelligence in the *Resident Evil* movie series. And though he had bestowed the moniker as a matter of personal amusement, there was no denying the unfeeling resemblance the woman shared with the fictitious computer construct. More simply, he didn't trust the woman in charge. And even though he couldn't say why, he had the sense that putting Waterford's database directly into Fichtner's hands wouldn't be a move in the right direction.

Ashley appeared at the doorway with the plate of raw burger patties. She smiled as she passed by, setting another beer in front of Cyrus on her way to the grill. Looking at the beer, Cyrus wondered where it had come from. There hadn't been any in the refrigerator the night before, and he knew Ashley was reticent to leave the apartment. She had explained that her exposure to the thoughts and minds of random strangers was difficult, but he sensed that her description was an understatement. Living in a city like Hennings, he realized, was very likely a daily challenge.

Pulling the heavy glass sliding door closed along its track, Cyrus guaranteed their privacy. While he took Ashley at her word that inside the apartment was bugged, he had thoroughly searched the balcony for any type of listening device and found it free from observation. There was always the chance that someone was using a parabolic microphone to eavesdrop from a neighboring building, but it was unlikely. The surrounding buildings were not as tall as Ashley's sixth floor balcony, and the first building with actual line of sight was too far out of range. Just the same, he took out his phone and began playing a streaming radio station to add background noise. It would help confound anyone trying to listen in from afar.

Lowering the lid on the grill, Ashley turned to see where the music was coming from. "I like that," she said. "Go with that."

The song was Buckcherry's, *Open My Eyes*. While his goal had been to subvert surveillance, he realized she appreciated the mood that it set. He couldn't help but smile. Even though everything she had known about the woman who raised her had been pulled out from under her over the course of the last few days, she still took pleasure in the little things.

Reaching out, Ashley put her hands on his chest. Her eyes met his. There was a sparkle of something he recognized as deep-seeded caring. The connection he felt when he looked at her was reciprocated, he was absolutely certain of it. Even if neither of them knew what it meant, somehow it was enough. At least for the time being.

"Thank you for giving me a chance to explain about William," she said quietly. "I promise, once I'm done you'll understand that everything he did was necessary. He's not the bad guy here."

Given what little he already knew, Cyrus was inclined to believe her; or, at least willing enough to give her the chance to explain. But knowing that William was regaining his strength was still troubling.

Cyrus and Ashley stood there for some time, lost in the moment. The connection between them was so tangible that it seemed like a living force. Just holding her in his arms and looking into her eyes was unlike anything he had ever experienced.

Suddenly, Ashley's pert wisp of a smile turned dark and ominous. "Why don't we look at the laptop," she said in a dry voice. "I saw something there that's been bothering me."

He shot her a questioning look. The scale of what she found disturbing had recently fallen into a rapid state of flux. Whatever she'd found must have stood out. It wasn't encouraging.

"I think my grandmother has other test facilities," Ashley explained. She didn't pull herself from his arms. Though she wanted to show him the records on the laptop, she seemed reluctant to leave his embrace. "As twisted as it might sound, she may have been treating William more kindly than we realized—at least comparatively speaking."

The implication made Cyrus's stomach knot and he suddenly felt a loss of apatite. "That bad?"

He saw her eyes grow moist at the thought. "I don't have all the details yet, but I found several mentions of neural implants being tested at a facility called Praxis. Something happened there recently. I think one of their test subjects escaped."

"Escaped? As in, being held against their will?"

Ashley nodded. "I'll dig deeper. If my grandmother is holding people prisoner, William will want to know."

Grinding his teeth, Cyrus wanted to know about it too. The Red Queen had mentioned Praxis when she revised his mission objective. What it was remained a mystery. "Praxis? It could be the name of the facility she's using, or it could be some sort of code name. Is there anything more specific?"

"Keegan Porter. Her name was mentioned. I don't know how she's related to the incident, but she was named in what little I've read so far. Cyrus, we have to do something. My grandmother is—"

A look of incredible agony flashed across Ashley's face. Cyrus saw her mouth slam shut and the muscles at the side of her jaw corded with incredible constrictive force. The pupils of her eyes dilated instantly, the irises growing larger and darker than he had ever seen. Her entire body went rigid in his arms and he caught her just as she threatened to fall.

Even as he lowered her carefully to the tile, Cyrus could see that her eyes were rolling back in their sockets. Her body began convulsing in some kind of massive seizure. Laying her out flat on the floor, he did the only thing he could given the sudden onset of whatever was happening; he circled around behind her and cradled her head to keep his hands between her skull and the hard balcony floor. Barring any residual harm from the seizure itself, he knew that he just needed to keep her from becoming physically injured while it played out.

The seizure lasted nearly two full minutes. It was the single most physically violent event he had ever witnessed, and he was powerless to stop it. But when the convulsions stopped and he looked at her eyes, they remained rolled back in her head. Even more troubling was the thick crimson blood running down her cheeks. Wiping it away and working his way back up her face to her eyes, he realized the source. The blood was flowing slowly from her tear ducts.

She remained unconscious, but she was literally crying blood.

His focus on Ashley, Cyrus failed to notice the five men who had silently slipped into her apartment. The group made short work of searching the condo, confirming that Cyrus and Ashley were alone. Finally ready to make their move, one of the men stepped to the edge of the sliding glass door and looked out onto the balcony. On cue, he slid the door open in a single, smooth motion. At the same moment, two of his teammates rushed out onto the patio. The pair of men stepped up behind Cyrus where he knelt, cradling Ashley's head. A single blow to the back of his skull caused Cyrus crumple to the tile without a sound.

…He never even knew what hit him.

Chapter 29

Mayflower Lab Facility
Hennings, South Carolina
3:52 p.m.

A burning scrape tore through Cyrus's arm, and he felt himself being pulled from the darkness. A tingling, pins-and-needles feeling spread through his body like a waterfall of burning liquid as he came back to the real world. His extremities felt as if they were being attacked. First his arms and hands, followed soon by a tightness in his chest that seemed like someone was sitting on him; then came his legs, ending finally when the pain reached his feet. But all of that paled in comparison to the throbbing pain in his head. No—throbbing didn't do it justice, he realized, as his mind struggled to understand what was happening. It was as if his head was being used as the puck in a professional game of hockey.

Opening his eyes, Cyrus was assaulted by the harsh glare of the room's fluorescent overhead lights. He smashed his eyes shut once more but the damage was already done. A lance of pain shot through his skull and he felt his stomach roil in response. It took focus to fight back a crushing wave of nausea.

"Well," he heard Gertrude say from nearby. "You're coming back to us ahead of schedule. It seems you're just full of surprises."

Trying to understand the comment, Cyrus fought against his instinct to once more open his eyes. He'd become aware of the restraints being used to keep his arms at his sides, as well as his legs, which were similarly secured below him. And he could tell without looking that he was lying on some sort of steeply inclined table. Still, he wasn't willing to risk exposing his pupils to the horrific glare just yet. The prospect of vomiting all over himself wouldn't improve his situation.

And what did she mean, *ahead of schedule?* And who was *we?* His first waking sense was that of something stabbing him in the arm. A burning sensation remained in the middle of his left forearm. Someone had obviously given him some kind of stimulant—he was sure of it. It explained his rapid and violent return to consciousness, as well as his body's apparent unwillingness to return to the land of the living.

But if she hadn't given him a stimulant, who did?

After taking a long, deep breath to steady himself, Cyrus slowly opened his eyes. They remained hooded against the glare of the harsh lights for several long moments while he squinted and looked around. He was restrained on an industrial grade medical gurney of some sort. It was assembled out of thick aluminum tubes, and he lay on a sturdy backboard that offered only a minimal amount of padding. The backboard was tipped on the gurney's frame, turning him about thirty degrees short of a fully upright position; reclined just enough to keep his head from falling forward while unconscious.

Ashley was bound hand and foot to a wheeled office chair not more than twenty feet away. But while his restraints were two-inch wide leather straps that were part of the gurney, she was held in place more crudely with a gratuitous amount of duct tape.

At least she was awake, even if she didn't look happy. She didn't say anything. Her look of hopeless resignation made him think they had been there for some time.

Walking up behind Ashley, Gertrude fixed Cyrus with a penetrating stare. She looked like the proverbial cat that had swallowed the canary. And when she stepped around Ashley's chair, Cyrus realized that the old woman was relying less on her cane than she had in days.

Perhaps most troubling of all, Cyrus recognized the large room in which they were being held. It wasn't Gertrude's own lab at the Mayflower Facility, but it was most certainly another of the labs. This one was outfitted differently, yet the high concrete walls and wide tiles on the raised floor were the same.

Behind Ashley there was a large bed. At the head of it was a massive machine, the likes of which Cyrus had never seen. It seemed that the bed would slide into the machine—similar to a MRI—but this was something more complicated. The bulk of the machine was far too large, while the look of the technology appeared to be generations ahead of anything ever seen in even the most cutting-edge hospital. While it was obviously some sort of imaging system, he had no idea what its true purpose might be.

A pair of hard looking men stood in front of the imaging device. They were dressed in street clothes, but Cyrus could tell at a glance that both were trained operators. Both had powerful builds and cold eyes. But they weren't military—at least they hadn't been recently. They stood casually, relaxed and overconfident. These were the type of men who were paid well to be on hand in case of emergency, but also the kind who lacked the discipline necessary to remain vigilant at all times.

Aragon Group, Cyrus concluded. Though familiar with the private security company as a whole, Cyrus had done a little extra research early into his first week of chauffeuring Gertrude around town. The day Cyrus went undercover as Gertrude's assistant his supervising agent, Greg Boone, had provided additional mission background. The package had included extensive research into Gertrude Waterford's financial history. Among the details of her spending, Cyrus had learned that his new employer had contracted with the Aragon Group at least a half-dozen times in the past. Aragon had provided personal security for Gertrude on a number of overseas trips and, interestingly, she used the same five-man detail each time she hired the group.

One of the men stood out from the other. There was something different about the way he carried himself, Cyrus realized. He had an air of authority. The head of the team, Cyrus thought. He became sure of it when he looked more closely at his dark eyes. They were experienced, emotionless, and betraying nothing. The man was studying him as if he were an exhibit on display in a museum or at a zoo. A pale scar bisected his left eyebrow and rounded the corner of his eye before disappearing into the skin of his cheek. The scar was a telltale sign that the man had seen action; but what had once been a tough and jagged slice in his flesh had obviously seen multiple operations to help hide the disfigurement. It meant the man wasn't as battle-hardened as his stare suggested. He was still a slave to his vanity, and Cyrus factored that into the assessment of his new opponent. When the time came, it would be critical to know his adversaries, and he felt confident he'd already gotten a solid read on the man leading Gertrude's security detail.

With the two men in front of him, that left three members of the five member team unaccounted for. Those three men and their locations would become important factors when he made his escape. Until then, he focused on learning as much as possible about his situation while watching for clues to the locations of the remaining three men.

A series of small computer stations flanked the massive imaging device, and the far left wall of the room was consumed by a enormous display screen. It was off at the moment, but it ran from the far corner of the room, ending just short of the massive sliding steel door that was the entrance; a door closed tight and presumably locked.

And four inches thick, he recalled.

The most chilling part of the lab was what Cyrus saw to his right. Deep wooden shelves that weren't at all in keeping with the cold clinical aesthetics of the lab consumed the majority of the right wall. The shelving unit was at least thirty-feet wide—maybe wider, since it extended past Cyrus's vertical gurney. It was made of oak and stained a rich, dark color that only made its contents all the more glaring. Each shelf was lined with glass jars pushed up against each other like books with only their binding showing. And while the jars were arranged in a seemingly random fashion that differed in every shape and size, each contained the same viscous, mostly transparent fluid. Each jar also contained a single organic tissue sample of some sort, though no two seemed alike. The front facing lower portion of each jar was labeled with only a small barcode.

Although Cyrus could recognize the samples as tissue, he had no idea what the jars represented. Ashley had said that Gertrude's work included vivisection. Apparently he was looking at the proof. The organic samples were enough to turn his stomach. Cyrus turned his head away so he could get a glimpse over his right shoulder. There the shelves had given way to massive cylindrical tanks that contained hundreds of gallons of the same liquid used in the smaller jars. Only the contents of these containers were not scraps of unrecognizable biological tissue as they had been in the smaller containers; these larger tanks contained twisted and contorted cadavers, suspended in the transparent solution.

The bodies, Cyrus quickly realized, were human—more or less. While they were disfigured in grotesque and horrible ways, they all had their head, two arms, and two legs—give or take. The bodies looked like some kind of organic mutation or cancer had been allowed to ravage them unchecked.

And while he could only see three such tanks from his position on the gurney, Cyrus had the sense that the horror show continued all along the wall behind him.

"My alpha specimens," Gertrude said simply in response to Cyrus's speechless examination of the freakshow. "Aren't they beautiful?"

Beautiful?

At first he thought she was being sarcastic, but judging by the proud gleam in her eye, Gertrude Waterford was entirely serious. She looked upon the display of barbaric aberrations with a mother's pride.

"You did this?" It was more accusation than question, and all he could bring himself to say. Never before had he been stunned beyond reason.

With a satisfied, egotistical smile, Gertrude walked slowly past the front of the display starting from the far end. She moved slowly, taking in each tortured body as if it were an independent piece of priceless art.

"The larger specimens were my earlier work," Gertrude explained, pointing to the massive canisters containing complete cadavers. She seemed to favor the samples in the smaller jars, though she showed substantial affection when she pointed to the twisted remains of the mutated corpses over Cyrus's shoulder. It was even more troubling because she was showing far more emotion for the samples than she had for her own grandchildren.

"Admittedly, crude attempts before science finally supplied me with the tools necessary to take my work to the next level." At that, she glanced at the smaller samples, not full bodies or even parts, but unidentifiable tissue.

"She killed William," Ashley said in a sad, hollow voice, speaking for the first time.

An image of Ashley laying unconscious on the cold tiles of her balcony flashed through Cyrus's mind. The violence of the seizure was unlike anything he'd ever witnessed. And the blood that flowed from her eyes? He'd never seen anything like that before. Though Ashley had described her connection to her brother only briefly, it seemed that severing the connection was as physically traumatic as it was mentally painful.

Cyrus cast an accusatory glance at Gertrude. He didn't actually expect the woman to deny her granddaughter's claim, but he was shocked when Gertrude simply shrugged it off. "He had become too difficult to manage," she said. "What can I say? He wouldn't leave well enough alone."

"My God," Cyrus virtually spat. "He was your grandson. How could you?"

While the question was meant to draw a response, he wasn't prepared for the look he received; Gertrude stood stock still, studying him for the better part of a minute. The entire time, her focus was cast upon him with laser-like precision.

Finally, Gertrude broke her gaze. But only long enough to readjust the positioning of her cane before slowly beginning her approach. "William and Ashley are *not* my grandchildren," she said.

If the statement didn't trouble Cyrus, then the questioning

glare she offered with the statement did. She wasn't trying to shock him, he realized. She thought he already knew as much—but that wasn't the point she seemed to be attempting to make. It was as if she was trying to gain understanding of some, as of yet, unspoken suspicion.

He had no idea what she was driving at.

"They have more in common with the specimens in these jars," Gertrude continued, further appraising his reaction.

Cyrus was adept at rolling with information as it became available. It was crucial to survival in undercover work. Still, he found the revelation almost as shocking as the callousness with which it had been revealed.

Ashley looked at her grandmother in utter bewilderment. Her gaze quickly gave way to shock. Several moments of silence followed, and while Cyrus tried to process Gertrude's admission, he could only guess what sort of stress it had brought upon Ashley.

The silence in the room seemed to last forever. Not surprisingly, it was Ashley who first found her voice.

"You raised us," Ashley said, accusation clear in her tone. "Mom and Dad died before we could walk and you took us in. How can you say that?"

Gertrude shook her head as if that were the most foolish thing she had ever heard. "You and William were twins, but you had no parents," she said with cold detachment. "You were twins, born and bred in a lab. *My lab.*

"If you have a mother or a father at all, surely I'm the closest thing to either."

Staring at Gertrude through wide eyes, Ashley didn't know what to say. Cyrus, on the other hand, was getting a better idea as to what was going on. Glancing over his shoulder, he took another look at the disfigured forms in the tall cylindrical tanks.

Alpha specimens.

That was what Gertrude had called the grotesque figures. His stomach turned another summersault as he realized that the birth of William and Ashley had been the result of a related experiment. "Praxis," he said aloud, as much for himself as for Gertrude.

"Of course," Gertrude said with a smile. "It's why you're here, after all. Is it not?"

Cyrus thought about how the Coalition had tasked him with the retrieval of Gertrude's database. It would contain all of her research, as well as a complete accounting of the atrocities she had committed. But somehow that didn't seem like the accusation she was making. He couldn't put his finger on it, but he didn't get the sense that she knew anything about the Coalition or their interest in her.

Meeting her eye, Cyrus remained quiet.

"I know who you are," Gertrude said with a smile. "There's no reason to hide it. Certainly not from me, of all people. I just want to know why I wasn't approached sooner. I've been waiting for so long."

While Cyrus didn't know what she was talking about, the gleam in her eyes told him that she wasn't referring to the Coalition. Beyond that, he needed more information.

"You think you've got it figured out?" Cyrus urged. He needed to get her talking if he was to have any chance at understanding what was really happening.

One more look at Ashley told him that she was on the verge of mentally checking out. The loss of her brother combined with the betrayal of her grandmother was potentially crippling to her on a psychological level. And to be told that she was nothing more than a walking, talking lab experiment? How did anyone process information as insane as that?

"You know about Praxis," Gertrude insisted. "And I've examined your genetic scans." She motioned toward the massive scanner at the rear of the room. "*I know who you are.*"

Making a show of pulling on his restraints, Cyrus shook his head emphatically. He'd been pulling at the bindings cautiously ever since waking and knew they couldn't be defeated through sheer force. Still, he pulled violently at the leather bands that lashed his wrists to the side of the gurney, rattling the cart loudly in the process. "Praxis? I heard you mention it on the phone once last week and again earlier this week. That's all I know. What is this all about? Why are you doing this?"

Gertrude was confused by his refusal to admit what she believed to be true. "Then why are you here?"

"What the hell are you talking about?" Cyrus snapped. "I'm a temp, for God's sake. I was hired as your assistant, you crazy bitch!"

Offering a devious grin, Gertrude shook her head. "I know that much isn't true."

Gertrude waved to someone who, up until this point, had remained hidden behind Cyrus. She motioned the unseen figure forward. A pair of men wheeled a gurney from the back of the room and parked it a dozen feet in front of Cyrus. A long, white sheet covered the contents of the cart but did little to disguise the form of the body beneath.

With a signal from Gertrude, one of the men lifted the sheet away from the battered and lifeless face of Lacy Osbourne. Though he hadn't seen her since their brief encounter when he interviewed for the position with Gertrude, Cyrus recognized her immediately.

"She didn't have a lot to say," Gertrude said with a dismissive shake of her head. She seemed less concerned with the loss of the woman's life than she was with the effort that had gone into interrogating her.

"But in the end, I believe it was because she honestly didn't know very much," Gertrude went on. "Still, what she did say was very helpful.

"The evening before you and I met for the first time, your CV appeared in Miss Osbourne's database for the very first time. She was certain of this," Gertrude said with inflection. "You see, I went through a fair number of applicants before you came along, and Miss Osbourne became well acquainted with the candidate pool before we were through.

"I find it curious that a qualified and, admittedly ideal candidate, should literally appear out of the blue. Don't you?"

Under normal circumstances Cyrus would've been inclined to remain silent when faced with such a question. It seemed as likely to be rhetorical as not, plus he was literally choking on the bile that had risen in the back of his throat at the sight of what Gertrude had done to Lacy Osbourne.

"I believe the term used was, *overqualified*," Cyrus said. He was doing his best not to grind his teeth with the statement.

Looking at Lacy's lifeless face, the only part of her that was exposed from beneath the featureless white sheet, Cyrus felt rage. He fixed Gertrude with a bracing stare that somehow contained every ounce of emotion he was feeling, and he growled the words, "Gertrude, what-have-you-done?"

The old woman staggered backward a full two steps at the horrified sound of Cyrus's voice, the look on her face as though she'd just been physically slapped.

Chapter 30

Mayflower Lab Facility
Hennings, South Carolina
4:17 p.m.

Standing still at the back of the room, Hondo listened to everything that was being said. Though he kept his distance, he remained just within earshot of the conversation at all times. Still, he had no idea what was happening. Cyrus was strapped to a gurney a dozen feet away, and as much as he wanted to let his friend know that support was on hand, he had yet to make his presence known. He was running his own play on Gertrude. He only hoped it was the right move. Infiltration operations were not his bailiwick, and the truth was that he didn't know what he was doing. Aside from the play he'd listened to Cyrus run on the crew in a bus garage on an earlier operation, he had no idea how to react when dealing covertly with an adversary. His experience had always consisted of direct combat. And at that moment, he realized how much he preferred combat to what he was doing now. The sneaking around, the lying—the constant fear of saying the wrong thing and being shot before he had a chance to defend himself...frankly, he had no idea how Cyrus functioned under such conditions.

Still, a debt was a debt, and when Cyrus called in his marker

Hondo had been quick to accept the challenge. At the time, he expected that infiltrating the security detail assigned by the Aragon Group would be the hardest part of the job. But he had followed Cyrus's instructions and made short work of vetting process. A third party—an independent contractor out of Miami—had provided Hondo his legend, or falsified work history, background and personal details, in tradecraft terms. All Hondo had to do was arrange a fortuitous *accident* for a member of the five man detail that was regularly assigned to Gertrude Waterford. For this, Cyrus had targeted Denton Stubbs, the 28-year-old field medic attached to the team. Using the forged work history and credentials that had been inserted into the Aragon Group's secure database, Hondo replaced the injured medic when Waterford requested her usual detail for a new assignment. The next thing Hondo knew he was in Hennings, South Carolina and part of a team charged with securing a hostile target on the 6th floor of the Templeton Tower building. The target turning out to be Cyrus shouldn't have been the surprise that it was, but that the identity *had* caught him so fully unprepared impressed upon Hondo just how ill-equipped he was for the work at hand.

It was a thought that ran through his head repeatedly while he listened to his friend being questioned. He knew only that another target had already been assassinated. The order was executed by another member of the team before Hondo was even aware that it had been given. It was another fact that weighed heavily upon him. Though he still didn't know who the target had been, the man's death was on his conscience. He'd been inserted into the security detail to provide support to his friend, but he had no idea if Cyrus would have had him prevent the sniper from killing the man at some railway yard. There had been no way to ask, even if he'd been aware of the order in advance.

The frustration of the assignment left Hondo with pent-up anxiety and no means of release. He stood in a sealed laboratory many stories underground with four well-trained and well-armed security operators; mercenaries, he corrected himself. But when he focused his attention on them more closely he found comfort, realizing that they lacked discipline. Each of the four men moved around the lab in a relaxed manner, secure in the false knowledge that they had the situation well in hand. These men were not as skilled as he first thought. The understanding brought him a degree of relief and renewed hope that things would break in their favor.

After arriving in the lab, Cyrus had been secured to the wheeled cart with thick leather restraints. Waterford had then decided to dismiss half of the security detail, sending them to the installation's commissary while she dealt with matters in the lab.

When Hondo realized he was about to be dismissed, he knew he needed to act and made a desperate play that he'd hoped would keep him in the room. He stepped forward and commented to Waterford that he had seen their target before. Unsure what direction to take his deception, he left the statement ambiguous at first. It was either the right thing to say, or entirely wrong.

Waterford's interest in his comment was immediately apparent, and Hondo knew he had gained room to work. He just wished he knew the right direction to take the lie. But when Waterford demanded to know what Hondo knew of Cyrus, he had a hint…pointing him in the proper direction. He explained that he didn't know Cyrus first hand, but their paths had crossed on an earlier security assignment. The concept was in keeping with his cover as part of the Aragon Group, so it seemed reasonable.

Hondo went on to explain in vague details that he had worked a four-man security job in Peru a year earlier. While there, he had encountered Cyrus. Though at the time, Cyrus had been working under a different name. He couldn't recall the name used, offhand, but the details of the mission didn't seem as important to Waterford as the fact that Cyrus had been in Peru and was using an alias. It was just as well, since Hondo was reticent to provide any additional details that might foul up his deception somewhere down the line.

He was already afraid he'd crossed into dangerous territory by hinting at the use of an alias, but the look he saw on the old woman's face at the mention of an alternate name and a vague location like Peru, made Hondo afraid that he hadn't set the hook deeply enough. Certain that he needed to stay in the room, he'd forged ahead, providing additional information against his better judgment.

The ploy had worked, and Hondo had been allowed to stay in the room. But it might have worked a little too well since Gertrude decided to keep the entire team on hand until she better understood the man she was dealing with. Once more Hondo was left to question how Cyrus could operate under such fluid conditions.

More troubling for Hondo was how his story might hold up once Cyrus was confronted with it. They hadn't agreed on the backstory, and the more he thought about it, the more Hondo realized how clumsy his tale had been. It was very likely to fall apart the moment he was put in front of Cyrus and forced to press the matter of their past encounter.

The one thing Hondo felt he'd done right since entering the lab was to inject Cyrus with a mild stimulant to rouse him back to consciousness ahead of schedule. He'd managed the injection without being noticed. The move hadn't been without concerns, though. Hondo had witnessed the blow that rendered Cyrus unconscious in the first place. Seeing as that there was a very high probability of a concussion, he feared for his friend in the short term as a result.

Whatever happened in the lab, Hondo knew that it needed to happen quickly. And, above all, he needed to get Cyrus and the girl out of there as soon as possible.

Chapter 31

Mayflower Lab Facility
Hennings, South Carolina
4:29 p.m.

"You forget," Gertrude continued. "I've seen the results of your blood work. I know who you are—I know *what* you are."

The accusation threw Cyrus for a loop. He took a long look at the woman and decided that she wasn't bluffing. She was referring to something specific. But whatever it was, he didn't have the slightest clue.

Blowing out an exasperated sigh, Gertrude signaled the pair of guards to move the now fully covered body of Lacy Osbourne out of sight. Retrieving a thin handheld tablet computer from a nearby cart, Gertrude tapped the screen and brought the device to life. It took only a few more taps before she retrieved the information she required. Turning the device toward Cyrus, she held it up in one hand. "Your test results," she accused.

Looking at the screen, Cyrus didn't see anything remarkable on the display. There were two sets of side-by-side DNA results with sections of the normal, short grey, black and white, horizontal bars highlighted in colored groups. But what he was seeing meant nothing to him. Below what he recognized as

DNA annotations were other groupings of codes and equations that were indecipherable.

Cyrus looked at Gertrude with a blank expression on his face. "Really? Is this supposed to mean anything to me? I wasn't hired for my understanding of biology."

"I'm not sure why you were hired at all," Gertrude snapped. "Clearly Voss and his clowns sent you to spy on me. Either that, or—"

The expression on Gertrude's face changed so suddenly that Cyrus wasn't sure how to interpret it. She turned her back and examined the display. Question was clear on her face. Lost in thought, she lumbered several yards across the floor before lowering herself into a very awkward and crooked position on a wheeled stool. Not bothering to adjust herself, she set the tablet on her lap and began rapidly tapping the screen with the fingers of both hands. Her cane, forgotten, fell to the floor with a crash that echoed in the confines of the large laboratory.

Cyrus watched Gertrude for at least a full ten minutes. She tapped and swiped fingers across the screen with reckless abandon. Clearly she was up to something, or maybe onto something was a better description. Whatever it was, it had consumed the entirety of her attention. While he waited, Cyrus continued to pull at the restraints that were cinched tightly around his wrists. It was futile effort since they hadn't given so much as a fraction of an inch since he first started working on them.

Finally looking up from the tablet, Gertrude studied him oddly. He didn't understand her stare; it was both foreign and clinical. He felt like she was looking at him for the first time, but it somehow seemed more like he was under a microscope rather than strapped to a bed in front of her.

After another uncomfortable stretch of silence, Gertrude

turned to Ashley who was still strapped to the chair a few feet to her right. "You really couldn't Read him, could you?"

The hatred in Ashley's stare was impossible to miss. And though Cyrus was sorry for the pain Gertrude had caused the young woman, he was at least glad to see that Ashley had derived strength from her false grandmother's betrayal. There was a cold determination in her eyes that made it clear she wouldn't be helping the woman in any way. The events of the last twenty-four hours might just as easily have caused the young lady to collapse; that she remained strong and functional spoke of some powerful inner strength. She would need it before they found themselves clear of the mess Gertrude Waterford had created.

"Do you really need to ask?" Ashley said in a cold dry voice. "Are you going to pretend that you don't have my home bugged?"

"Like you pretended that you could Read him when you couldn't?" Gertrude countered.

Fire danced in Ashley's eyes. Had she not been bound to the chair, she would've sprang from it and torn the old woman limb from limb—Cyrus was certain of it.

"You spent a great deal of time together after that," Gertrude continued. "Were you ever able to Read him? Did you ever get any kind of sense from him?"

At first it looked like Ashley wasn't going to answer. It was the only way to fight back against the woman who had taken so much from her. But then she seemed to think better of it. Cyrus realized that Ashley had given a great deal of thought to the very same questions that Gertrude was now asking.

Shaking her head slightly, Ashley avoided meeting Gertrude's eye. She wanted to understand almost as much as her grandmother, but she couldn't bear to acquiesce to the woman in the process.

"And William couldn't Push him," Gertrude concluded. If she was aware, or even cared about Ashley's feelings on the matter, it didn't show.

"And I know damn well that he tried to Push you," Gertrude said, directing the statement at Cyrus. "He only attacked the lab when he couldn't Push you into doing the job for him. He must've tried like hell, too. But he couldn't do it.

"The question I should've been asking was; what makes you so special? No one has ever been naturally resistant to William or Ashley. I developed the neuro-dampener so I could protect myself from their abilities while they were growing up." Gertrude subconsciously massaged the tiny patch located behind her ear.

Cyrus knew that something had happened recently to alter the delicate balance on which Gertrude relied. William had somehow recently become more powerful. It was the only way to explain how he had been able to subvert the patch Gertrude's security team wore. He wouldn't have been able to attack the underground facility without first finding a way to defeat the countermeasure.

"*So why are you so special?*" Gertrude asked again.

Cyrus offered no response. He'd grown tired of her games and was looking for a way to end all of it. At one point he'd been curious about these questions himself, but that curiosity had passed. Nothing remained except anger, as he set a cold gaze upon Gertrude Waterford.

"There's nothing special about me," he said at last. "This is all in your head. You've lost your mind, Gertrude, and you're hurting good people. It's time to end this."

Continuing as if he hadn't spoken, Gertrude held up the tablet display once more. "This is the answer," she said. "It's all

XANDER WEAVER

right here. The work is too perfect, too refined to be Voss's people, and well beyond anything Onyx can produce. They don't have the technology. No one has the technology for this. Tell me about *Arlington*."

"Arlington?" Cyrus asked. "What's Arlington?" He sensed the weight in the word, the damage it could do, but it held no meaning for him.

After studying him for a long moment, Gertrude seemed confused by his response—or perhaps the sincerity of it. She raised a hand and signaled to someone standing in the background, someone located behind the vertical backboard where Cyrus was restrained.

When the man stepped into view, Cyrus felt the blood surge through his veins. He'd been waiting to find the face of the last man in Gertrude's security detail, and when Hondo stepped into view it was a tremendous relief. Though Cyrus had arranged for Hondo to insert himself into the team, he'd only contacted the people necessary to make it happen before having to go dark once more. He had no idea if Hondo had been successful in arranging the accident for the team's medic, let alone whether he had successfully infiltrated the team.

"This is Mister Fenway," Gertrude introduced. "But I believe the two of you have already met."

Cyrus felt his heart race once more at Gertrude's accusation. If she was aware of their relationship, things wouldn't end well for either of them. He would be responsible for getting his friend killed. Still, Cyrus maintained his best poker face and sent a questioning look in Gertrude's direction. "Excuse me?"

"Peru, about a year ago," Hondo clarified. "Does that ring any bells?"

Cyrus was surprised. He'd run into Hondo in Peru about a year back. Hondo's Delta team was working to secure a mining operation that had been plagued by sabotage and theft. Cyrus was working undercover at the mine at the time, tracking shipments of a new and exceedingly rare superconductive material that was a byproduct of what was being extracted from the same company's silver and gold mines.

The overlapping operations were responsible for bringing Cyrus and Hondo together for their first encounter. It was odd for Hondo to reference the incident in front of Gertrude, he thought. Particularly since both of their operations were highly classified at the time, and as far as Cyrus knew, remained so. If Hondo had told Gertrude about Peru, it meant something.

His mind spinning, Cyrus realized his friend's play and quickly went with it. He smiled. "That's right, I remember you. A year ago? Sounds about right." He needed to make conversation and give Hondo a chance to explain what line he'd run on Gertrude. He realized that Hondo needed to establish a shared past of some kind, and though he didn't know the reason for it, he knew his friend wouldn't improvise the precarious maneuver without a damn good reason. And it was Cyrus's responsibility to play along.

"You go by a different name now," Hondo accused. "And it makes me wonder... Why is that?"

"I'll admit," Gertrude interjected. "That part has me curious, as well. Why would you use one name in Peru and another here in the States? And how does that factor in with your test results? I was certain that it made you a part of Arlington, but that doesn't fit with what I see in the examination of your telomeres."

Now Cyrus was completely lost. He was only vaguely familiar with telomeres, and it meant that Gertrude was referring to his physiology again; more specifically, his biology. As best he could recall, telomeres were a sort of protective end cap for chromosomes that shorten with each cell division. It was essentially part of the aging process. But he had no idea what Arlington was, or how it was related to telomeres or Gertrude's examination of his chromosomes.

"You're a perfect genetic neutral," Gertrude said, as if the vague words explained everything. He felt her eyes probing him for some kind of response, but all he had was honest confusion, which is all he could offer in reply.

"Genetic *neutral?*" Cyrus asked. "*What in the hell does that mean?*"

Again, he felt her eyes probing him for signs of deception, but he knew she wouldn't find any. He was entirely lost. He had no idea what her accusation meant.

"You really don't know do you?" she said quietly. The question was a statement, more to herself than to him, as her mind attempted to work through the facts. He wasn't sure Gertrude was even aware she had said it out loud.

"The human genome contains a little more than twenty-four-thousand separate genes," Gertrude explained. "Through examination and extensive experimentation, I've discovered that certain sequences of genes activate abilities that are generally latent or dormant. Think of these genes as tiny genetic light switches, to put it into crude terms that you can understand."

Crude was good, as far as he was concerned. He just wanted some answers.

"When you flip one on, something might happen to the host body or something might not," she continued. "But if you flip the proper sequence of switches? Well, then the extraordinary latent abilities of the human body and mind begin to surface.

"The first trick is to locate the proper switches. Or, more accurately, the proper sequences of switches," Gertrude continued, "In the past, it's been a crude process of trial and error that has resulted in truly unsatisfactory results."

With those words, she motioned in the direction of the large glass tanks over Cyrus's shoulder, and when his eyes met with the visual example of what she referred to simply as *trial and error*, Cyrus felt the acid roil in his stomach, and the pure and utter rage build in his mind. Those monstrous mutations were the result of her playing with her so-called genetic 'light switches', and the idea sickened him. It seemed a great deal like a person playing God.

"On the very rare occasion," Gertrude offered a sly smile and glanced in the direction of Ashley. "The results were much more positive, and quite impressive."

Ashley's abject horror was clearly visible on her face. She stared at the tortured and disfigured twist of limbs and flesh inside the massive glass tanks, and Cyrus knew that she was realizing the same thing he was. Those tanks literally contained her brothers and sisters. They shared DNA and were early attempts at what Ashley and William would eventually become. The sad truth was that those failed specimens were more her family than Gertrude Waterford had ever been.

At first, it looked like Ashley was going to be physically sick. Her eyes moved from tank to tank off into the distance, further supporting Cyrus's supposition that more horrors were present in additional tanks beyond his sightline. But when Ashley's gaze shifted and fell on Gertrude once more, it had resolved into a visceral mask of pure hatred. Cyrus suddenly fully realized Gertrude's motivation for killing William Waterford. While the look in Ashley's eyes clearly expressed her silent desire to see Gertrude removed from the earth, William had possessed the unrestricted power to make that desire manifest. Once William had demonstrated his ability to defeat the patch Gertrude wore, his fate had been sealed. He had become a danger that the old woman could no longer afford.

"But, based on what I see here," Gertrude said, interrupting Cyrus's thoughts. "You're absolutely unique. It actually explains why Ashley can't Read you and why William couldn't Push you."

There was a supremely satisfied smile on the woman's face that told Cyrus his test results also represented something more to her. And as much as he hated to further fuel her ego, he needed to understand the ramifications of his own genetic sample.

"What?" Cyrus asked in a dry, reluctant voice. "What do my test results tell you?" he insisted.

"They tell me a great deal," Gertrude said. Her immense satisfaction was practically written across her face. "They tell me that you're something special, *and* they tell me that you were never subject to Darwin's laws. But, most importantly, the results of your scans will advance my research by decades."

Cyrus didn't understand how. "You're saying that I have genetic markers similar to what you've been producing in your experiments? That I have the genetic make-up necessary to read minds or influence thoughts?"

He didn't buy it. He had never experienced anything even close to that in his entire life. If he were pressed, the only thing that could be considered special about him was his near perfect memory. But it was a far cry from the sort of supernatural abilities Gertrude was trying to invoke in normal people.

Gertrude laughed at Cyrus's question; not just a chuckle of amusement, she laughed hard, until she had grown short of breath. "No," she said at last. "You have no abilities of the sort! You appear to be a perfect genetic *neutral*, the antithesis to everything I've worked for. It's actually what makes them unable to influence you," she explained. "Every switch I flipped in them to activate their latent talents? Those same switches are set to the exact opposite in you.

"It makes you immune to their abilities, but it also makes you the ideal roadmap for my future research!"

The smug smile on Gertrude's face triggered a rare response in Cyrus. He felt an uncontrollable rage welling up within him, and for once he had no desire to check his emotions and maintain any degree of self-control. Before he even knew what he was doing, he found himself pulling savagely at his restraints. Though they offered very little play, his arms thrashed violently at his sides, and his legs kicked and smashed against the thin padding of the gurney's mattress.

Cyrus surprised himself with his own feral, vicious desire to crush the life from the old woman. She was more a monster than anyone he had ever met. And that was saying something, given the type of people his work put him in contact with.

Realizing his rage would do him no good, Cyrus was about to back down when he caught Hondo's movement in the corner of his eye. Hondo had stepped near, drawing Cyrus's focus. He gave Cyrus a quick wink, seeming to encourage his frantic effort. And while Cyrus didn't know what his friend had in mind, he went with it. His effort of bucking and thrashing against the restraints doubled in violence.

"Ma'am," Hondo said over the racket emanating from Cyrus's fit. "If this man's as important to your work as you say, maybe I should sedate him before he does serious damage. He's already taken a hard blow to the head; he's likely already suffered a concussion. At this rate, he's liable to have an aneurysm."

Surprised by the violent outburst, Gertrude quickly gave her approval.

* * *

Watching the medic carefully, Ashley had been struck by the unusual thoughts moving through his mind. While the members of the detail were concerned with other matters, this man was focused entirely on helping Cyrus escape his restraints. At first she was certain that her grandmother—that Gertrude was messing with her, and put the medic up to forcing these strange ideas to the forefront of his mind—but Ashley quickly realized that is wasn't a trick. At least not on Gertrude's part. Somehow Cyrus had managed to get a friend inside the underground lab, and that man was trying to help them escape.

Throughout Gertrude's conversation with Cyrus, Ashley had been eavesdropping on the thoughts of everyone in the room. While Gertrude's mind remained firewalled thanks to the patch she wore behind her ear, and Cyrus's was still beyond her mental reach, she was able to listen in on Cyrus's friend, Hondo, and the four other members of the security team.

Two of the security men were bored beyond reason, looking forward to concluding their work with *the old woman* and more or less figuring out how to spend the money they were making on this assignment. One of the others was preoccupied with thoughts of the underage Vietnamese girl who constituted his 'girlfriend for hire', and the fourth guard was obsessing over his perverted co-worker with the Vietnamese hooker girlfriend.

It was a sick bunch, and a perfect example of why she hated her ability to read minds. Today was the one day that it seemed to be working to her advantage. She saw Cyrus's eyes grow cold in a way she'd never before witnessed, and a moment later he began thrashing against his restraints. She didn't need to Read him in order to know that he wanted to kill Gertrude every bit as much as she did.

But then she heard the voice in Hondo's head. Hondo's first concern was for Cyrus and that he might hurt himself in the futile effort. He had suffered a blow to the head prior to being brought to the lab? That was news to her, and she realized that a great deal must have taken place while she'd been unconscious. They had called it a seizure. She wasn't sure what happened, but she felt like a part of her soul had been torn from her body—and she blamed Gertrude for that.

Hondo had quickly seized on a clear plan. He suddenly reversed his position and wanted Cyrus to continue the assault on his bindings. If he could convey the message to his friend, he thought he could convince Gertrude to let him sedate Cyrus. It would be an opportunity to slip his friend a weapon—possibly even free him from a restraint in the process.

It was a great plan, Ashley realized. But there was no way for Hondo to communicate the idea to Cyrus with everyone watching. While she searched for a way to assist, Ashley felt a sudden surge of relief from Hondo and realized he had somehow secured Cyrus's participation in the plan. She had no idea how he had done it. Though she had been watching the entire time, she hadn't witnessed the communication. Thankfully, neither had anyone else.

Gertrude gave Hondo permission to sedate Cyrus, and Ashley watched as the man retrieved a small wheeled cart from a few feet away. He pushed it up beside Cyrus's inclined table and placed his medical bag on top. But she felt her stomach drop when she realized what Hondo had in mind. There was no way the he could pull it off at the moment. Certainly not while everyone's attention was focused on the two of them.

Ashley felt rage at the trouble her grandmother...the old witch, had caused. A burning hatred was consuming her, and even though her own desire to kill the woman sickened her, she refused to fight back the urge. At that moment she realized that her pain and anger held the key to Hondo's plan being successful.

Throwing all of her hatred and rage into an attack on her own bindings, Ashley kicked and tore at the duct tape that held her to the office chair. The tape held, but the wheels began to clatter against the floor as she rocked back and forth in her fight against the tape. All of the effort created a tremendous amount of noise and pulled attention from Hondo and Cyrus.

Unwilling to ease her efforts for even a moment, Ashley put every ounce of her energy into the fight. The tape continued to hold but the chair was quickly upended and she went crashing to the floor. The impact knocked the air from her lungs, but even with her mind deprived of oxygen, she managed to continue the violent effort. She fought and rolled in the chair, smashing its arms against the floor as two of the guards descended on her, fighting to find a grip and restrain her.

But the girl was not about to give up.

Chapter 32

Mayflower Lab Facility
Hennings, South Carolina
4:44 p.m.

It took only a moment for Hondo to load a syringe with the proper dose of the sedative. Although everything taking place was improvised, Cyrus still felt confident that he knew the plan Hondo was preparing to set in motion. If Hondo was going to do what Cyrus suspected, everything would take place in full view of Gertrude Waterford and four highly trained men who were loyal to her pocketbook. Simply put, there were too many eyes on them for Hondo to make his move. The risk of being caught was too great.

But when Ashley shrieked in a fit of rage and then followed it up by sending herself smashing to the floor, she managed to divert all but Gertrude's eyes at a critical time. At first Cyrus wrote the coincidence off as an act of fortuitous timing, but he immediately realized his mistake; it wasn't luck at all. Ashley had been fully aware of Hondo's plan, even if Hondo didn't realize that she was on board. She'd pulled the thoughts from his mind as quickly as they had formed, and even more impressively, she had improvised the necessary distraction all on her own.

Still raging against his restraints, Cyrus saw that Gertrude had managed to keep a suspicious eye on him despite Ashley's efforts. Hondo didn't look back at her before he plunged the needle into Cyrus's flesh and emptied its contents with a single powerful stoke of his thumb across the device's release. Maintaining the act, Cyrus made a few more powerful pulls against his wrist restraints and offered just one more kick of his right leg before sagging against the raised backboard with a drunken roll of his eyes. Though his head was lowered, further acting out the effects of the nonexistent sedative, Cyrus saw Gertrude turn her attention in Ashley's direction.

"Now," Cyrus whispered to Hondo.

With a single stroke of the razor sharp scalpel from his medical kit, Hondo severed the leather restraint binding Cyrus's left hand. On his upswing, he slipped the handle of the scalpel into his friend's grip before stepping around the gurney and drawing his firearm. Four shots—a pair of lethal torso strikes to each of the men stationed near the closed hallway door.

Not having time to cut himself free, Cyrus discarded the scalpel and settled for snatching a 9mm H&K from an open flap inside Hondo's medical pack. Hondo had made a point of making the weapon's grip visible while he worked to ready the sedative injection. Still bound by both feet and his right hand, Cyrus fired a pair of shots into the chest and abdomen of one of the guards standing over Ashley. The man was just starting to draw his weapon. The force of the impacts sent the man toppling off to the side and, unfortunately, provided a moment of additional cover to the last remaining guard who'd been in the process of raising Ashley's struggling form from the ground. The guard ducked behind her, using her as a human shield.

A second later, Hondo turned a hundred and eighty degrees and brought his weapon to bear on the last guard, but he had no better line of sight than Cyrus. The guard cowered behind

Ashley who was still taped to the chair. He adjusted her with ease, thanks to the chair's caster wheels, making sure to keep himself out of the line of fire.

The entire attack had taken all of four seconds. Gertrude had stumbled back and fallen in the commotion and lost her cane in the process. It lay three feet in front of her, askew on the tile floor and out of reach. Her hands were shaking so bad, it was no wonder she couldn't stay on her feet. That was fine as far as Cyrus was concerned. A fall on her ass was only the start of what she deserved.

"Nobody moves!" the guard bellowed. His voice had squeaked in a fairly undignified way that conveyed his full understanding of the situation. He had reached around the back of Ashley's chair and lodged the muzzle of his gun in the flesh between her neck and collarbone. A bullet discharged at that angle was certain to tear through half of her major organs.

The guard continued to adjust the angle of the chair by fractions as he scooted backwards across the floor on one knee, pulling the chair and Ashley with him. He didn't make any further demands because he didn't need to. It was a standoff. At least for the time being.

Hondo kept his weapon trained on Ashley and, by extension, the man hiding behind her. Cyrus knew he wouldn't fire. Even for an expert marksman the shot was too risky. Gertrude sat motionless on the floor, now in the room's middle ground and about forty degrees out of the line of fire. She seemed to sense the precarious nature of the standoff and was unwilling to move for fear of setting catastrophe into motion. It wasn't likely in fear for her granddaughter, Cyrus understood. Those misconceptions had come and gone. At that point, Gertrude was simply worried that one of the bullets had her name on it.

The only one willing to move was Cyrus. He set the 9mm aside on the wheeled cart and retrieved the discarded scalpel. It took a single slice to free his right hand and two more before he had regained the use of his legs. He picked up the gun with his free hand and stepped off the small ledge that supplied his footing on the inclined table—his eyes remained locked on the guard crouched behind Ashley. When the man's eyes met his, Cyrus held the scalpel out to his side and opened his hand. The razor sharp surgical instrument struck the hollow floor with a clatter.

"It's over," Cyrus said to the guard. "Is this contract worth your life?"

The man didn't answer. His back was to the large imaging device at the other end of the room. He had no means of further retreat.

"Let her go and you can walk out of here, free and clear," Cyrus persisted. He made a point of phrasing the suggestion as a command rather than a question. The point was to show the man that there were no options here. It was a basic hostage negotiation tactic but, at this point, Cyrus lacked the primary tool critical to all successful negotiations.

Patience.

He wasn't feeling particularly indulgent at the moment and realized that making that clear to the man with the gun might be advantageous.

"I'm making you an expiring offer," Cyrus continued. "Lay down the gun, get up, and walk away. It's that easy. I won't shoot you, and I won't follow."

"You're not in any position to make demands," the guard said at last. "I'm the one with the gun."

"You're the one with the gun until I walk over there and take it from you." There was a cold edge to his own voice that surprised even Cyrus. He needed to scare his opponent into submission, and he had only a bluff to work with.

"You try it, and I'll pull the trigger," the man stammered.

Cyrus heard the uncertainty in the man's voice and knew he was making headway. He needed to press the issue before the man could rationalize his situation.

"If you pull that trigger, you're dead for sure. I'll drop you where you stand." Cyrus added harsh inflection to his voice to drive the words home. "The only way you walk away from this is if you lay down arms, and you do it *now!*"

When a response wasn't immediate, Cyrus knew he needed to act decisively or risk the situation spiraling further out of control. Though his breath was locked in his throat, he steeled himself and refused to let even a fraction of his indecision or fear show. His eyes still locked on the man who was peeking around the terrified form of Ashley, Cyrus gnashed his teeth and took a brisk step forward.

His leg extending forward in the initial step, Cyrus was shockingly aware of every ripple and whirl in the grip of the weapon in his right hand. He didn't even have the weapon cradled or sighted as he would have if he were ready to take a shot. It was at hip level, nowhere close to firing position, and that was the point. He was betting everything on intimidation more than the immediate threat of violence.

Besides, if a shot needed to be fired Hondo had that covered. He stood ready to fire the moment the man broke cover in the slightest. This was all about getting the gun off Ashley.

Before his single stride was complete, Cyrus saw the guard pull the gun from Ashley's neck and point the muzzle harmlessly off to the side. Two fingers instantly went up on Cyrus's left hand, a signal to Hondo not to take the kill shot.

"Toss it away," Cyrus said calmly. He continued to close the distance on Ashley and his opponent at a steady, unhurried pace.

The guard's weapon clattered across the tile by the time Cyrus was within ten feet of Ashley's trembling form. Cyrus kept his weapon at his side, signaling the guard to his feet with a simple wave of his hand. The guard, now fully compliant, did as instructed.

After retrieving the guard's weapon, Hondo pulled the man aside and went about restraining him. Cyrus knelt before Ashley and smiled. "He was willing to pull the trigger," she said in a quiet, horrified tone. "I heard him thinking it, clear as day. I thought that was it—I was sure of it!"

Sliding a very small scalpel along the arm of the chair, Cyrus cut Ashley free. She looked down at the blade in his hand, confused. Following her gaze to the larger scalpel he'd dropped dramatically to the floor before advancing on the gunman, Cyrus grinned.

"How?" was all she managed to say.

He shrugged. "I've had this little blade for a while," he admitted. "But they had the restraints cuffed so close to my hands that I couldn't do anything with it. I was going to use it to make my move until he showed up." Cyrus tipped his head in the direction of Hondo who was still dealing with the sole surviving guard.

Though he didn't think it was possible, Ashley's eyes grew wider. "Wait—you didn't know your friend was here?"

Cyrus laughed. "Things have been happening kind of fast. Cut me some slack, would you?"

At first he didn't know if she was going to laugh or cry. The tears that had welled up at the corners of her eyes finally washed down her cheeks, and she broke out in a sputtering, exasperated laugh.

Cutting the last of the bindings away from her feet, Cyrus helped Ashley up. He followed her eye line to where Gertrude still sat on the floor. For his part, Cyrus had been keeping the woman under constant observation in his peripheral vision. He knew that Hondo was doing the same. But since the moment she'd stuck the floor following the outbreak of gunfire, Gertrude hadn't moved an inch. In fact, she was only now pulling herself to her feet.

As soon as Ashley's attention fell on Gertrude, Cyrus could tell that the woman had already decided how she would try to spin the situation in her favor. He couldn't imagine what angle Gertrude could possibly use to justify the atrocities she'd committed, but he knew that he was about to find out.

Gertrude met Ashley's eye with a defiant stare and an upturned jaw. "I suppose you expect me to—," she began.

Ashley closed the gap between them in five quick steps and delivered a right cross to Gertrude's proud jaw, sending her crashing to the floor once more. The woman hadn't yet realized what hit her, before Ashley was standing over her fallen form, seething with rage. Ashley looked like she was sifting through hundreds of things she wanted to scream at the hideous woman, but in the end, she said nothing. Rocking back on her heels, Ashley took another look at the old lady lying in a crumpled heap before turning silently, and walking away.

A wide satisfied smile spread across Cyrus's face, as he took a long look at Gertrude. Deciding that she wouldn't be going anywhere for some time, he turned and walked away as well.

"What do we do with this guy?" Hondo asked when Cyrus walked over. He had his gun in one hand and the restraints that bound the wrists of their prisoner in the other.

"Cut him loose," Cyrus said without hesitation.

Hondo looked at him as if he'd lost his mind.

Cyrus shrugged. "It's not his fault. He just took the wrong job. When push came to shove he did the right thing and stood down. We'll honor our end of the bargain and let him walk. I think it's the right thing to do."

Cyrus realized the guard was looking at him over his shoulder. The man seemed as surprised as Hondo with the decision, but Cyrus met his eye. "Call it professional courtesy," he explained. "Sometimes it's how we deal with a bad situation that proves who we are in the end. You did the right thing. Now we will too."

Epilogue

Hennings, South Carolina
9:05 a.m.

Reluctant to ask questions, Ashley had tried to satisfy herself with listening to the terse conversation between Cyrus and Greg Boone on their drive to the Rockefeller Federal Building. The truth was that most of what she learned hadn't come from the abbreviated discussion between the two men, but from the thoughts of Greg Boone in the long silences that had filled the car over the course of the fifteen minute drive.

From what she'd pieced together, Boone and Cyrus worked for some sort of low profile law enforcement agency. No one had actually mentioned the name of the organization, but the word 'coalition' had crossed Boone's mind on several occasions. Beyond that, she didn't know much about the group, its goals, or its jurisdiction. Only that Boone wasn't happy to learn that Cyrus had involved her, *a civilian*, or that he had insisted she accompany them to visit Gertrude first thing this morning.

"Did the guards say anything about last night?" Cyrus asked Boone. He sat in the passenger seat of the rented Jeep Cherokee while Boone drove, allowing Ashley to listen in from her spot in the backseat.

Boone shook his head. "Waterford was in the infirmary until

just before midnight," he explained as he drove. "Their attending physician wanted to keep her in medical for observation all night, but I pushed the matter on your suggestion. Why were you so keen to get her back in her cell, by the way?"

There was no humor in Cyrus's voice when he replied, "That woman is a piece of work. You know the type, always looking down her nose at everyone? I didn't want there to be any confusion about her situation by the time we saw her today. Believe me, a long night on a shitty jail cot will do her good."

Even from the backseat Ashley could see the smile appear on Boone's face. He nodded. "Then this should do the trick. I talked with her doctor last night. It seems Ashley packs a hell of a punch."

Boone's eyes went to the rearview mirror and met hers. "You destroyed the dental implants on the left side of her jaw and knocked out four of her teeth. For a while they thought they might need to wire her jaw shut."

Cyrus turned in his seat and was relieved to see that she wasn't upset at the news. He didn't say anything but he did offer a prideful smile that made her heart race. She'd been feeling uneasy with the situation since Boone's arrival. Cyrus had referred to the man as his 'training officer', but hadn't explained exactly what that meant. All she knew was that Boone had arrived in town late the previous night. If Cyrus were some kind of trainee, she couldn't understand why he would have been sent undercover with no support. She didn't know much about law enforcement procedures, but it seemed incredibly unorthodox.

Where Cyrus had offered very little by way of explanation when it came to Greg Boone, he had been happy to introduce her to a man he referred to simply as Hondo. That was it. She didn't know if that was the man's first name, last name, or just a nickname, and neither had been inclined to explain. As Cyrus put it, Hondo was a friend from "a ways back." Cryptic at best, and again, neither man offered greater detail. But once Cyrus and Hondo had secured the situation at Gertrude's lab, things had settled down significantly.

Cyrus had contacted the local FBI field office. The FBI had the facilities needed to take Gertrude into custody; likewise, the staff responsible for the lab's security were also taken into custody. As Cyrus had explained, he would be surprised if any of the hired help knew the true nature of Gertrude's work, but he needed to cover all possible bases. For that, he utilized local FBI resources. It was a decision Boone was quick to criticize as soon as he'd picked them up at Ashley's apartment.

"Bringing the FBI in on this was a bad call," Boone chastised. "You know how they are about compartmentalized information."

Cyrus didn't respond at first. He continued looking out the passenger side window as they drove through city streets. "What would you have done in my place?" he asked at last. His tone was entirely neutral. If Boone expected to start an argument over the matter, Cyrus wasn't engaging.

It was Boone's turn for a long moment of silence. "There should've been a field team standing by. It was important to keep this all in-house."

"Why? The Red Queen wanted a copy of Waterford's database. Things escalated and Waterford went off the reservation. Based on her psych profile, it was unanticipated. You know how these things go. She was going to kill me and Ashley. Matters spiraled and I didn't have the resources to round everyone up on my own. Besides, you love pulling rank on the Feds."

More than the words coming from Boone, Ashley was reading far more questions as they moved through his mind. That was the first time she realized the truth of the situation. Cyrus hadn't told Boone what really happened. He'd kept the truth of her abilities out of his report and it had led to holes in the story that could definitely be potential problems for his career.

"You were supposed to retrieve her research," Boone acknowledged at last. "You're telling me that, over the course of almost two weeks, you *never* had a chance to access the information? You didn't learn *anything?*"

"I didn't even get access to the research lab until twenty-four hours before everything went to hell. And even with my access, I couldn't login to the database. Only Gertrude had access to that, as far as I can tell. I was going to use her terminal to pull a database dump the first chance I had—but, again, things went pear-shaped before I had the chance."

Ashley caught what she thought was an accusatory glare from Boone following Cyrus's statement, but his mind Read entirely blank. It was as if he were on the fence when it came to believing Cyrus's story. He wasn't predisposed in favor or against Cyrus. In fact, he seemed to be entirely neutral, while suspicious at the same time. It made her wonder exactly what sort of work this Coalition really did. The sense she was getting from Boone was that, despite his looks, he was a very intelligent and dangerous man.

"Pear-shaped?" Boone asked. He looked back at the road and gave the comment some thought. "That's the other part of this that's not really working for me. You said Waterford just went off the reservation? Something must have triggered it."

"Her grandson, William, broke into the lab," Cyrus clarified. "He was looking for proof of his grandmother's work. That's what sent her over the edge. After that, she just flipped."

"But why? What was William after?"

A sudden shortness of breath gripped Ashley. She felt on the verge of a panic attack. Cyrus was trying to provide a detailed account of events without letting his people know about the extrasensory abilities instilled in her and her brother as the result of Gertrude's work. It seemed only a matter of time before he was caught in the deception. She knew he was putting a great deal on the line to maintain her secret, and she suspected that it was for more than just privacy. She didn't know what a clandestine government organization would do with a mindreader, and she didn't want to find out.

"Ever heard of The Order of Origin?" Cyrus asked.

Boone shot him a quizzical look. "The crazy cult out east?"

"William was a member. For whatever reason, it put him at odds with his grandmother. I never got the full rundown, but she pretty much went bat shit crazy over the whole thing. From what I could tell, William joined with the cult about the time Gertrude really went off her rocker. She had him institutionalized at some place called 'Tuttle Heritage'. I haven't had a chance to look into the place, but based on the way he described it, it's no Betty Ford. She basically just put him on ice and wrote him off."

Pulling the Jeep to a stop at a red light, Boone sat quietly and drummed his index finger on the top of the steering wheel. When the light went green, he didn't react. The car behind them sounded its horn and snapped Boone from his trance. "And you think the old lady's gone round the bend?" Boone asked after they'd driven another block.

"You will, too, when you meet her." There was no humor in Cyrus's voice. "She thinks her grandkids have superpowers, for God's sake." He turned and looked squarely at Boone before continuing, "Worse yet, she thinks she *gave* them those superpowers. She was so terrified of William that she had him murdered. She's certifiable."

There was a long silence again. Ashley sat silently in the backseat feeling fairly certain that both men had forgotten she was there. It was just as well. If someone asked her a question, she wasn't sure she could answer without revealing how terrified she'd become. She was waiting breathlessly for a sign, *any* sign, that Boone was buying Cyrus's tale.

With a sigh, Boone shook his head. "That's just great. So, even if we get our hands on Waterford's research it's probably useless anyway. Wonderful."

More than Boone's words, Ashley sensed the conviction of his thoughts. His mind was already working on a way to salvage the operation and moving to other concerns, like how he was going to explain the details of the failed mission to someone named Monica.

Ashley had the sense that something life-altering had just transpired, though she wasn't sure exactly what or how. A dreadful concern had grown deep inside her gut over the course of the car ride, and she realized it was entirely related to the shadowy organization Boone referred to as the Coalition. Whatever it was, Cyrus didn't want them anywhere near her or Gertrude's work…and his worry spoke volumes.

* * *

The Rockefeller Federal Building
Hennings, South Carolina
9:19 a.m.

The elevator ride to the fourth floor of the Federal Building took no time at all. Ashley's silence hadn't escaped Cyrus's attention, but he was reluctant to say much to her in front of

Boone. The less he knew about their relationship the better. It would only cause him to ask additional questions and look more closely at the details of the mission in the final report. Still, as they stepped off the elevator, Cyrus saw that Ashley's normally pale complexion had grown even grimmer; it was the thought of facing her grandmother—facing Gertrude once more. He reminded himself again that they actually shared no blood relation.

The three of them walked up to the main desk, and Boone explained to the clerk that they were there to see Gertrude Waterford. He'd phoned ahead and was informed that she'd already been placed in holding room number two and was ready when they were.

Boone signed his name to the necessary paperwork followed by Cyrus and then by Ashley. Cyrus knew that Boone wasn't happy about bringing Ashley along for this part of the process, but Cyrus pushed the issue, explaining that Gertrude was a stubborn woman and it would be beneficial for her to see that Ashley was actively assisting in the investigation.

Buzzed through a secure doorway behind the reception counter, they met up with a man in a suit who led them down a hall and around a corner to another short section of hallway lined on each side with three doors. The doors were labeled I-1 through I-6, respectively. 'I', standing for interview, the politically correct, twenty-first century euphemism for interrogation. Cyrus shook his head. They might change what they called the rooms but the tough questions asked on the other side of the doors would always remain the same.

Cyrus watched as Boone tapped the six digit combination into the crude mechanical lock on the door's knob, and then followed his mentor through. A few paces past the threshold, Boone froze in his tracks. This caught Cyrus off-guard; stepping to the right, he peered around Boone's shoulder. There, sitting at the interrogation table with her wrists cuffed to the steel restraining bar, was Gertrude Waterford in a baggy pale blue jumpsuit. She sat upright in a hard steel chair, her chin sagged low against her chest, and frothing white foam fizzed on her lips.

Boone cursed and circled the table to check the woman for a pulse. Cyrus ducked out into the hallway to call for assistance, as Ashley stood at the corner of the doorway and watched the scene with no emotion whatsoever.

Building security locked down the entire facility in record time…but it didn't matter. Whoever had delivered the fatal dose of poison had made their escape before the alarm was raised. But the fact that someone walked into an FBI field office and accessed a locked room in order to kill a suspect in custody was a significant matter. Cyrus knew there would be an investigation. Still, for his part, Gertrude's death simplified things. He no longer had to worry about how her debrief would differ from his. And, with her gone, burying her research would become a much easier matter.

Even with all the positives, however, Cyrus was left wondering *who* could walk into the heart of a secure government building and deliver a fatal dose of poison without being caught? There was no chance that the old woman smuggled the poison in herself. If she had the opportunity, she would've killed herself down in the cell block. Plus, there was no question—the old woman was just too proud and far too vain to do this to herself. She was the type who would make sure to show how intelligent she was to one and all—even if her audience was in a courtroom, deciding whether or not she could live.

Even more concerning to Cyrus was, who had something to

fear with Gertrude Waterford in federal custody? Whoever it was hadn't ever appeared on their radar. As far as anyone knew, Gertrude Waterford was the end of the investigation.

Apparently, that wasn't the case, after all.

* * *

The Templeton Tower Building
Hennings, South Carolina
8:45 a.m.

When Ashley opened the door of her apartment, the smile that greeted Cyrus went a long way toward staving off the stress of the morning. Prior to parting the previous night, they had decided to meet first thing to cover some remaining details. It was a thinly veiled excuse to see each other again and the best they could do under the circumstances. Both felt a powerful connection, while at the same time realizing that Cyrus's time in Hennings was coming to an end. In fact, Ashley had asked him to stay the night but it had been impossible. Cyrus knew that he was already drawing scrutiny from his superiors, and he couldn't risk them looking into his work anymore than they already had.

So their morning meet had to be enough. Plus, Cyrus's day had started with some unexpected news that he felt compelled to share. Just when he thought he could put this entire case behind him, another complication was quick to rise from nowhere. The confusion would not end with the death of Gertrude Waterford. Well...assassination would be a better description, Cyrus decided. Someone had managed to walk into a secure government building and poison the woman while in a locked holding room. Worse, review of the security footage had yet to explain how the killer had reached Gertrude, or how he had made his escape.

He took a deep breath, putting those questions on hold as

he relaxed in the warmth of Ashley's smile. Placing her hand on Cyrus's forearm, she guided him into the familiar surroundings. "Nice to see you again," she said with a playful smile. "I can't help thinking that it would've been more...*efficient*, if you'd just stayed the night."

With a groan and a roll of his eyes, Cyrus let her lead him into the sitting area where they dropped closely together on the sofa. "Efficient, huh? I would've had a hard time explaining that to Boone. He showed up at my door first thing this morning."

He saw suspicion in her eyes. "Yeah," he confirmed. "More bad news. Someone broke into the Mayflower Facility last night. Gertrude's fileserver was erased, and then destroyed for good measure."

"I thought the lab was being guarded!"

"It was," he continued. "Around the clock by a detail of five agents. Still, someone made it in and out without being spotted. All of the data's gone. There's nothing left."

"How is that possible?"

"Exactly. And how did someone kill Waterford? You can bet the two events are related."

Ashley went silent, apparently giving the matter a great deal of thought. The entire series of events was troubling—the sort of thing that Cyrus would normally lose sleep over. But not this time. He'd reached a point where he wanted nothing more than to put the entire case behind him. Though he wasn't sure why. For some reason, the reality of Gertrude's experiments had unsettled him in a deeply personal way. That was saying something, when he worked with thieves, smugglers, killers and bureaucrats on a daily basis.

Pulling a small evidence bag from his pocket, Cyrus held the contents up to the light. It took a moment for this to catch Ashley's attention, and he realized just how distracted she was with all that had happened. At least he wasn't alone in his discomfort. Though, if *he* found the entire case unpleasant, *how* would she be feeling? This case involved the entirety of her life. She'd lost her brother and the woman she believed to be her grandmother. Furthermore, she was the product of some insane scientific experiment. The fact that she was even functional at this point spoke to her resiliency.

Ashley took the bag from his hand for a closer look. Inside was what looked like a business card. But rather than the name of a company and someone's contact information, the card had only the word 'Origin' written in large block letters. Inside the letter 'O' was some kind of stylized series of interconnected lines that looked like some twister version of an atomic symbol. He could tell by her stare that she didn't understand.

"This was found with Gertrude's body," Cyrus explained. "It's literally the calling card of The Order of Origin, the church group your brother was a part of."

Ashley glared at him. "You can call it what it is, a cult. Don't sugarcoat it." She flipped the card over and seemed disappointed to find it blank. "You think this was some kind of retribution for the death of my brother?"

"You tell me," Cyrus said with a shrug. "You two had a connection. You said you somehow knew when he was being held at that mental institution. I thought you might know more about this cult, or at least William's involvement with the group."

After an extended moment of silence, Ashley seemed to find the words for what she needed to say, even if she was reluctant to speak them. "My connection to Will is—*was*—a hard thing to describe. I don't think most people have the capacity to even attempt to understand it, so I've never really tried to put it into words."

She looked him in the eyes and studied him before continuing, "I guess that doesn't matter now. You're not at all like *most people*. If anyone can get it, it'll be you.

"It's like when you wake up in the morning, and you know that it's raining outside before you even open your eyes. You can't hear the rain and you can't see it, but you know that it's there. There's no real question about it, it's just sort of a sense you have, even if there's no way to explain it. Or, when you slip on the ice—the way your arms cartwheel to gain balance and your entire body reacts in an effort to right itself, even though your mind can't accurately process what's just happened. Some things, movements, reactions, are just natural, hardwired responses. You don't have to do anything to learn it, it just comes naturally. It's a part of you.

"It was like that with Will. For as long as I can remember we just had this innate connection. We were in our teens before we even realized that we had something other people didn't. It was just that natural. It was most obvious with strong emotional responses. For example, when I was scared—I mean *really, really scared*, Will would know it. It was funny because, when that would happen, he would call to check on me. I guess it was the sort of thing that can make two people extremely close."

Cyrus nodded. He was getting a feel for the nature of their connection. It was exactly the kind of situation that would make siblings close, become vital parts of each other's lives. "Did the connection only apply to fear?"

"No," she smiled and shook her head. "It covered pretty much the whole range of emotions. Anything that was extreme. Happy, sad, excited, nervous—we were linked." She rolled her eyes and shook her head again. "For better *or* worse."

He was afraid he might be intruding on something private, but after seeing the curious expression on her face, Cyrus was compelled to ask.

Ashley blushed, but met his eye. "I sort of freaked when I got my first period," she said quietly.

"And?"

"And good old Will got pulled along for the proverbial ride." Ashley's sad smile quickly spread before finally blooming into one that reflected nothing but joy. Tears welled up as she looked off into the distance recalling some far off memory. "He tried to play it down, but I think that experience scared him more than it did me in the end," she laughed.

"Oh! But he got me back years later," she continued. Her cheeks turned a deeper pink, almost red at the thought. "When he lost his virginity."

Cyrus burst out laughing. Ashley chuckled, wiped away the tears and joined in, her laughter growing more infectious.

It was fascinating, Cyrus realized. He had always heard stories about twins having an innate link between them, but nothing like this. Ashley went on to explain how things worked in greater detail. While they could sense the emotions of the other, that was the extent of it. And the link faded with distance. William had taken a trip with his class at one point; it had been the first time they had been separated by a great distance. At one point Ashley had felt her connection to her brother falter and she'd become terrified. Ten minutes later the phone had rung. The call was from William, concerned for her safety as he, too, had felt their connection break.

"Twelve hundred miles," Ashley said with a smile. "That's what we worked it out to be. For whatever reason, we're connected as long as we're within twelve hundred miles of each other."

"But why?" The question had escaped his lips before he thought better of it.

"No idea," she said. "Even Gram—even Gertrude couldn't figure it out. She understood what it was about our genetic make-ups that contributed to our abilities, but she never understood our connection."

Cyrus wasn't so sure. The way things had played out in the end, Gertrude understood Ashley and William's abilities because it had been her research that had triggered their talents. Gertrude had lied about so much. He found it almost impossible to believe that she didn't know more than she'd admitted when it came to her would-be grandchildren. They were her lifelong Guinea pigs, after all.

"You're skeptical," Ashley said with a grin.

"I thought you couldn't Read me," Cyrus countered.

She laughed. "I don't have to Read you for that. I'd like to think that I've gotten to know you."

"I guess I just feel like it's a mistake to underestimate anything that Gertrude said or did. You knew her a lot better than I did, but I still wouldn't put anything past her. It's just that, with her research destroyed, there's really no way to be sure of anything."

Ashley slid her hand inside of his and gave it a squeeze. "What if there was a way to know for sure? What would you do?" she asked.

The question confused Cyrus. He didn't see the point of her *what if*—not unless she knew of a backup when it came to Gertrude's research.

"If you had access to Gram's research," she pressed, "what would you do with it?"

"What?"

"I mean, how would you use it? Would you try to understand it? Would you take it back to your people like they told you to? Would you use it as evidence in the investigation?

Or would you try to understand what she meant when she called you a genetic neutral?"

Clearly Ashley had given the idea considerable thought. Cyrus, on the other hand, had not. He'd gone against orders and declined to steal a copy of the database earlier. But once Gertrude had been in custody and the lab had been locked down, the matter was out of his control. He'd been forced to choose between Gertrude's research and Ashley's life. At that point, there hadn't been any consideration necessary. He had taken Ashley out of the lab and used the FBI to lock down the research facility. In doing so, he knew the data would end up in the hands of the Coalition, but it was an unavoidable consequence. He'd had no choice but to secure the lab.

"Are you telling me that you have a copy of the database?" Cyrus asked in a quiet voice. He wondered if her questions were rhetorical. If she had the information, it wasn't unreasonable for her to want to know what would happen to it.

Sliding from the sofa, Ashley went to the massive bookcase on the east wall of her apartment. Finding a shelf at eye level, she pulled three hard covered books out before retrieving a small portable hard drive from the space behind them. She padded back to the couch silently on bare feet and once more slipped into her spot beside Cyrus.

"I guess I could've wrapped it," she said with a mischievous grin before handing him the drive.

Taking a closer look at the small black data enclosure, Cyrus didn't know what to say. He hadn't anticipated the turn of events. "How?" he finally managed.

"William transmitted the data to me when he broke into the lab," she explained.

That much Cyrus already knew.

"I had it on my laptop, I showed it to you. And Gram took

the laptop when she sent the goon-squad here to get us right after. But she didn't know that I made a back-up as soon as the download was complete."

Cyrus just stared at her, shocked and impressed. He knew that Ashley's apartment had been under surveillance for years, even though it was something Ashley had only recently become aware of. While he knew she'd been out on the patio when she downloaded the data transmitted by William, at some point she had needed to bring the drive inside and hide it, all within full sight of her secret observers. How she had accomplished it, he had no idea. And as much as he wanted to know, he decided that some things were better left to the imagination.

Besides, he didn't think that referring to her 'around the clock observers' would be conducive to their conversation. While it was only one more personal violation she'd suffered at the hands of Gertrude Waterford, it was a big one, and the sort of thing a young woman was likely to take very seriously.

"So what will you do with it?" Ashley asked.

It was a simple question with no simple answer, Cyrus realized.

"Unless you have a better idea, I'm going to sit on it for the time being," he decided. "There's no way I'm turning this over to my people. We're the good guys and all, but I just have this nagging suspicion that this data would end up in the hands of someone who is all too happy to pick up where Gertrude left off. And I won't have that on my conscience."

"What about what she said? Don't you want to know if it's true? Don't you want to know if you're like me?"

That brought a vague nod from Cyrus. "Right now I'm writing that stuff off as the ravings of a deranged megalomaniac. I'm not going to lose sleep over it. Besides…genetic neutral? That sounds profoundly vague. I'm not buying it.

"And if I change my mind, maybe I can find someone trustworthy to take a look at the data. From what I understand, there are only a dozen or so people in the world with the level of knowledge needed regarding this kind of thing. But where there's a will, there's a way. Maybe someday."

Ashley seemed satisfied with the answer, if a little surprised. Maybe even a little disappointed, he suspected.

"What about the Order of Origin?" she asked. "What happens to them?"

Cyrus slapped his leg and smiled. "Fortunately, they're not my problem. The card left on Gertrude's body means that someone will be looking into them much more closely, but it won't be me. To be honest, if they *did* kill good old Gert, they likely did it in retaliation for what happened to your brother. And a big part of me isn't all that upset to see the woman gone after all she's done. So I'm washing my hands of everything. Case closed."

"Just like that?" She was surprised.

"Do you think I should go after the cult for what they did?"

She shook her head. "I sort of want to send them a fruit basket for what they did, but I suspect that would surface in the course of the investigation. I think I'll concentrate on finding a new place to live."

Now it was Cyrus's turn to be surprised. "You're moving? What's wrong with staying here?"

"Aside from the fact that the entire building is owned by the deranged woman who pretended to be my grandmother? The woman who locked my brother in a mental ward before having him assassinated? Aside from all that, she's dead. It's time to find a new place."

"I only ask because I did some checking," Cyrus said with a pacifying smile. "Old Gert didn't have any other living family members and, as it turns out, while you and William were not blood relatives to her, she was your legal guardian in the eyes of the law."

A furrowed eyebrow conveyed Ashley's silent confusion.

"You are Gertrude Waterford's sole surviving heir," he said bluntly. "Congratulations. You're the new owner of this building."

To Cyrus's amusement, Ashley was struck speechless.

"Not just this building either," he went on. "Apparently, she had a fair number of real estate holdings throughout the city, and more than a little money stashed away for a rainy day. It will all be yours once it clears probate. I know it's no conciliation after everything you've been through, but you're about to become a very wealthy woman."

After taking a moment to process the news, Ashley shrugged and seemed to push the thoughts from her mind. Cyrus was surprised when she didn't ask how much money he was talking about, but she seemed truly not to care. In that, he discovered one more thing that was profoundly attractive about her. She'd gone through some major ups and downs, but she seemed to have the type of disposition that would see her through the toughest of times.

Slipping in closely beside Cyrus, Ashley nuzzled herself beneath his arm. He felt the warmth of her body as she placed her head against his shoulder. Leaning back into the sofa, he propped up his feet on the coffee table and wrapped her in his arms. He had one or two days left in town at most…and they both knew it. After that, things would become more difficult. But, as they had been since the moment they met, both were on the same page and content to make the most of what time they had while they had it. Something good *had* come from all of the death and chaos and they were happy to celebrate any victory they could.

For the first time in a very long time, Cyrus had the sense that he was right where he was supposed to be. Every nagging question, every concern seemed far away and unimportant.

"You know," Ashley said. "If I'm as wealthy as you say, you could quit your job and become my full time boy toy...I'm just saying..."

Cyrus Cooper will return in
Rogue Faction

Acknowledgments

An amazing amount of effort goes into the production of a single novel. Despite the name on the cover, this book wouldn't be what it is without the support and contributions of some very special people. After months of work, somehow saying 'thank you' just doesn't seem like a strong enough sentiment. That said…I'm going to give it a try.

First, I would like to thank Amy Lignor for her work as Editor. She did an amazing job with this manuscript in an incredibly short period of time, and helped polish it into something far stronger than it would've been otherwise.

Likewise, I offer my heartfelt thanks to Kane Gilmour and Seeley James. Kane helped me with a book that will be released later in this series, and in the process I learned a great deal. His help on that novel is reflected throughout this one in ways too extensive to list. I have Seeley to thank for his extensive notes on a late draft of Dangerous Minds. His comments brought a precision to the final draft that I find profoundly satisfying. For both of your efforts, I am exceedingly grateful.

Next, the folks who were exposed to early drafts and beta copies of this book receive a huge 'thank you'. The contributions of these individuals cannot be overstated because they were my critics as well as my cheerleaders. These are the contributors who helped me with the early edits—the truly

messy, down and dirty, revisions that took place before I was ever willing to show the book to a professional editor. These are the people who know how very far this manuscript has come and what it took to make it what it is now. Thus, 'thank you' to Terri and Wayne Manke, Jamie and Julie Dresser, and Wenzel Roessler. You made the long hours spent putting this book together worthwhile.

I owe this book's cover design to Lee Roesner from Paradigm Graphic Design. We all know that a book really is judged on its cover, and Lee did a fantastic job developing not only a cover for Dangerous Minds, but also a cover theme that will be used for the rest of the series. Lee has the kind of design talent that makes art look easy.

Last but not least, I want to thank my wife, Carrie. More than any other single person, she championed this book as well as those that will follow. Not only has she tolerated my constant "what if's?" and "how about's?", but she made those conversations as enjoyable as they were fruitful. And for all of those early drafts that my beta readers were exposed to, no one saw this book in a more feral form than Carrie. She is the first to read everything I write, and first to help me revise and refine it. Her contributions to my work are beyond compare.

Thank you, Carrie. For all that you do, and all that you are!

About the Author

Thank you for reading, "Dangerous Minds." This is the first novel in the Cyrus Cooper thriller series, and I am looking forward to delivering a fantastic journey to readers.

I'm Xander Weaver, and this is my debut novel. As a lifetime fan of thrillers, as well as science fiction, I took the opportunity to blend both genres in order to create excitement and adventure, with a sci-fi 'kick'. There are three more books in production at the moment, with book #5 currently in the planning stage. So, if you enjoy this story half as much as I did while writing it, please look for the follow-up adventures in the near future.

If you would like to be notified of future book releases in advance, you can sign-up via my website at www.XanderWeaver.com. And you can rest assured that your personal information will never be sold or traded.

While I'm working on the newest thrill ride, I frequently post updates to my Facebook (Weaver.Books): http://bit.ly/fb-xander and Twitter (@XanderWeaver): http://bit.ly/twitter-xander
Follow the progress and join in the fun!